"I see that you do not like this, cadet."

"Get used to it," she said. "It is your training."

Without giving any indication that a punch was coming, Falconer Joanna jabbed Aidan in the nose, and he felt something break. She hit him again in the same place, and the pain was so bad he could not see straight—or, rather, he could see too well, in too many images. The third punch knocked him to the ground.

He looked up to see Falconer Joanna standing over him.

"Are your through yet, nestling?"

He tried to sit up, and she gently pushed him down. This time he stayed there.

"This one might test out all the way," she said to Falconer Ellis, who now stood beside her. As she spoke she was putting on the falconer gloves, whose star-shaped studs caught some light and sparkled. She held each glove, palm side toward her, directly in front of her face as she pulled it on. Her face grimaced as she stretched it tight. "He does not, as you saw, give up easily. Let us keep track of him—make his stay with us especially hard."

# BATTLETECH®

## LEGEND OF THE JADE PHOENIX
### VOLUME 1

# WAY OF THE CLANS

## ROBERT THURSTON

A ROC BOOK

ROC
Published by the Penguin Group
Penguin Books USA Inc., 375 Hudson Street,
New York, New York 10014, U.S.A.
Penguin Books Ltd, 27 Wrights Lane,
London W8 5TZ, England
Penguin Books Australia Ltd, Ringwood,
Victoria, Australia
Penguin Books Canada Ltd, 2801 John Street,
Markham, Ontario, Canada L3R 1B4
Penguin Books (N.Z.) Ltd, 182-190 Wairau Road,
Auckland 10, New Zealand

Penguin Books Ltd, Registered Offices:
Harmondsworth, Middlesex, England

First published by Roc, an imprint of New American Library,
a division of Penguin Books USA Inc.

First Printing, August, 1991
10 9 8 7 6 5 4 3 2 1

Series Editor: Donna Ippolito
Cover: Bruce Jensen
Interior Illustrations: Jeff Laubenstein
Mechanical Drawings: Steve Venters
Copyright © FASA, 1991
All rights reserved

**RoC** Roc is a trademark of New American Library, a division
of Penguin Books USA Inc. BATTLETECH, FASA, and the distinctive BAT-
TLETECH and FASA logos are trademarks of the FASA Corporation, 1026 W.
Van Buren, Chicago, IL 60507.

Printed in the United States of America

To Rosemary and Charlotte

# Prologue

## A Kind of Fate

At different moments—say, the night before a battle begins or the night after a love affair ends—the Commander usually seeks a quiet place. Unlike most Clan warriors, he looks for isolation rather than camaraderie when in the grip of an emotion. This time he does not choose the cockpit of his 'Mech or a dark place in a forest. This time he goes to the inlet of a quiet lake with an abbreviated beach whose quietly lapping water is only four or five steps from the edge of the woods. He sits, back against the stump of a tree (burn marks and missing bark suggesting that the tree had once, like him, been a battle victim—except he had survived). He watches moonlight sketching intermittent highlights on the few ripples in the water, listens to the weak breeze almost shyly send ripples of sound through the woods behind him.

In a book that had been burned in battle, a book that the Commander had carried with him into the cockpit of a 'Mech whose shards had been scattered across the landscape of some embattled planet he no longer recalled, he had read a story that he wished he had memorized. In it a father mourned a son killed in battle. The battle had been primitive, a war over some nonsense about which side possessed some valued object, the death the kind of tragedy that was not quite a tragedy (no falls from great heights, no individual ravaged by a single, identifiable character flaw). The war had been a thousand accumulations of sorrow, a thousand rewardings of honor. Like most wars. The boy had died because someone else had made a mistake. After the boy had saved someone— a friend, a lover, a child, an enemy (there were so many stories, the Commander thought, how could puny details be remembered?)—he had been killed by a projectile from whatever weapon belonged to that era. His father dug him out of a battlefield pile of corpses, the smell of blood not yet become the stench of decay.

The father looked at the tortured face of the boy. His eyes still seemed to stare with life, but now they gazed at some point just past the father's shoulder and not into his eyes. A thousand memories, a thousand fragments of the boy's life, rushed into the father's mind. The moments went from the cradle and childhood frolics to the important experiences of growing up, through all the choices that seemed to lead directly to this pile of corpses, in a straight line of events with a strange sort of inevitability to them, a kind of fate. And of course, in the world of the father and his son, it *was* fate that had guided them. Fate was the point. Fate was the last remaining expression in the boy's eyes, which the father now shut with gentle urges of his fingertips.

That was not the end of the story. Events had propelled the father into a deeply complicated plot where in some ways he redeemed himself from a taint and in some other ways reconciled himself to his son's death. Whether or not the father survived, the Commander could not recall.

The Commander, however, had survived. His special talent, survival.

His Clan upbringing had long interfered with his understanding of the story and, for that matter, many other stories in many other books from among the volumes he had so long ago discovered in that Brian Cache where he had done such dreadful and enervating duty. The concept of father had initially troubled him. What was a father? Naturally, he understood the technical meaning of the word, but what did it really mean? What had it meant for the devoted father of the story?

The Commander, the offspring of genetic engineering, of genes from a sacred gene pool, had several father figures but only knowledge without awareness of his actual father. All he could fall back on was imagination to understand any concepts about natural parents in the books he had read. He had been raised with others also genetically matched, in a sibling company, a sibko. He had a fine understanding of what siblings felt, but how could he have really comprehended the sorrow of a parent over a lost son or daughter? At least back then, the concept had puzzled him. Now he understood it better. Now it was easier even to feel. Now it was his own private sorrow, not only previously unknown but forbidden to be known.

The idea of fate was easier to comprehend. The Clans had a notion of fate, though it differed from the fate portrayed in the story. A Clansman tried to control his fate, measuring it methodically against the vagaries of chance. Everything in life required a bid. If a man was good at bidding, he controlled his fate. A successful bid in warfare meant he led his warriors into battle, planned the execution of their maneuvers, planned the battle itself, reacted to chance interferences with the skill of a battleworthy strategist, beat chance with the action of his adept-at-strategy mind, overwhelmed what fate appeared to have in store. Of course, for the other warrior, the pilot in the cockpit who saw fate rushing right at him, the outcome of the engagement, the loss, undoubtedly seemed like fate.

Clan officers met before a battle and bid for the honor of fighting it. It was an intricate and complex procedure. The first officer to bid removed one or more of his units from the battle strategy. The next bidder had to duplicate that move, then up the ante by eliminating a unit or more of his own or by replacing a strong unit with one ranked below it. A 'Mech could be substituted for an aerospace fighter or five Elementals, the Clan's genetically bred, battle-suited infantry. Bids flew back and forth until one commanding officer was left with low bid, the bid below which no fellow officer could commit personnel and materiel. But a bidder could not hold back a low bid for too long. An opponent might beat him to it, making the winning bid he had intended and leaving him back on a DropShip, watching his rival lead his forces into battle. There was no position so uncomfortable as sitting in a plush DropShip chair observing the military triumphs of the officer who had beaten you bidding.

All Clan men and women took delight in the victories of others, but no success was more satisfying than that of the warrior doing the winning. A certain regret inevitably crept into one's praise for others. It was not envy that fueled it, nor was it loss of face. Every Clansman respected the wagering skills of a good officer, and there was no shame attached to losing a bid. But there was another kind of loss of face, a kind the Commander well understood. It was the loss of face within oneself: the realization that one had not quite made the grade. That was the true loss of face, when you gazed at yourself in the mirror of your mind and had to look away.

The Commander remembered a fellow warrior who had graduated from all levels of training spectacularly, had risen through the ranks rapidly, had become one of the youngest Star Captains in the history of Clan Jade Falcon. But he had proved to be inept in the prebattle ritual of bidding. Too often he gave away too much manpower in his desperate attempt to gain the bid. Undermanned, he fought too many losing battles or marginal victories, endangering his troops and materiel. Though one of the fiercest warriors ever to charge an enemy, the man's bidding deficiencies finally cost him his command, even lost him his 'Mech. When he finally met his death in battle, he was not a victim of fate but of destiny. The Captain's genes were not passed on in the gene pool so sacred to all warriors. But what point was there in a warrior's living and dying if his genes were not judged worthy of the gene pool?

The Commander knew that when one controlled the key aspects of his destiny, fate did not matter. There was no fear of fate among the Clans. As he had read in a Clan saga, in a passage he could not quite remember accurately:

Fate sits high in the bidder's chair
Trying to subdue the Wolf Clan
And failing;
Trying to outbid the Ghost Bears
And losing;
Trying to make the Jade Falcons listen to reason
And listening instead.

What was he doing, thinking about fate at all? He always tended to become dangerously reflective before battle, allowing his mind to wander around his past. Too many books, too many stories with unsettling doubts in them, too much reflection altogether. His life had been difficult, much of it, with failure, shame, loss, hard success. But he had struggled through it all. Survived.

Some people said they would change nothing if they had their lives to live over. As for the Commander, he would not repeat a moment of it—well, maybe a moment here and there—even if it meant forsaking his present high position in the Jade Falcon chain of command. Too many events had warped his thinking, too much hardship had made him the perpetual outsider. Of the Clan, yet outside of it.

I have read too many books, he thought. I am beginning to think like one. And we cannot have that.

Still I would like to go back in time, confront myself at the moment I began training, tell myself the mistakes to avoid. I could bargain for myself a more ordered life, bid for the kind of existence I should have had.

Ah, the training.

They had been young, so young, mere children. He might have been wise beyond his years at the beginning of training, but still only a child when the rough-hewn, rough-clad instructor-officers had taken him and the others in hand. Sculptors of people, yes, even more sculptors of the mind, they had remolded him, part by part constructing him and the others like the vaulting of a great cathedral, making them the buttresses of their units, their Star Clusters.

In the Commander's memory, the others were young, too, but (at least in his mind, now) somehow younger than he. Where were most of them now? Some, of course, were dead. The Clan did not recognize the sanctity of life, one of those Terran and Inner Sphere concepts he had read about; all Clan warriors could be fodder, and rightly so, as long as their deaths forwarded the goals of the Clan. War and the Clans made a good combination, especially in their heartlessness toward human life. There was no sanctity to it all, only survivors. The 'Mech won or the 'Mech fell, that was what happened.

But if a messenger were to bring him word now that Marthe had been killed, if he had had to meditate on her passing while sitting on this beach and staring out at this roughly sketched lake, he would have been sad. Un-Clanlike, he would have been sad.

The Commander had survived. That was the final result. The Clan was as proud of its dead warriors as its live ones. The courage of all justified the Clan. He had learned to accept the Clan, his Jade Falcon Clan. He had even come to love it. It had taken time, but it had begun the day he and the others stepped off the hoverbus onto the cold (even through heavy boots) ground of the training center on the Jade Falcon planet of Ironhold.

# 1

Across the great expanse of a grassless, rocky plain, other vehicles were also arriving, each dumping new trainees—from uncharacteristically anxious sibkos—onto the landing site, where in threatening packs, the training officers awaited their charges, their next set of victims. These strange-looking men and women hardly seemed to notice the newcomers. Instead, they talked among themselves, their barked-out words frequently interrupted by raucous laughter. They often pushed against or elbowed each other in ways that looked to Aidan neither friendly or even human. They were more like hawks crowded together in a cage, each ready to start a bloody battle if nudged out of place by another.

In spite of the cold, the blasts of wind that had reached even into the hoverbus to chill its passengers, these warriors, these combat survivors, were scantily dressed, unlike Aidan and his sibko, who had snuggled into tunics of thick animal hide, broad-brimmed fur hats, and light but well-insulated leather boots.

Each training officer wore what had apparently once been a fatigue jumpsuit, but with ragged holes in the sleeves and torso and with the legs cut off unevenly, exposing lower limbs that were bare down to light, low-slung boots. Sleeves were shortened, too, just below the elbow. Over the cutaway jumpsuits, some wore fur tunics, the only apparent concession to the intense cold.

On the chests and sleeves of the jumpsuits were many patches, some indicating rank, some indicating past units in which the warriors had served, some indicating battle achievements. A few of the officers wore thick gloves, the well-padded kind used in falconry.

It made Aidan recall the first day he had launched his favorite bird, a peregrine he had named Warhawk. Standing on the crest of a promontory, he had been sending her out to hack—to fly free and obtain that sense of liberty so essential to a bird that would spend most of its life tied to blocks or carried on the wrist-end of a padded glove. Hacking was a practice of all those in the Jade Falcon Clan who had chosen to honor their name by cultivating the ancient art of falconry.

Aidan had spent the rest of that morning hoping that Warhawk would return. Of course, she had, proving to be one of the coolest, most successful hunting falcons in Aidan's sibko.

But that was long ago. Today, stepping onto the ground of the training site, tension overwhelmed him. On his side, on the side of the sibko, there was closeness, trust, the answering of needs. On the other side, on the side of the training officers, there was indifference, danger, contempt. However, there was also—in the occasional sidelong glance and in a certain bodily stiffness—a sense of the enemy ready to spring.

Aidan looked over at Marthe, found her staring at him. Though her eyes were calm, he knew her well enough to perceive in the uneasy set of her full-lipped mouth (shaped so much like his) that she was just as apprehensive.

Sibkos rarely met their genetic donors. At the time the first ilKhan, Nicholas Kerensky, was instituting the first genetic programs, theorists warned him that contact between donors and their sibko children could cause dangerous influences. They were especially wary of what they called unhealthy parental inclinations. Such feelings, they advised, had to be eliminated so that the genetically created warriors would not suffer the personality complications and character flaws that could so easily lead to the mistakes that lost battles and failed whole campaigns. By law the donors must be the best warriors society could offer. The best warriors should, they reasoned, not even want to see their sibspring (a linguistic corruption of ''sibling offspring'').

Though everyone in the sibko had the same genetic background and resembled one another, Aidan and Marthe looked more alike than either of them resembled any of their sibkin. They were the only ones who had the high forehead tapering down to a narrow chin, a shape akin to a perfect triangle. It was said the look came from their maternal side, and was the famous appearance of Star Commander Tania Pryde, many of whose combat and sporting exploits were excitingly recorded in Clan Jade Falcon annals. She was still among the Bloodnamed, but like all warriors who had reached the age where custom dictated they must retire from combat, she was fulfilling a noncombatant assignment somewhere or retired into another caste.

Less was known about Galaxy Commander Ramon Mattlov, the paternal contributor of the genes for Aidan's sibko. Rumor had it that his exploits were as impressive as Commander Pryde's, but the accounts had somehow not found their way into Clan or sibko lore. Aidan had been told that he and Marthe resembled Mattlov in their height and slimness. They were the tallest members of their sibko, with Marthe topping Aidan by only a few centimeters.

However, the characteristic that really set off the pair was their eyes—blue as the summer sky on the planet Circe and just as deceptive. As a Circe storm could seem to descend on the planet from nowhere, a swirling tempest preceded only by the slightest change in the serene skies, the calmness in the eyes of Aidan and Marthe when confronted by opponents was the lull that preceded their storms. That serene moment before they sprang into action often gave them the edge against an adversary of equal skills.

Aidan shivered. Even in the thick garments he wore, the harsh wind blowing across the plain made him feel exposed. The other members of his sibko appeared to be shivering, too. They had been instructed that the only clothing they could bring to training camp was what they wore to the landing site. Some of Aidan's sibkin had put on a couple of extra layers; now he wished he had, too. The cold air discovered any ingress into clothing, any place where the material did not quite meet the skin, then rushed in to thoroughly chill every epidermal surface.

"I do not trust any of those non-kin," said Bret, the smallest of the group. "Non-kin" was a term that differentiated their sibko from other sibkos and, for that matter, *any* assembly of people outside the sibko. These unkempt, ill-dressed, indifferent officers, for example.

Bret's smallness had seemed to guarantee his early elimination from the sibko, but nobody had counted on his tenacity, courage, and the discipline that had made him exercise for hours every morning. Now he had a strong and muscular body, and the others relied on him for leadership, as much as fiercely independent sibkin could accept *any* leader.

"They have planned something for us."

"What, Bret?" Marthe said.

"I do not know, but based on how vicious and unfeeling those who will train us are said to be, I suspect their casual indifference right now is a fraud to hide something devious instead."

"I doubt they will make us stand here for long," Aidan commented. "It would not be Clanlike."

"Clanlike? Are you being sarcastic?" Bret asked.

He was, but Aidan did not want Bret to know that. Bret, who had no concept of the humorous, often commented that Aidan treated life too lightly. The smaller boy had been so intent on his own survival in the sibko, his own proof of kinship with the others, that he never understood a joke. Around a campfire, on hunting expeditions, his laughter always rang false, the laughter of a serious person trying to blend in with others by following their ways. The only jokes he ever told were ones he had heard from others. His nervous manner and the catches in his voice when he delivered punch lines made his listeners doubt his understanding of the joke's humor. The sibko needed Bret's shrewdness and quick decisions at those times when the entire group was being tested, so they excused his lack of humor.

"Neg," Aidan responded. "I am being factual. We are not often allowed relaxation, *quiaff?*"

"Aff. You know what I think? I think they are testing us right now. See the sidelong glances? They are assessing us, I am sure."

"And at the same time agitating us, quiaff?" Marthe said.

"We should try to look calm," Rena said. "Show we are ready for them, ready to be warriors."

Rena was unusual among Aidan's sibmates. Though a

bit overweight, like all the survivors of the arduous customs, testings, and retestings of a Clan upbringing, she was in good physical condition. Rena liked to use her unimposing appearance to catch people off guard. She could flip an attacker over her well-muscled back, then wrestle him to the ground faster than anyone else in the sibko. The wrestling was often a prelude to coupling, which she carried out with a similar athleticism. Aidan often let himself be tossed by her, in prospect of having the painful blows evolve into amorous caresses.

"I believe Rena is right," said Bret. "Best to ignore them. How about a team-tussling session? You all up for it?"

There was immediate agreement among the sibko's dozen members. Automatically splitting into their usual three teams, they squared off. Team tussling was both an exercise and a game that, Aidan had once noticed, harmlessly ritualized the kind of grand melee that occurred during a Trial of Position.

Team tussling had developed naturally out of the sibko's intense gymnastic competitions. Once any such activity started, all members of the sibko wanted to be the best at it. In a tussle, they used acrobatic talents along with the combat skills they had been learning, it seemed, since they were trying to kick their way out of their cradles.

The ritual began ceremoniously. Two members of each team formed a "chair" with their hands while another stood on or sat in it. Aidan was certain this beginning had originated from falconry. In a team tussle, the competitors were launched just like the birds. Bret stood on the surface offered by his team's quartet of thinly gloved hands, then his holders hurled him forward. He executed a single flip in the air, landing in front of Rena, who was thrown forward from a sitting position, rolled into a somersault, and then landed at Bret's feet just as he came down.

This opening was well-ritualized by now. Rena grabbed at Bret's ankles. Bret anticipated the move and jumped aside, landing in the path of the first-out acrobat from the third group, a stocky, quarrelsome young man named Endo. He had entered the fray by leaping from his holders' chair onto his hands, "walking" a few steps, then flipping onto his feet just in time to give Bret a hard chop to the side of his head with hands that Endo had hardened with practice on any material he could find. Each member of the sibko had a fighting specialty; chopping with his hard-heeled, calloused hands was Endo's. Bret reeled sideways and encountered Rena driving her shoulder into his midsection.

Aidan watched with the other members of his team, as always nervous and eager for the moment when they all could enter the battle. At one time, team tussling had been simply a boisterous free-for-all. Refinements had gradually been introduced until the game evolved into its present form, where—in imitation of the Clan's military bidding procedures—each team sent out its minimum effective force, one fighter, to do battle for a precise two minutes before the others could join in. If that single fighter was rendered ineffective by an opponent (a difficult task when there were three or more teams) or, as sometimes happened, was knocked out cold, that team was defeated and its other members were not allowed into the mock but hard-fought combat. This was the overwhelming fear of the tussler, that he or she would work up all the restlessness and energy necessary for a good scuffle and then be deprived of the chance to let it out. Aidan, not the best gymnast of his team, was unable to offer a stylish opening gambit for the beginning of tussling, and so rarely went out first. He hated these moments of being denied battle.

Marthe, beside him, was equally restive. She liked a good fight as much as Aidan and never shied from it. In their sexual encounters, she had shown similar appetites, which was why she was, among all the members of the sibko, his favored partner for coupling. Unfortunately, others felt the same and getting to her was often more arduous than a team tussle.

A sibko survived, they had been told often enough, on its ability to function as an effective unit as well as on the intensity of its internal competitions. A sibko member was always battling, on the outside and the inside.

He looked over at Marthe. The back of her left hand was against her hip, and she was rubbing it nervously up and down against the rough material of her short trousers. The skin visible between her trousers and her high boots was prickly with goose bumps. He glanced down at his arm, which was also showing the effects of the cold. A few more seconds, and if Rena stayed true, he could get warm by mixing it up in the center.

Rena almost got caught out by Endo, who, by throwing himself onto his back and kicking his legs high, knocked her off balance. Endo then rolled into the back of her legs and flipped her over his hunched back. She landed, uncomfortably, her head pressed against a large rock, her eyes less than clear but not dazed, her right arm under her body, her left flailing ineffectively. Endo, who moved quickly in spite of his stockiness, jumped on her and nearly pinned her, but his head was snapped back by Bret, who, by the rules of the game, could not stand by and let one individual defeat another. In a team tussle, a physical exercise as much as a competition, it was forbidden to win by allowing your opponents to defeat each other. Inactivity was inglorious.

The whistle-signal came from the Timemaster, in this case Dav from Endo's team. Screaming like hawks, the others ran, leaped, twisted, and elbowed their way into the melee.

Aidan rushed right at Tymm, a clever but stolid infighter who could often be dazzled by diversionary tactics. At almost the last second before Aidan would have rammed into Tymm (and received a skillful defensive blow in response), he veered away, as if his choice for combat were someone else. He ran another three steps, stopped, and—without looking at Tymm—launched himself sideways while bringing up his elbow, making contact with the side of his opponent's jaw and sending him off balance. A quick kick to the back of Tymm's knee and he fell to the ground, where Aidan quickly placed his right hand firmly but safely against Tymm's neck to hold him down. This act, held for five seconds, signified Tymm's defeat. Aidan had no time to watch Tymm get up and slink away, for he had to cope with Orilna, the skinny but lithe martial-arts specialist. She was just a bit off with a chop to the back of his neck, and he merely stumbled a few steps, recovering in time to block her elbow strike, then deal her a just-barely slowed-down punch to the stomach. She took the blow well, not even doubling up, but her next attempt, a weak heel-palm strike, was obviously affected by his attack. Bending low, Aidan tackled her about the waist and wrestled her to the ground, his arm gripping her through her right leg, the back of his forearm against her chest. He was just about to do the five-second mock stranglehold on Orilna when a booming voice drowned out the sounds of the scuffle.

"STOP THIS IDIOCY!"

The voice had so much of the sound of command, the sharp consonants of authority, the drawn-out vowels of wrath, that Aidan froze in position, his hand reaching for Orilna's neck, his other arm still entangled in her legs. Orilna, too, like all the other sibko battlers, stopped fighting and tensely held still.

Aidan looked up to see a trio of training officers, two of them with arms akimbo, the third gesturing wildly as he spoke: "Is this harebrained sibko, this fluttering nest of eyasses, so foolish as to think a demonstration of its belligerence would in some way impress us?" Eyas was the word for a hawk just taken from its net before it could fly. "You are children still, *quiaff?* No doubt you spit up your cereal and go behind rocks so no one can see you defecate. Has there been a mistake, comrades? Have they sent us a sib-nursery instead of a sibko on the verge of becoming warriors?"

The officer to the speaker's left laughed raucously, a sound analogous to the roar of a sudden Circean wind. When she spoke it was in a voice that, if anything, was louder than her colleague's: "Freebirth! If these whelps are our training unit, I think I will make myself a bondsman to the laborer caste, because what use will be there in going to war? With novices such as these, we might as well bid for surrender as combat."

The third officer started to pace among the sibko. Aidan saw that his fellow sibkin were like statues, each commemorating some fighting pose or other—fists reared back, struggle checked in sometimes absurd tableaux, legs locked in what seemed like physically impossible knots. He relaxed his grip on Orilna and sat back on his haunches. Orilna did the same. Some of the others shifted position.

The third officer, a man whose complexion was so bad that he seemed a genetic anomaly for the warrior caste, made odd sounds of disgust in his throat. "You call this fighting?'' he finally said in a gravelly voice. ''This is horseplay. It is soft, too soft. You call your caresses punches? Go home and spend your days among the fields of flowers, coupling and quoting the pornographic sections of *The Remembrance*. Create a freebirth in a real womb.''

Aidan nearly vomited, so insulting and obscene was the third officer's last remark. Among warriors, any reference to freebirths or the freeborn was the deepest curse, the most profound of insults. To be born from the womb of woman was disgraceful. Male warriors could sire children with a woman from another caste, but the child would then be freeborn, a word synonymous with lowborn in Clan society. Warrior fathers never spoke to their freeborn children. There was no meanness in it; they were merely indifferent to their bastards.

''You,'' the third officer said, pointing toward Endo. ''What is that on your lip? Do you grow vegetables there perhaps?''

Endo instinctively felt for the sparse group of hairs that he called his mustache. He was so proud of it.

The second officer now strode among them. ''Facial hair is forbidden for cadets,'' she said. ''You will shave that off by tomorrow at dawn or we will pluck it off hair by hair.''

For a moment, Endo looked as though he were experiencing the sensation she described. Aidan ran his hand along the underside of his smooth chin, fearful that he might have grown a beard there and forgotten it.

''Stand up!'' the first officer suddenly shouted. ''All of you!''

All members of the sibko were on their feet within an instant, standing stiffly at attention.

''I am Falconer Commander Ter Roshak, but until you are yourselves warriors, you are forbidden to refer to me by name or by rank. You may not, in fact, address me directly or refer to me when talking to anyone else. The same holds true for your other officers, Falconer Joanna.'' The woman officer nodded. ''And Falconer Ellis.'' A grunt from the other male officer. ''Falconer Joanna, explain semantic code.''

Ter Roshak was a tall man who held his left arm strangely. Slightly curved, but not in an anatomical way, it seemed to cling to the side of his body as if attached there by invisible wire. It barely moved as he spoke.

Falconer Joanna, bellowing instructions, wove her way among the trainees. "You must give full attention to us when we address you, but you must not respond to us. If words must be delivered, you must couch them in indirection. You do not understand what I mean. I will demonstrate."

Suddenly she stood in front of Aidan. She was a head shorter than he, but the difference in height diminished in no way the intensity of her gaze. Her eyes were blank, almost colorless, mean. Palms together, she held gloved hands in front of her face, tapped them against her chin. They were falconer's gloves, thick, decorated with sharp-pointed metal stars. The stars no doubt denoted some kind of military information, something about the military division called a "Star" in Clan fighting units, unless they merely represented the vanity of Falconer Joanna in some way.

"You are a tall one, cadet, *quiaff?*"

"Aff."

"Aff? What do you mean?"

"As you said, Falconer Joanna, I am tall."

She slapped his face hard, using the back of her right-hand glove effectively. He felt the points of some of the stars dig into his skin. Her eyes stared into his, probing for a reaction. Except for the first startled moment, his eyes held onto their characteristic coolness. Long ago he had vowed never to let his guard down for anyone, in or out of the sibko.

Falconer Joanna continued to glare into his eyes, without blinking. It was now a battle of self-control. Her mouth hardly moved as she spoke to him: "You spoke to me! You addressed me by name! You must respond to our direct questions, but never in any way talk *to* me. You must talk as if to the air. Do you understand?"

"Yes. This cadet must talk to the air. As he is doing now."

"You learn quickly, eyas. We weave among you cadets like the harsh, relentless winds of Ironhold," she said softly. "You follow our orders, immediately doing whatever we command. What is you name, eyas?"

"Aidan."

"Aidan. Put your arms around me, Aidan. Around my shoulders."

He was about to protest, but realized that meant addressing Falconer Joanna directly, offering an independent comment, so he did what she said.

"Good," she said. "A bit slow, but obedient. But you are like a tentative lover, holding your body away from mine. Come closer. Good. Your arms are strong, eyas, muscular. But I can take you."

She brought her arms up through his and roughly broke his grip. She hit him in the stomach, digging her glove in deeply so that the points of the stars scratched his skin beneath the thick hide of his clothing. He doubled over, he had to, and could not blink back the tears that sprang into his eyes. But despite the pain ravaging his insides, Aidan looked back into Joanna's eyes, refusing to show her even a hint of it. She seemed ready to hit him again, then suddenly backed away.

"You have falcon's eyes, cadet," she said quietly. "I will be watching you."

Aidan cursed inwardly. His first minutes in training and he had caught the attention of an officer with a fierce temper and a strong punch.

Nearby, Falconer Ellis was dressing down Tymm and giving him a series of punches on his arm and chest. Tymm looked about to cave in.

Then Falconer Commander Ter Roshak strode into the middle of the group, bellowing: "Can we send these little birds back to their nests? My time here on Ironhold must have some meaning. I will not waste it on a doomed project."

Up close, as close as Aidan was willing to look out the corner of his eye, Ter Roshak was an odd-looking individual. His face seemed made of jagged rock, with many signs of erosion. The eyes were hard to see beneath the overhanging cliff of his brow; his mouth a forbidding mountainside cave. Emphasizing the analogy of stone was the man's hairlessness, just a few blades of hair growing around his nearly shapeless ears, and none visible on his arms and legs, as if the ban on hair had included limbs as well as face. The falconer commander had seen more of life than Aidan ever wanted to, probably most of it in the cockpit of a BattleMech.

"Shall we test them, Falconer Commander?" asked Falconer Ellis, his terrible voice eager for something. Aidan could not tell what, but he immediately dreaded it. The man's pockmarked skin, its apparent malleability a strong contrast to Roshak's hardness, reddened with anger, or perhaps it was merely the assault of a wind that seemed to get more turbulent by the minute.

"Test them? Of course we will test them. I would do it myself but I can see in your eyes, falconers, that you would prefer to bid for the privilege."

As Roshak strode toward his subordinates, Aidan realized why the man's arm had appeared odd. It was not his real arm, but a prosthetic creation. He must have lost his arm in battle.

"It is not a bidding situation, Commander," Falconer Joanna said. "Twelve to one is too great odds even for warriors like myself and Falconer Ellis. However, I would be willing to divide them up seven to five. Seven for me, five for Ellis."

Ellis grunted. Aidan could hear the insult in the grunt, but was not sure how to interpret it further.

"Seven, Falconer Joanna? You are tired today, I suppose? I will take on eight of these paper-thin warriors, leaving four for you to toy with."

"Eight might be a strain for *you,* but I will offer nine. What say, Falconer Ellis?"

Ellis smiled and looked smug. "Nine? Bargained well and done, but I should add that I think Falconer Joanna has typically overstretched her ambition. So nine it is, Joanna. I will flick off the other three like flies."

Gazing at the bemused expression of the new trainees, Ter Roshak shouted at them: "You three!" He pointed to Bret, Orilna, and Quenel, who had the most muscular-looking body of the sibko. Muscular-*looking* but, oddly, less adept at feats of strength than many of the others. "Those are yours, Falconer Ellis. All of you: Show me your best. No cowardly holding back of your blows out of misplaced respect to an officer. We do not accept ritualistic respect. That is for freeborns. We prefer only that respect due us, that we have earned. That should be clear enough, even for nestlings like you. Falconer Joanna? Falconer Ellis?"

The nine chosen members of the sibko moved closer

to each other, all of them facing Falconer Joanna nervously. About fifteen meters away, Ellis' trio was grouped similarly. Aidan felt Marthe's shoulder against his; the shorter Endo stood slightly in back of him.

"You seem to cower, eyasses," Falconer Joanna said, a pleased smile on her face. "Are you screamers, taken too soon from your nest, tender of the hood, pulling at the jesse, unable even to be at hack safely?" The terms belonged to falconry. Being at hack was the time of liberty and exploration before the bird was trained to the hunt; a jesse was the leather thong that tied a hooded bird to its block during periods of inactivity. Aidan thought the comparison uncomfortably apt for cadets and even trained warriors.

"You heard the commander. Fight, you freebirth mutants. Fight, you sib-bastards." Another low term, sometimes used when it was discovered that there were inferior strains in a sibko's genetic makeup.

Aidan looked past Joanna at the many other groups of trainees in the huge field. Some of them were now in furious activity. Some were assembling to march, others were already marching away from the landing site. In the distance he could see a brawl going on. Closer by were two groups, whose members were lying on the ground, with training officers urging them back to consciousness and mobility. The wind had died down, but the air was still bitter cold. Far away he noticed for the first time a chain of ragged mountains that looked like a line of teeth—littered, he feared, with the bodies of erstwhile trainees.

"You!" Falconer Joanna shouted, pointing to Endo. "There is no use in hiding behind your fellows. Step out, cadet!"

Endo walked around Aidan. He was obviously trembling, though it was more likely because of the frigid temperature than fear. No doubt he did feel fear, like Aidan, but it would be unsib to show it, especially to a warrior like Joanna.

Endo opened his mouth as if to speak, but Falconer Joanna's scornful glare made him think better of it. "Remember not to address me," she said softly, then, with a punch that was not at all telegraphed, she hit him in the stomach. Not just hit him, but dug her fist into his extra flesh as hard as she could while grabbing his hair and yanking his head back. She was still wearing her metal-studded falconry gloves. Recalling his own pain when Joanna had gut-punched him, Aidan winced to think how the blow must hurt Endo. "You are allowed to hit me, surat." Surat was a loathsome word, the name of a disgusting, monkey-like creature. "Hit me, surat. Hit me." Endo reared back and, grunting, attempted a roundhouse right that, if successful, would have addled Joanna's brain for a moment. But she was too quick for him. She blocked the punch and dug her fist into the exact same place on his belly. Endo's face turned red. She pushed him away. He stumbled backward, gasping for breath.

Standing straight, Falconer Joanna ceremoniously removed her gloves and casually tossed them onto the ground. "I do not need these, not against nestlings like you." She squared away, her body loose and ready. Her eyes scanned the still-standing members of the sibko, who now had edged together. Passed out, Endo was splayed out on the ground in front of them.

Suddenly Joanna ran at the group, yelling, "This is a free-for-all. Fight, you drooling fools!" She hit Bret with a forearm chop across the bridge of his nose, then she head-butted Tymm while kicking back at Orilna, making contact in a spot that might have been more painful to a male but nevertheless made Orilna double up.

"Do you still suck the metal teat, cadets?" Joanna yelled. "Fight me!"

Both Aidan and Marthe accepted the challenge. Aidan leaped at Falconer Joanna, his arms flailing as a diversionary maneuver. She brought up her arms to block the expected blow, but at the last minute, he drew his arms in, lowered his head and butted her just below the breasts. He had been aiming for her stomach, so when his head hit her at rib cage, he was momentarily stunned. Marthe, in the meantime, maneuvering from a position to Joanna's left, missed a grab at her neck but managed to get hold of her upper arm. As Marthe twisted the arm back, Joanna laughed. "Tug and tussle do not work here, whelp." With no trick, no diversion, with just a demonstration of her own strength, she brought her arm back to its former position, then—moving so quickly that

Marthe was caught by surprise—Joanna flung her body at Marthe, knocking the cadet backward with a shoulder blow that caught Marthe at the tip of her chin. As Marthe reeled back, eyes dazed, the now-recovering Aidan saw that she was definitely out of the fight. With a yell that would have frightened an ordinary person, he rushed at Falconer Joanna. The cry did not, of course, faze Joanna.

Leaping, letting out a scream that *did* scare Aidan, she sent him dizzy with a kick to his head. Around him the sibko had come to life, and as he fell, they all tried to pounce on the falconer. Reacting quickly to evade their smothering assault, she managed to make contact with her fists, elbows, knees, feet, head—all her destructive body parts dealing blows that bruised, stung, and pained, even injured, her attackers. Wading back into the melee once she was free, Joanna quickly dispatched the remaining sibkin and soon stood over a groaning, squirming mass of cadets.

She stared around her, her cruel eyes daring any of the downfallen to try again.

Aidan tried again.

He stood and rushed toward her with all the strength left in his legs. As he reached her, she brought her forearm up to ward off a weak blow that he had intended as a feint, but then he brought around his other arm slower than he wanted and she dealt him a punishing backhand right without bothering to ward off his attack. Another couple of solid punches, and Aidan was down on the ground again.

Above him, her eyes sent out the dare again.

Aidan dared.

Pulling himself to his feet, swaying from side to side, he clasped both hands together and, running forward, managed to hit Joanna on the side of her face with the joined hands. The impact seemed to surprise the falconer, who had arrogantly made no attempt to defend herself against his onslaught. She stumbled sideways, but regained her footing and turned to him, smiling. The smile was peculiar. Though her eyes retained their scornful cruelty, her smile was pleased. It seemed almost appealing. She walked toward him, the smile becoming friendly. She held out her hand.

"I see you do not like me, cadet. Good. I admire your tenacity."

With her outstretched hand, she took his and held it for a moment. Then, releasing his hand, without rearing back or giving any indication that a punch was coming, she jabbed him in the nose with her other hand, and he felt something break. She hit him again in the same place, and the pain was so bad he could not see straight—or, rather, he could see too well, in too many images. The third punch sent him back to the ground.

He looked up to see Falconer Joanna standing over him.

"Are you through yet, nestling?"

He tried to sit up, and she gently pushed him down. This time he stayed there.

"This one might test out all the way," she said to Falconer Ellis, who now stood beside her. As she spoke, she was putting on the falconer gloves, whose star-shaped studs caught some light and sparkled. She held each glove, palm side toward her, directly in front of her face as she pulled it on, grimacing as she stretched it tight. "He does not, as you saw, give up easily. Let us make his stay with us especially difficult."

Her compliments gave Aidan no pleasure. He was not sure he wanted her approval. He *was* sure he hated her.

She might have said more about him, but things blurred and he passed out.

He was probably not unconscious long. The next thing he knew, he and the others were being hauled to their feet by their now businesslike training officers.

Aidan felt around in his tunic pocket for something to wipe away the blood he tasted along his lips. He found nothing. He must be content to let the blood dry. His fellow sibkin were all standing now, looking confused and in pain.

"Well," Falconer Commander Ter Roshak said as he strolled among the sibko, "Joanna and Ellis have taught you something already. There is more to combat than your acrobatic but rather absurd struggles. A BattleMech does not move gracefully, nor is its jumping particularly acrobatic. Entertain us no longer with your morning exercises. We expect real effort from you, not ballet. Falconers, line them up and march them out."

Pushing and shoving, the falconers managed to get the sibko into two swaying but relatively even lines. Joanna saw to it that Aidan was beside her, at the head of one of the files.

"It is a long walk to your barracks. You will march every step of the way. In double-time."

Aidan could not imagine walking for long, much less marching, but as soon as Joanna gave the command, he put his left foot forward briskly, and with hatred of Joanna keeping him going, he somehow kept up with her. He had to. Whenever he did not, she kicked his nearest leg with the sharp metal toe of her boot.

At one point, just after they had joined a mass of other marching cadets, Joanna tapped him with her glove and said softly: "You are mine, cadet. You may resist and I sincerely hope you do. I will destroy you or make you the best damned MechWarrior of all these sibkos. I will probably destroy you. You will fail."

Her words angered him.

"Never," he said defiantly.

She pulled him out of line and threw him to the ground. "You are *not* to address me or any other officer. Understand?"

He had not forgotten that rule. He had chosen to answer Joanna. Without looking at her, he stood up and ran to catch up to the others, retake his place in line.

The march was long. There were times when Aidan felt such pain in his legs that he could only take one more step. Then another step after that. Every muscle in his body had discovered its own private, selfish ache and was competing with the others to be the biggest single pain of his lifetime.

He began to walk with his eyes closed, sensing direction and pace from the sibkin in front of and back of him. Finally, there was a shouted halt. The two falconers now stood in front of them, eying them with distaste. Ter Roshak had disappeared. Aidan could not remember seeing him at any time during the march. He tried to relax his body, but he could feel every bruise Joanna had left there, plus some pains that could not logically have come from her assault.

Joanna took off her gloves and hooked them in her belt. A frail-looking man in a Tech jumpsuit brought her a towel. She pulled it out of his hand roughly, even though he was offering it to her. He seemed not to mind her rudeness. Methodically she wiped away sweat from her body, first burying her face in the towel, then scraping it against the back of her neck and vigorously rubbing down her glistening arms.

She threw the towel down to the ground, where the Tech quickly picked it up and retreated. Joanna meanwhile eyed the new trainees contemptuously. For a moment her gaze stopped at Aidan and she nodded.

For years he had spent most of his time with the sibko and their sib-parents, older warriors whose combat was behind them. They were in charge of the education and training for the sibko's childhood and adolescence. The sib-parents had been tough, but the sibko had come to love them. He felt he would never feel such affection for Falconer Joanna. He was too frightened of her for that. It was the first time in his life he had felt fear of another. Looking around him, he saw his fear duplicated on his sibkin's faces, as if imprinted there, a new expression upon faces that already resembled each other.

They were assigned their barracks, a thin-walled wooden building with visible cracks through which the wind blasted. The falconers told them to get undressed and get some sleep in their assigned bunks. There would be uniforms in the morning and the beginning of training. "After tomorrow," Falconer Ellis said in his rough voice, "today's activities will seem like frolic to you."

Inside supposedly indestructible boots, Aidan's feet felt less eternal. When he released them from the footwear, arches ached, toes were bloodstained, heels showed calluses the size of pebbles. After undressing, he literally fell onto his bunk, whose thin, uncomfortable mattress stank of the fears and misery of the generations of cadets who had been, it seemed to him, condemned to this place at other times. Even with a scratchy blanket wrapped around him, he could not get warm. He wished he could go to Marthe, snuggle up to her for warmth, take her in his arms and—Aidan was asleep before he could take this comforting, if not warming, fantasy to its logical conclusion.

# 2

"**A**nd that world was named Strana Mechty by Katyusha Kerensky. The name comes from her native Russian. What does it mean, class, in our language?"

With the loud and forceful responding style that had been drummed into them since the first classroom session of their training eight months ago, the cadets of Aidan's sibko shouted, "Land of Dreams!"

Aidan sat ramrod-straight in his chair. Slumping was severely and publicly punished by Falconer Instructor Dermot, who took great glee in whipping a chalkboard pointer against the back of students' necks. Aidan chose to mouth the response while facially faking the strained-tendon, angry look that should accompany such a yell. He wondered why chanting was acceptable to Jade Falcon training officers. Even though one could not address them individually, a chanted group response was allowed. What good was the procedure if it did not give the cadets any opportunity to ask questions, to engage in the kind of give-and-take exchange that would clarify information and ideas? The cadet class seemed, after all, so much in the dark about *everything*.

At the first class session, Dermot had explained, "Intellectual questing is for the scientist caste and the teacher subcaste. Ambiguity is so much mental garbage in a warrior's mind. The mind that questions anything other than prebattle strategy, the mind that allows meaningless or extraneous considerations to interfere with bid-cunning, delays responses, therefore delays action. A passing thought might interfere slightly with the move of a thumb toward a control-board toggle, or the snap of reaction to an enemy counter-strategy, or lead to misperceiving a fellow officer's bid. Idle speculations waste time. Too much lost time and the battle is lost. To paraphrase an old Terran saying: For want of a thought, the battle is *won*. At least when the thinking intrudes on warrior instincts.''

Such views meant something to Dermot, but Aidan could not stop thinking, could not stop questioning. That had been his curse even when growing up in the sibko . . .

"Your eyes are layered,'' Marthe had said to him once when they were quite young. He could not remember what they had been doing or what had provoked the comment. He seemed to remember that they held hands while sitting on a flat hillside rock, watching their sibkin fight a mock-battle with crudely crafted wooden weapons.

"I look at your eyes, Aidan, and I always see something beneath them. Another layer that the eyes I see are hiding. Then sometimes that layer appears, and yet another layer seems to lie under that one. It is as if secrets are hiding secrets in your eyes, a whole network of deceptions and secrets in your brain that we only glimpse occasionally in your eyes.''

"I suppose that would be true of all of us.''

"No! No, it is not. No one here has eyes like yours.''

"What about your eyes, Marthe? We look alike, they say.''

"We resemble each other, true, but not in the secrets in our eyes. I have no secrets. You know that. You can see that. Come, Aidan, admit it. Look into my eyes. You see no concealment there.''

He nodded. "Yes, it is true. Your eyes are what they call open.''

"As am I. As are all of us, except you. I love you, Aidan.''

"We all love each other. That is the way of the sibko.''

"I love you beyond the way of the sibko.''

"You are talking about layers again.''

"I suppose I am.''

"Then you have secrets, too, after all.''

"I suppose I do.''

He had understood her well, had bantered with her only to avoid the subject. One of his secrets, one that he trusted was not revealed in his eyes, was that he loved

Marthe in return, unreasonably, outside the way of the sibko. He dreamed of her and of them alone together. How unsib, the others in the sibko would have said. Unsib or not, in his dreams they often no longer belonged to their sibko—or any sibko. He would never admit that to Marthe. With its implicit violation of siblaw, it might shock her too much, destroy the permissible closeness they already had.

"We can't have such feelings for one another, Marthe. The sibparents say that love, even the passing desire to be alone with *one* specific person, is a freebirth feeling."

Her face darkened momentarily, as did the visages of Aidan and others in the sibko at the mere mention of the awful word, freebirth. "I know," she said. "We are not supposed to love one another. We are supposed to love *all*."

"And we do. Do we not?"

"I suppose so. But the love for all is not the same as—"

"Do not even say it, Marthe."

And they stopped saying it, but the need that Aidan so often felt for Marthe's company, to the exclusion of the others, continued. He wondered if Marthe felt the same uneasiness at violating what was, after all, the way of the Clan.

# 3

The season had changed at least three times since they had come to Ironhold. As the cadets listened to Dermot, who was now droning on about the Exodus from the Inner Sphere, the hot, humid air was difficult to breathe. This oppressiveness, in turn, made concentrating on Dermot's dull lecture nearly impossible. Aidan felt sweat accumulating under his training uniform, a jumpsuit of rough cloth that chafed against his hot, damp skin every time he moved. He believed that the uniform, which had been issued to everyone in sizes either too small or too large, was intended as just one more adversity on the list of many calculated discomforts of warrior training. His uniform, too small when he got it, now seemed even more so. Not only had he grown a few centimeters, but had been adding muscle on muscle from the intensive physical training, long, seemingly pointless marches and drilling, and hard, demeaning labor that were part of the military routine for the cadets. The material of the uniform was being stretched thin.

He longed for a larger uniform, or at least an airier one. Right now he did not know which was the worse, listening to Dermot or his uniform's chafing, a sensation just marginally more pleasant than rolling around naked on a bed of pumice.

Dermot was offering his regular catechism on Clan history, beginning with General Aleksandr Kerensky's carefully planned Exodus from the corrupt and quarreling star empires of the Inner Sphere. Unable to restore the Star League as a political entity, he had led his people to this new sector of the galaxy where, after overcoming many hardships and uprisings, he had set up his new government on the planets of Arcadia, Babylon, Circe, Dagda, and Eden. (Aidan had been hearing this ancient history from, it seemed, his cradle days, and perhaps even since the canister, the sibko's slang term for the artificial womb from which he and all his siblings had been born.) After the Exodus, it had been necessary to conduct a shakedown of the forces. Societies did not survive on the skills of warriors alone, so it became necessary to relocate three-quarters of the Regular Army and Navy personnel. Eventually this demobilization led to the formation of the castes, as new skills had to be learned and new duties assumed by the warriors without portfolio who had been judged not quite good enough to remain in the general's service.

The demobilization, it turned out, was not simple. Characteristics essential to warriors did not always blend in smoothly with normal society. Some warriors became yojimbos, a word whose origin was buried in past history. The yojimbo's escapades on several Clan planets became nettlesome. Many became outlaws, roaming the countryside looking for any kind of work that would make use of skills no longer really in demand. Occasionally someone might hire them to serve in a private army, and a few employers had problems that only a bit of muscle and military expertise could solve.

It was a hard time, the time of the yojimbo, a transition period between the end of the Exodus and the beginning of the Clans. Restlessness and rootlessness, disorientation caused by the hardships of the new worlds and the yearning for the old worlds, led to individualism. If not for for the wisdom of Nicholas Kerensky, this dangerous trend could have created political divisions among the settlement worlds that would have been as destructive and violent as those that had disintegrated the Star League into the quibbling and chaotic dominions of the Inner Sphere.

Dermot's drone rested heavily on the oppressive air as he described how the Clan worlds were expanded into a nearby group of stars called the globular cluster. It must have been an exhilarating time for those who were there, but Aidan, at this remote distance in time, could not concentrate on the dry history of it all. He wanted stories, not a recitation of facts. Stories of heroes and yo-jimbos, warriors and villains.

They had been very young. It was in the time when the sibko was still full, before the first eliminations of its members through failed tests, lost trials. They were all young hawks then, nestlings at hack but not willing to fly too far away from each other, much less the sibparents. One of the cadre of sibparents in charge at that time was named Glynn. She was a tall woman, one against whom Aidan and Marthe were later to measure their own considerable height. They would become taller than Glynn, but not until they were well into their adolescence. By then, Glynn, too soon dead, was no longer around to be measured against.

Glynn had wanted to be a warrior but had failed in the middle training stages. Everyone in the sibko adored her and thought her the loveliest person ever created. Later they saw that she was not beautiful, but merely pleasant-looking, with a bland face that was too gaunt and wonderful yellow hair that was too stringy. They made up stories in which she defeated formidable, firebreathing monsters and slaughtered hordes of barbarians.

Aidan sat beside Marthe. Even at that early time, barely out of the toddler stage, they were friends. The child Aidan had never seen a more beautiful face than Marthe's.

"Mifoon faced his adversaries, who were lined against him across the wide boulevard," Glynn was saying. This story was one of the many she knew about the legendary yojimbos. Whatever the tale, the protagonist always had the strange, almost absurd name of Mifoon.

"In the line of villains, Mifoon recognized at least four who had once been of the noble yojimbo caste." The sibko knew there had been no caste system at the time of the yojimbos, but they allowed her the fancy because she equated the wandering fighters with warriors, as if they had been precursors of the Clan system rather than aimless, out-of-work warriors, disenfranchised by Kerensky edict.

"With his right hand holding the whip the Ice Queen had given him and brandishing Toshiro with the other"— Toshiro was the name of Mifoon's magical sword, awarded him for valor by General Kerensky, who had ordered him to rid the land of the new villainy—"Mifoon screamed the falcon cry and rushed down the boulevard toward his antagonists who, in turn, were speeding toward him." (Glynn also gave Mifoon characteristics suggesting he was a precursor of the Jade Falcons, and therefore someone extra special.)

"First he faced the wicked merchant Canfield, who directed the barrel of a laser pistol toward Mifoon, his finger closing on the trigger. Quickly Mifoon released Toshiro. The sword, true to its mark, sailed toward Canfield. The merchant could not get out of the way and Toshiro sailed into his chest, sending blood flying out and along its blade." (The children oohed and aahed, as they always did when the hero disposed of a villain. They also thrilled at the kinetic movement with which Glynn punctuated her stories, holding a hand to her chest to "feel" the sword implanted there, flying with her arm on its return to Mifoon.)

"Canfield fell and the sword returned to Mifoon's hand, the blood on it magically dissolving. Mifoon, out of the corner of his eye, saw the yojimbo Pablo rushing at him, his eyes filled with rage at how Mifoon had killed his lover Susan in the moonlight raid on Brender Camp." (Glynn's eyes suddenly duplicated her hero's fearsome rage.) "Mifoon knew he could not bring his sword around to be used effectively on Pablo, so he flicked the Ice Queen's whip, with its heat-guidance tip, at the on-rushing adversary. Of course it caught Pablo in the neck, first bouncing off it, then wrapping itself tightly around his neck and choking him to death." (Glynn's eyes bulged at the feel of an imaginary whip on her own neck; she seemed to expire as the whip tightened, then her eyes shot open, sending some of the children reeling backward in fright.) "Stepping over the body of Pablo, jerking the whip off the dead man's neck, Mifoon now turned to greet the attack of the evil—"

"Glynn!" It was the voice of sibparent group leader Gonn, who often destroyed her stories with his uncanny ability to find the secret place where they had gathered, then interrupting at an especially crucial part. "Telling your lies again?"

Suddenly the formidable Glynn seemed to shrink, her

shoulders sliding in as if on runners, her good posture turning into a postulant's supplication. "They are not lies," she said in a small voice. "They are stories."

Gonn scoffed. "Stories are lies. It is demonstrable, you know that. If you fill the sponges in their heads with unsubstantiated legends about roving malcontents, they could become malcontents themselves. That is not the way of the sibko, *quiaff?*"

"Aff," she responded weakly. "Not the sibko's way."

"Or the way of the Clan, *quiaff?*"

"Aff. Not the Clan."

"Truth unites us, *quiaff?*"

"Aff. United by truth. Truth the binder of belief."

"Very good. Belief the underpinnings of truth, the destroyer of pallid myth."

As they went through their ritual, Aidan—and perhaps the others—grew restless. He wanted more story. He wanted to know what had happened to Mifoon. That might not be the way of the sibko, or the way of the Clan, but it was the way of Aidan. . . .

# 4

Dermot, who read poetry in a halting voice that tended to obscure the import of the words, was now reciting a long segment from *The Remembrance,* the wonderful saga whose verses, simple on the page but resounding when recited by one who could convey the epic sweep of it (anybody but Dermot), described the founding of the Clans, how Nicholas Kerensky had restructured society after planets had been ravaged by those who thought land equated with power.

Nicholas Kerensky took over his newly won dominion armed with a plan to forge a new society out of the disparate populations that made up the Exodus survivors. By mining the resources of its own diversity and channeling the energies of its warlike inclinations, the reborn society would unify his people into a force capable of achieving his greatest dream—a return to the inner Sphere to reestablish the Star League, the form of government that had once existed there. Everything directly connected to the Inner Sphere was suddenly banned, while nationalistic ties to the past were discouraged.

The Clans themselves had their origins earlier, during Nicholas' exile on Strana Mechty, when he had reorganized his armies into twenty groups, or clans, of forty warriors each. Within each clan, Nicholas decreed smaller units, what another age would have called platoons. Each of these sub-units was composed of five warriors and was eventually termed a "Star," the image presumably based on the conventional five points in the usual star symbol. Later, when the Clans had grown to their present massive proportions, the star imagery was continued and much of the organization was still based on quintuple segments.

The reorganization of society involved resettling outsiders into the various clans, a move that tended to further destroy nationalistic leanings. (Dermot's voice was itself resettling down into its deepest, most boring register, the voice whose vibrations Aidan seemed to feel so deeply through his body that they gave him back pain).

As the class recited the names of the Clans in unison and in precisely clipped words, Aidan's thoughts drifted off again, even as he stayed right in rhythm with his classmates . . .

Only a few days before the sibko had left for the training cycle, Aidan and Marthe had gone grave visiting. First, they went to the grave of Warhawk, whom Aidan had buried just outside the cemetery fence, then marked with a stanchion so that he could always find the site again. Warhawk's death had been unfortunate, the result of a malicious member of another sibko who thought he could bring honor to his own group by flinging a stone at the falcon. If Warhawk had not lost the sight in her right eye in a brutal skirmish with a renegade hawk, she might have seen the stone coming and executed one of her incredibly beautiful swooping arcs away from it. But the shot had been true, and Aidan watched her seem to come to an abrupt stop in the air, then drop to the ground like a lead weight. When he found her, her body still, her neck twisted and seemingly stretched, he had gone into a rage, found Warhawk's murderer, and nearly sent him to his own grave. For a while, an unpleasant feeling between the two sibkos led to many skirmishes (which Aidan's sibko usually won, led by his fierce charges, his punishing blows), but the conflict ended abruptly when the boy who had killed Warhawk was himself slain in a fight within his own sibko.

Now, he found, it was difficult to tell exactly where Warhawk lay beneath the ground. The mark was still on the stanchion, but it seemed to Aidan that something about the ground had changed, that in some way its configurations had shifted or that the way he remembered them had altered. Now there was grass where none had previously been, and that complicated his search even more. He wanted to place his feet along the sides of the burial site, a silly ritual that he always performed during each visit to Warhawk, but this time it was impossible. As he stared at the spot where the grave might be, he fingered the edge of his leather vest at the place where Warhawk had often bit and nibbled. Bite marks were still there, rough and frayed to Aidan's touch.

"Do not be sad," Marthe advised. "We are leaving here soon and may never come back. If we do, the fence may even be gone or rearranged to suit new dimensions of the graveyard. We lose boundaries all the time, *quiaff?*"

Next they went into the cemetery and searched out Glynn's grave. Dav, the most artistic member in the sibko, had carved out a fighting sword on top of the grave marker, so it was easy to locate. In the shelter of a bushy tree, the sword seemed to thrust out of the ground, as if the corpse beneath was holding onto the hilt from inside the tomb. The shadows cast by the tree created the illusion of fresh bloodstains along the blade.

Standing silently by the grave, Aidan thought of Glynn's wasted death. One day a roving band of bandits had come too near the sibko, which was undergoing extended wilderness-survival training, camped in some geodesic domes abandoned by another sibko whose members had gone on to the next stage of their training. Gonn, an insecure military strategist at best, had panicked and set up a perimeter defense outside the encampment. It was clear to Aidan that the bandits might have passed them by if Gonn had not drawn their attention.

Aidan remembered lying on the ground, his hand tightly clutching the low-powered laser pistol that had become standard issue for the sibko after its tenth birthnoting. It could not kill, but it could cause extreme discomfort, as Aidan learned when Peri, the sneaky little runt of the siblitter, had shot him during a mock infantry exercise. The beam caught Aidan in the neck, sending a steady pain through it that was worse than any headache or muscle spasm he had ever endured. The pain made his eyes tear up and he fell to the ground. Peri, fearful that her toy had been set too high, ran over to him. When she saw that he was still alive, she laughed triumphantly. That was Peri's way; she exulted in her victories and let her victims know that she was happy to have defeated them.

In spite of his pain, Aidan had grabbed Peri about her legs, tipped her over, and disarmed her of the toy laser pistol, which he then held to her head. At that moment he had wanted to give her a headache the equal of the pain she had inflicted upon him. Fairness won out, however. Aidan accepted the skirmish victory as his due, sending the now-frowning Peri back to the assembling area with other defeated child-warriors, all waiting for their next turn in the battle game.

Aidan watched the bandits come toward the entrenched sibko. He could hardly make out the features of their faces, so begrimed were they with the dirt of the road that it looked as though they'd been wallowing in mud. Their clothes were mostly old and ripped, though here and there a bandit wore relatively clean, new-looking garments, probably booty from their most recent raid. The hair of the man at the head of the pack was tightly wrapped in a trio of short pigtails that bounced against his forehead with each step. Three pigtails identified him as the antikhan, a title that marked his rebellion against the warrior caste (he had no doubt been a disgraced warrior or failed warrior cadet). The word itself showed contempt for the rigid political structure of the Clans, each of whose leaders was called a khan, while the leader of all the Clans was given the exalted title of ilKhan.

Each member of the attacking horde seemed to grow in size as he or she came nearer. It was an optical illusion, Aidan knew, but the front ranks of the bandits were nevertheless populated by bulky, thick-muscles brutes who looked like warrior caste flush-outs.

Aidan, remembering Glynn's latest Mifoon adventure, took aim at the bandit leader's forehead and waited for him to get as close as possible before firing. Sibparent Gonn, who was in charge of weaponry training, had told Aidan that his main flaw as a marksman was that he was always the most eager to fire and most ready to fight in the entire sibko. Therefore, Gonn said, he should train himself to use proper caution. Aidan was now trying to be cautious, while his finger longed to pull the trigger and blast the bandit leader between the eyes. (According to Gonn, Aidan was one of the two or three best shots in the sibko, too).

He would have fired, and he would have stunned the leader and perhaps averted the attack if it were not for Glynn. No one ever had a clear notion of why she did it, though Gonn would later say the fanciful tales she told had chipped away too much battle armor from her mind, and that she probably thought she was some roving yojimbo out to save the local community from ravagers.

At any rate, Glynn marched past the line of sibko-defenders. With her height, she seemed like a giant stepping over ordinary people, especially with all the members of the sibko prone and looking up at her with awe. As though her long legs propelled her with a life of their own, she headed right for the advancing horde, which came to a halt at a signal from the tri-pigtailed leader.

The leader watched Glynn's approach, no doubt noting that the only weapon at her disposal was a sheathed sword that bounced rhythmically against her thigh just as his pigtails had danced against his forehead. He smiled, revealing surprisingly white teeth. With the rest of his face obscured by dirt and grime, the smile seemed to exist on its own, almost as if it floated in front of his face, an eerie smile without a link to anything else.

A few steps in front of the leader, Glynn stopped and said something to him. Her words did not carry back to the sibko, most of whose members now stood and, defying Gonn's cautioning, had begun to move toward the bandits. While not losing sight of Glynn and the bandit leader, Aidan chose one of the bandits, a surly-looking, stocky, bearded man on the right flank, as his quarry if a battle erupted.

The bandit leader's killing move was nearly undetectable. His right hand had rested in front of a scruffy vest, quite casually, then suddenly he had drawn a knife from somewhere in his clothing and raked it across Glynn's neck. Aidan got a sense of some blood spurting as Glynn fell, but by then his rage had taken over and he rushed toward the stocky bandit he had selected. As he came close, he realized he could get a shot at the bandit with his pistol, but he also knew he did not want that. It would be too easy. For his own sense of revenge, he had to make the man suffer.

The bandit came at him. He, too, had found a knife somewhere on his clothing and was brandishing it like a tiny sword. Knife or sword, no conventional weapon could frighten Aidan. In their hand-to-hand combat training lessons, he and the other sibko members had been well-drilled to respect a weapon but not to fear it.

Switching the pistol to his left hand, Aidan used it to deflect the downward arc of the bandit's knife. Before his adversary could recover, he grabbed the man's wrist with hands whose muscles had been strengthened by long calisthenic drills supervised by sibparent Gonn. Aidan had squeezed resilient materials, performed a dozen types of exercise ritual, hardened the skin in martial-arts demonstrations. As a result, he—like the others in the sibko— could do wonders with just bare hands. Aidan could feel the bandit's wrist break as he snapped it backward violently. The knife fell out of the man's hand. Kneeing the stocky man in the stomach and doubling him over, Aidan quickly snatched the knife off the ground and waited patiently for the man to straighten up. It would have been too easy to plunge the knife into the bandit's back. That would have been too much like a proper Clan death, the noble demise of a warrior who, even though a member of the bandit caste, could die in battle. But if the man were to die, there must be shame attached to it, especially after the bandit leader's almost casual slaying of Glynn.

As the bandit straightened up, he made a quick lunge at Aidan, who neatly sidestepped the man, sending him plunging forward and down, his face in the dirt. Ironically, it was Glynn who had drilled him in this very same battle-footwork.

Aidan stepped backward. He sensed, out the corner of his eye, a movement toward him. Another bandit, a short, thick-legged woman with fire in her eyes, raced toward him. Her fighting skills were no better than those of the man on the ground, and Aidan was able to strike the side of her head with the barrel of his pistol. He could have stabbed her, but he was saving the bandit's knife for its owner. She collapsed and he saw, as the fire in her eyes went out, that she would be at least momentarily unconscious.

Turning back to the bandit, he saw the man trying to

heave his bulk upward. With no further reason to toy with him, Aidan kicked him in the side, sending him back to the ground. Assuming the look of contempt taught him by Gonn, he forced the bandit to roll over with further kicks, then stared into the man's now-frightened eyes. Aidan was revolted by the man's look of fear. Showing such emotion had no doubt contributed to this man's failure as a warrior, if indeed this particular freebirth had ever been a warrior.

Aidan did not care to savor the act of killing. It was necessary but repulsive to him. Quickly, he brought the bandit's knife down toward his face. The man tried to turn his head sideways, but Aidan knocked it back with his pistol, then he plunged the knife into the victim's open mouth, forcing it deep. The bandit's eyes widened in pain. Blood followed the knife blade out of the man's mouth, then—watching the horror in the dying man's eyes—Aidan finished him off. With the same casual, almost indifferent motion the bandit leader had used on Glynn, Aidan slit his throat.

Looking around him, Aidan saw that the battle was over and that they had won it. The survivors among the outlaw band were running from them, and the bodies of the less lucky were strewn about the improvised battlefield. Like Aidan, other members of the sibko were standing and surveying the damage they had done. Many of them hovered over the corpse of the bandit leader, who had more than the requisite wounds in his body to bring about an agonizing death.

For a moment, he saw the scene as it might have looked from the viewpoint of the enemy. The bandits had lost a fight with a raging horde of *children*. That would damage the pride of the survivors. It was the first battle, other than planned ceremonial skirmishes, that Aidan's sibko had ever won. And the cost of it was Glynn's death.

When Aidan arrived at the side of Glynn's corpse, where the sibko was assembling, his body was still trembling and his stomach still bouncing around inside his body from the exhilaration and disgust of his first killing. Looking at Gonn, he saw that lines of tears ran out of the corners of Gonn's eyes. Aidan could not tell whether they were angry or sad tears. No one ever could, or did, know what went on in the group leader's mind.

LAUBENSTEIN·91

Their other sibparents had seen to it that Glynn was given a proper ceremonial funeral, marked with a few rituals that normally belonged to those who had attained warrior status. After the funeral, Gonn was severely reprimanded and removed from command over the sibko for having lost control of it at a key moment, even though the sibko itself was praised for its bravery. He was demoted to menial tasks, which he did desultorily. Then, one day, Gonn drowned in a river alongside which the sibko was camped. Some wondered if he had committed suicide, although direct suicide was rare in the Clans. Few clansmen or women ever chose to kill themselves, except through recklessness in battle.

Though Aidan had despised Gonn for his cowardice against the bandits, he nevertheless felt some grief upon hearing of the man's death. A few years earlier, a different kind of Gonn had taken Aidan under his wing—under his falcon wing, a catchphrase he used often—and helped with the training of Warhawk.

One day Gonn had found Aidan trying to pull some broken feathers from Warhawk's wing. The falcon had been in a mysterious fight somewhere, apparently with a bird nearly as tough as she, and she had returned from the fray much the worse for wear. Many feathers were tattered, with others severely damaged and attached by only a few remaining strands of quill.

"Silly child," Gonn had said. "Do not pull out feathers that way, no matter what shape they are in. Do you not know that when they are taken completely out, you can be sure that they will not grow again at next molting, and perhaps at no future molting?"

"No, sir. I did not know that. I—"

"None of your excuses. Warriors do not try to find reasons for their failures. That is not the way of the Clans." The way of the Clans, another catchphrase, was one all the sibparents used. "As you do in so many other ways, you show yourself not ready even to imagine yourself a warrior. I doubt that you will go that far, for all your fancy achievements. And you will not answer now, *quineg?*"

"Neg."

"Now here I will show you what to do. It is called imping."

Gonn took Aidan, who held and soothed Warhawk, to his quarters, at that time in their existence a hastily put-together shack, whose sides and roof were made of the durable caldo leaf, which grew abundantly on trees in that particular part of Circe. The shack was like all the places Gonn had ever lived, cluttered and strewn with debris from his life. Using a set of needles that he kept in the kit-bag that always hung from his belt, he selected some three-sided needles of various sizes. Reaching into a box under a strange-looking work-desk cluttered with tools whose uses Aidan could not begin to imagine, Gonn took out a spray of falcon and hawk feathers. He told Aidan he had saved them from the molt of many of the damned birds that the sibko kept.

Taking the first needle and holding it up to the light streaming in from the open doorway, Gonn examined it closely, then measured the old feather against it. He told Aidan they would match old feathers with Warhawk's real feathers. As Aidan clutched Warhawk firmly but gently, Gonn went to work on the bird. With the delicate strokes of a surgeon, working the knife slowly, he cut away the feather at the point where the fracture occurred, then on the remaining section he fashioned an oblique edge. Leaning away from Warhawk, he took the old feather and sliced its edge off. With nimble fingers, he checked to see that the edges of the true feather and the old feather fit together neatly and that the remade feather would be about the same length as those around it. Inserting the needle into Warhawk's real feather, he fastened the old one to it, gently pushing the false feather onto the real one until the break between them was hardly noticeable. Satisfied with his handiwork, he leaned back and said:

"There. That will suffice until Warhawk's next molting. The needle is treated so that it will attach to the inside of each feather and hold it securely. Now, let's do some of the others."

Aidan and Gonn worked together for several hours. It was the only time when Gonn had seemed even remotely human to Aidan. His grave lay somewhere in the graveyard, but Aidan and Marthe refused to visit it.

For three years afterward, Aidan dreamed of the man he had killed in battle. Variations on the act made the dreams even more frightening than the actual experience.

In some dreams, the victim fought better and was not so easily killed. In the ones from which Aidan woke up in a cold sweat, the victim was about to win.

The other graves he and Marthe searched for and found that day were of the sibko's dead, the ones who had died in trials or been the victims of disease or accident. These were few, however. Most of the now-absent members of the sibko had simply failed tests and been sent to other areas where they were integrated into other castes. No one ever really lost face in Clan society. Any momentary shame was made up for by assuming a useful life in another caste.

Now there would be shame, Aidan thought, as he tuned back in to Dermot again. It is a bad thing to have to leave a sibko before training, but it was a lifelong embarrassment to be dismissed from warrior training. True, one could join a new caste like the earlier flush-outs from sibko training, but the knowledge would always remain that one had been on the verge of becoming a warrior, the highest caste of all. People who talked to you, however cheerfully and respectfully, would never quite be able to forget that you had suffered the ultimate ignominy, the removal from warrior status. The few failed warriors whom Aidan had met while growing up had seemed to be exoskeletons covering no body, as if the inability to be warriors on the outside had dried up the inner self and turned it to dust. These individuals performed their caste roles well enough, even admirably, but something was always missing. Aidan did not want that kind of life. He could *only* be a warrior.

Dermot was describing the controlled breeding program, telling how the exalted Nicholas had seen the need to go beyond the normal birthrate to quickly create a race of the finest warriors. All the strife had severely depopulated the Clan worlds, and drastic action was necessary. Therefore, Nicholas had created the systematic eugenics program by which the 800 warriors in the Clans donated genetic materials to a type of baby factory that the scientists euphemistically called "Homes." These Homes specialized in combining the best traits from individual genes in the sperm and ova to make children who, it was hoped, would become warriors with the skills of their donors and without the negative characteristics that had caused so much strife and rebellion among the early settlers of the Clan planets. Raised in artificial wombs, each generation would, with the process of testing and retesting, become even freer of defects and more able than the generation before it.

With each Clan raising children assigned to sibling companies, or sibkos, the population growth that Nicholas envisioned began occurring quickly and in exponential fashion. Though not everyone in a sibko actually made it through the years of grueling tests to become a warrior, and some died trying, those who were assigned elsewhere made important contributions to the rest of society. As strong leaders and superintelligent citizens, they tended to take control of other castes. It was axiomatic that a trueborn was more likely to succeed in Clan society than a freeborn.

Aidan could barely keep up with the chanting responses that Dermot required. He was thinking of the trueborn-freeborn conflicts throughout society on the various settled planets. Out there, he had heard, where the life was nonwarrior and nonsibko, there had been some blemishes on the visage of Nicholas Kerensky's idealized society. For the most part, the basic divisions of society, trueborn/freeborn, the hierarchy of castes, service castes/worker castes, scientist caste/all other castes except warrior, warrior and everybody else, were maintained. Some planets were run so well that, it was said, very little trouble occurred. Critics of the social structure, and there were many, especially among the educated class who stayed on at universities, complained about the urge toward conformity that the caste system seemed to foster routinely and the lack of freedom for the individual. However, nobody ever listened to anyone in the teacher class, and so their ideas were merely additions to the clash of theories and philosophies that interested no one but the academics.

Dermot's current drone was on the subject of the codex, the meticulous record of a warrior's life from his first successful test to the day he died in a cockpit or in some other useful social role. It was in the analysis of the codex that scientists found genetic histories so worthwhile that the individual warrior's genetic materials might be retained for the gene pools.

"That is your goal," Dermot was saying, as he had said so often before, "the achievement of the ultimate honor. Imagine your deeds living on in history—that is, like a book, and like a book, fading with time. But being passed on genetically to the next generation. That is a taste of eternity, your line forever in the great Jade Falcon annals."

Aidan wanted to ask what in the name of the venerable Nicholas were the Jade Falcon annals. He had never seen any. There were no texts that bore that title. He wanted to ask Dermot that question and many others, but he would be punished for asking any question directly. Even when one used the proper channels, writing a set of questions at the end of written work, the instructors usually accused them of overwhelming stupidity.

Dermot was beginning to rub his hands together, usually a sign that he was close to the end of his lecture. Aidan's body tensed, ready to leave the stuffy classroom and get to some physical training. He did not like to sit still for so long.

Suddenly a hand grabbed him by the back of his neck. He did not need to squirm around to see whose. Only Falconer Joanna ever seized a neck like that and squeezed so hard with the tips of her fingers, and usually she did it to Aidan. Why she had taken such a dislike to him, he was not sure, but at times he would have preferred to crawl under and be crushed by the giant foot of a 'Mech than have anything to do with her.

# 5

"**I** see you are not listening," Joanna said, her voice a hissing whisper. "You pretend, but your mind is elsewhere. You may speak to me on this, eyas. I am right, *quiaff?*"

"Aff," Aidan just barely squeaked out, his throat suddenly contracting to its smallest possible dimensions.

"Come with me."

Her hand still tightly on his neck, Joanna led him out of the classroom. His sibkin watched passively, as they had to. General orders decreed that they must show neither approval nor disapproval of any disciplinary action from a training officer. As Dermot had explained in one of his few plain-spoken observations, in the middle of a battle there was little point in registering emotion because a warrior already had enough to do. Aidan did not have to look back to know that Dermot would nod at the class and they would follow Joanna and Aidan outside. They were all going to the "Circle of Equals," the place where falconers settled disputes among themselves and distributed in-camp punishment to their charges.

Releasing her grip on his neck, Joanna shoved him violently over the row of stakes that marked the rim of the circle, then—her stride long and graceful—she walked in after him.

He was supposed to feel terror, he knew. But in eight months of training, Joanna, Ellis, and the specialist-falconers had all had their shot at him and, for that matter, everyone in the sibko. Any mistake, however trivial, was worth a blow to the midsection. Any talking out of turn was excuse for a cuff to the back of the head. Any major stupidity or minor rebellion was worth a thrashing in the Circle of Equals.

In the Circle a cadet could hit back at a falconer, could even speak to the officer. However, the cadet had to be prepared to accept the consequences of any utterance. Aidan, in all the times he had been there, with all the beatings he had endured from people who were, after all, more skilled in all phases of combat than he, had never spoken a word to the aggressor. He would not give Joanna and her fellow officers that satisfaction.

For warriors, each battle in the Circle was considered to be an "honor duel," a fight similar to a Trial of Position, the major ritual by which warriors won bloodnames and cadets made their final test to graduate to warrior status. Yet, in the training environment, the name Circle of Equals seemed a misnomer, a cruel joke. No cadet in Aidan's sibko had gone into the circle as an equal. Instead they were victims, the targets of old warriors who desperately needed to keep their aggressive skills honed.

He was certain Joanna was not in the least disturbed about classroom inattention. She had seized him as an excuse to take out some fierce inner rage on someone. Unfortunately, Aidan was her most frequent choice for that job. Ever since he had defied her that first day, she had kept at him, haranguing him, rousting him out of bed at night to perform irrelevant guard duty, finding a new insult for him every day, calling him the worst names, singling him out for punishment at the slightest and sometimes imagined infraction, favoring him with her favorite insult, calling him "filth." Though anyone might draw the name from her lips, Aidan was awarded it on a regular basis.

It had rained the night before and his boots seemed to sink into the muddy ground, as though it were a quicksand ready to swallow him up after he suffered the ignominy of defeat at Joanna's hands. No, he thought, it was not right to think that way. It was not the Clan way to envision *defeat* in any battle. Perhaps, though, it was the cadet way. From the time they fell out of their bunks in the morning until the time they were pushed back into the barracks late at night, cadets were made to feel low and inferior. Joanna and the others continually harped on the fact that only a few of them would make it to the final test, the Trial of Position that could win them promotion to warrior status and earn them a specific rank according to how successful their trial was.

Joanna stared at him balefully for a long time, displaying contempt like her own personal banner. Then she abruptly turned and walked back to the rim, where Ellis awaited her with a bundle in his arms. Taking the bundle from him, she lay it on the ground. It was wrapped in heavy brocaded cloth whose surface depicted images of swooping falcons in bright colors and stark design. To underline the sacredness of the intriguing package, Joanna began to unwrap it with slow, deliberate motions, as if according to an ancient rite. When the corners of the cloth lay flat to the ground, Aidan still could not perceive the contents. Looking up at Ellis and receiving a nod from him, Joanna respectfully lifted two identical objects from the cloth and held them gingerly in her arms.

The rest of the sibko had left the classroom, and with Dermot hovering nervously behind them and moving around the diameter of the circle, they watched the central actions intently. Aidan spotted Marthe staring only at him, her eyes so cool that, with the empathy they shared, he could easily see her anxiety.

Joanna stood up. Approaching Aidan, she held the pair of objects over her head, yelling to the crowd, "You may have seen whips before, children, but none like these." She cracked both whips, and their sound was explosive. "These thongs are of the toughest leather and their handles are perfectly balanced. Not only that, but each is equipped with a guidance system that, like a missile, finds its target, even when your arm is so weakened that you can only flick out the whip feebly. A useful personal weapon when you are faced with survival on a backwater planet or when your 'Mech is down and the enemy is closing in on you. Like so." She leaned down close to the ground and, with no perceptible wrist or arm movement, sent the whip thong flying toward Aidan's feet. Before he could move out of its way, it had wrapped around both ankles and flipped him over. He landed on the ground with some impact, and the pain of it surged up his spine. Some of the members of the sibko laughed, but it was not mocking laughter, it was a laugh of relief at not being the victim of the demonstration. At one time or another, each one had been knocked over by some attack or other by a training officer, and they did not at all mind watching it happen to someone else. (More than once Aidan had wondered whether the tactics of their trainers were not intended to strike at the sibko's closeness, to dislodge them from long-held loyalties.)

As Aidan sat up, the whip thong still wrapped around his legs, he saw the mix of terrible emotions that had come onto the faces of his sibkin. Bret's look was scornful, a judgment on Aidan's penchant for getting into trouble. Peri's was mocking, an I-hope-you-really-get-it-this-time kind of look. Endo was smug, probably thinking that he was punished in the Circle much less than Aidan or any of the others. Orilna was more withdrawn, but she already had poised her body, as she often did, into a battle pose. She would, while standing still, imitate the bodily moves of Joanna, whom she admired beyond logic. Freda, who drew punishment almost as much as Aidan, was already grimacing, ready to absorb all the pain empathically. Only Marthe's face showed much concern for Aidan's plight. She hated Falconer Joanna almost as much as he did.

Behind the agitated group, Falconer Commander Ter Roshak stood impassively, as he usually did. He rarely participated in training but frequently observed it. Although he usually did not speak to cadets, it was said that he called in the training officers each night and gave them trenchant critical lectures laced with scorn and obscenity. Every once in a while during the training period, Aidan had looked up to see Ter Roshak staring piercingly at him, a suggestion of anger in his eyes. His strange face often seemed to take on different looks, different aspects, as mountainsides did during the changing light of day.

As Joanna pressed a button on the handle of her whip, the thongs were abruptly released from Aidan's ankles. They glided back toward Joanna, who was clearly guiding their flight. At the end of the trip, the thong straightened and slid back into the handle. "A beautiful hurting machine, eh, class? Repeat the words after me. A beautiful hurting machine."

"A BEAUTIFUL HURTING MACHINE."

"If you think kill, you will kill."

"IF WE THINK KILL, WE WILL KILL."

"If you have a boot, you crush your enemy."

"IF WE HAVE A BOOT, WE CRUSH OUR ENEMY."

"If you have a hand, you strangle your enemy."

"IF WE HAVE A HAND, WE STRANGLE OUR ENEMY."

"If you have a club, you bludgeon your attacker."

"IF WE HAVE A CLUB, WE BLUDGEON THE ATTACKER."

"If you have a knife, you stab your foe."

"IF WE HAVE A KNIFE, WE STAB OUR FOE."

"If you have a gun, you shoot it."

"IF WE HAVE A GUN, WE SHOOT IT."

"If you have a tank, you roll it over the opposing ranks."

"IF WE HAVE A TANK, WE ROLL IT OVER THE OPPOSING RANKS."

"If you have an aerofighter, you bomb them."

"IF WE HAVE AN AEROFIGHTER, WE BOMB THEM."

"If you have a 'Mech, you win."

"IF WE HAVE A 'MECH, WE WIN."

"You are always the victor."

"WE ARE ALWAYS THE VICTOR."

"When the blood is spilled, the bloodname is earned."

"WHEN THE BLOOD IS SPILLED, THE BLOODNAME IS EARNED."

"We are the Clan."

"WE ARE THE CLAN."

At the end she held the pair of whips high over her head, harsh beams of light coming off the metal studs in her falconer gloves, and Aidan was certain that her voice made the outer walls of the school building shake. If not for his intense control over his physical body, it would certainly have made him tremble.

But he no longer feared Falconer Joanna. At first he had, but each insult, each beating, cut down fear rather than increased it. Ter Roshak, on the other hand—Ter Roshak, who had never addressed Aidan, for all the times he had stared at him—was for Aidan an object of continual fear who even terrorized his dreams.

Turning toward Aidan, who now stood, Joanna tossed him one of the whips. She purposely made the arc so that it would fall just short of Aidan's easy reach. But he was used to her devious ways and instinctively took a step forward. With an awkward lunge that almost made him lose his balance and fall, he caught the whip by its handle. Surprised by how light it felt, he quickly learned how to position his fingers, with his thumb locating the simple controls. Setting his face in a proud grimace, he pressed the button that released the thong and watched it fly upward, toward the sky, the line of it sure, its graceful arcing a pleasure to watch. Aidan felt a slight vibration in the handle and heard its quiet hum. Flicking his wrist and making the whip snap, he felt as if he had been using this weapon for ages. Yet, it was the first time he had held a whip of any kind.

"Look toward me, filth."

The haziness of the air around them, which made the sun seem to fill the sky, made Joanna indistinct. Her body had no clear outline, her features the vagueness of an unfinished portrait. But the whip she was now raising was as detailed as a technical drawing in a manual. Aidam almost expected to find lines leading away from it to outlined boxes containing sentences of technical explanatory detail.

Joanna's arm barely moved as she flicked her wrist and sent the thong of the whip flying toward him. It came so fast that he scarcely felt its physical contact as it grazed against his cheek. It stung terribly, but he used his best resources of control to keep his face from displaying any reaction. Touching his face with the back of his hand, he felt the small cut. When he looked at the hand, he saw a trace of blood along his knuckles. Bret, who hated the sight of blood, might have blanched if similarly cut, but Aidan allowed his mouth to form a pleased smile.

"You do a good imitation of a piece of animated garden statuary, filth. Will you fight or are you the classic coward portrayed by those monuments?"

Aidan shrugged. The shrug was a calculated insult, a wordless response to Joanna's words. Any hint of defiance infuriated her. She flicked out the weapon again, but this time Aidan was prepared. Acting instinctively, he brought up his whip, tabbed the button and allowed

the thong to entangle with Joanna's and divert it away
from its target, apparently the middle of his body. She
cursed under her breath and tugged the whip backward.
Because her whip was tied up with Aidan's, she was almost able to yank Aidan's whip out of his grip, but he,
gaining quickly in knowledge of the whip's controls, released its contact with Joanna's and drew it back toward
him. It settled about his feet in a symmetrical coil. There
was no time to take another moment to learn, Aidan realized. He must attack before she did, even if he was
unsure how to manipulate the weapon. Drawing up the
handle so that it was virtually aimed at Joanna, he pressed
the button while thrusting forward. The whip thong sailed
across the gap between them. Though slightly overshot
and slightly too high, it nevertheless made contact with
the side of Joanna's forehead, rocking her sideways. She
brought her own whip around, snapping her arm with the
same fierceness as the whip's own snap. Its thong
wrapped around his neck and jerked him forward. At the
same time, she used her free hand to catch the thong of
his whip as it descended toward her. It was an astonishing move, one Aidan could admire even while in the
midst of being strangled by a narrow strip of the finest
leather available to a warrior for anything other than a
uniform.

Though Joanna had obviously relaxed her grip on her
whip, the pressure of the thong itself did not diminish.
It slowly squeezed tighter. Aidan felt his eyes begin to
bulge out. Everything around him was taking on a firmer
definition, a more pronounced outline. Outside the Circle, the sibko appeared to share the same frightened expression. He sensed Marthe tensing, wanting to rush into
the Circle, but the sanctity of the Circle would hold her
back. Ter Roshak studied the fight intently, but his gaze
was cold as ever.

Aidan found himself consciously trying to force his
tongue backward as though, in some mysterious way, it
could intrude itself into his slowly closing throat and
somehow reverse the impending strangulation.

As Joanna walked toward him, her grip on the whip
loose except for the tight hold her thumb kept on the
control button, her eyes were icy. The offer of death was
in them, with no promise of mourning. And why should

she mourn? She had often said she could see a cadet die in a trial or combat within the Circle of Equals without caring one iota about the corpse's former skills, potential, or training achievements. It only took one loss, one mistake, one flaw, one irritable, murderous training officer to mark the end of a cadet or at least flush him or her out.

Aidan was surprised by how coolly he was perceiving his situation, even as the bright sun above him seemed to be slowly going out. He tried to find some air someplace, but there was none.

"Stop this, Joanna!" someone cried. Her eyes became fierce and it was apparent she would happily arrange the speaker's demise next. Aidan had enough presence of mind to look down at the whip handle, where she still held onto the button. The flesh around her thumbnail was very white so that the natural color of the skin around it was like a dark frame.

At that moment, the world seemed about to blink out as Aidan began to lose his sight.

Then the pressure stopped and he felt the thong recoil off his shoulder as it fell away. Eyes closed now, he felt his knees buckle and an overwhelming need to fall came over him. He resisted it. He could not fall at Falconer Joanna's feet. That would please her too much. Somehow, straining leg muscles, overtaxing back muscles, obtaining some strength from the sheer fantasy of the effort, he remained standing.

As he gradually opened his eyes, he heard the speaker again and recognized the voice as Falconer Ellis': "You kill too easily, Joanna. It is not right, not for this one. This one will surpass us all."

Ellis now stood beside Joanna, his hand on her wrist. The whip, apparently forced out of her hands by him, lay like a docile snake at his feet. It was a surprising move on his part, a violation of Circle procedure and Clan protocol. Nobody was allowed to enter the Circle during a battle, except for Falconer Commander Ter Roshak.

The two training officers seemed to go out of focus for Aidan. He could barely concentrate on them. But he had to. If he looked away, he might lose consciousness and wind up on the ground, his body coiled as ignominiously as the fallen whip.

Suddenly someone grabbed his arm. His head turned sideways laboriously, as if his neck muscles had gone rusty. He looked into the badly sculptured face of Falconer Commander Ter Roshak. Glancing down, Aidan saw that his arm was being clutched by Ter Roshak's false hand. That might explain the pain that was now surging through his arm, unless of course it was simple weakness that would have suffered from the least grip. In a way, Aidan was glad it was Ter Roshak's prosthetic hand that held him. He would have had to try to wriggle out of anyone else's grip; with Ter Roshak, it was a clear impossibility so Aidan could relax in his bondage and merely wait to see what would happen next.

What happened next was that Joanna wheeled upon Ellis, in her eyes and voice a hatred so intense that even Aidan, groggy as he was, could see that the emotion was not born at just this moment. It had been building up for some time.

"An honor duel then, Falconer Ellis?" Joanna said.

"It does not have to be."

Ellis' response was mere ritual, the offer of an opportunity to settle a dispute without conflict. This allowed a warrior who was either under the influence of an overwhelming emotion, a bad substance, or a mistaken notion to withdraw honorably from the issue of the duel. Warriors, however, rarely took a step back, and Joanna had always made it clear that a weak act of honor was to her an act of dishonor, whatever the Clan codes said.

"An honor duel then?" she said.

"Honor duel," Ellis responded, nodding.

"Mechs fully armed."

"No. The woods, a single weapon, your choice."

"No. No weapons. Just you and me. Here. Now. To the death."

There was a slight hesitation on Ellis' part before he said, in a voice louder and firmer than hers, "To the death."

"Well bargained and done."

"Well bargained and done."

Aidan had never heard the bidding process spoken so rapidly, concluded so easily. There had been no sense of strategy, just offers from instinct.

"See what you have done, cadet?" Ter Roshak whispered. "Fate allows fools like you to precipitate events that end in futile catastrophe."

Aidan wanted to protest that he had not precipitated anything, that Joanna had wrenched him out of a classroom for her sport. But it would be his head to address the Falconer Commander, especially when Ter Roshak was in such a foul mood.

"Fool!" Ter Roshak cried. He tightened his grasp of Aidan's arm, then lifted him off the ground and hurled him away, over the line of the Circle of Equals, into the midst of his fellow sibkin, who now backed away from him as if he were suddenly diseased. Even Marthe kept her distance, her feet shuffling nervously as though she could not decide whether to direct them toward Aidan or away from him. He hated that. Before, she would never have considered away.

# 6

For a long while Aidan just sat on the ground, his gaze fixed on an odd pattern of rocks that seemed deliberately centered between his legs. Aware that no one in the sibko was allowed to comfort him, and probably did not want to, he ignored them by concentrating on getting his head cleared and on watching the rocks. His head stubbornly refused to clear, and his vision went in and out of focus. Whenever the rocks came into focus, he tried to look up to see what was happening around him and in the Circle of Equals, but the slightest movement of his head returned him to dizziness. The sensation was something like looking into firelight: everything became hazy and there was pain where intense illumination struck the retina. He would have tried to shake his head clear, but after doing it once, the pain it caused had nearly knocked him out completely.

The pattern of the rocks was irregular, which fascinated Aidan. He realized that if one were to isolate any group of rocks strewn across the ground of this exceedingly rocky planet, one would find any number of irregular patterns. The regular pattern would be the exception. Nevertheless, everything *else* about life was in such a fixed pattern that he never, until now, thought much about irregularities. Growing up in the sibko, days and nights were arranged, schedules were kept, a regular process of regular progress was meticulously noted and recorded so that a warrior's codex, his or her lifetime in a collection of data, could be maintained. If this entire process were to be significantly violated, Aidan was certain that the Clan would devise some other pattern to replace it. Patterns were all, all was pattern. Had not Dermot said that last week? The sibko itself was a pattern, created out of patterns in a gene, itself a pattern in a cell. Their differences were minimal, their similarities praiseworthy. A sibko joke: DNA means Don't Need Anything. (The use of the forbidden contraction seemed, to childish minds, a bit of rebellion, and they loved to say it.) They did not need anything because all was planned for them. Their lives were table arrangements, utensils in the right place, at the right angles next to a perfectly arranged set of plates. Training on Ironhold merely continued the regular pattern.

He could discover no pattern in the rocks, and that troubled him. With his training, he should be able to see the pattern in *anything*. He picked up one rock and placed it down again so that it formed a triangle with the two other rocks, so that there was at least one pattern amid the anarchy. But it didn't satisfy him, the triangle. It was more out of place than the irregular setup had been. Because he had formed it, he could not help but concentrate on it. Now the triangle was taking on too much importance among the other rocks. He picked up all three rocks and tossed them away, refusing to note where they fell.

The sounds coming from the Circle entered his consciousness, but he refused to look up. He did not want to see what was happening there, not even when it was Joanna who screamed in pain. Her pain gave him no satisfaction. By rights, he should want to see her writhing in agony on the ground. He should want to see her deeply tanned skin stained with her blood. He should want to see her neck broken or her limbs hanging uselessly. But those prospects were just as repulsive to him as was Joanna herself. He did want to see her dead, or even hurt.

What he would have liked would be for her to tell him that he had done something well. It was wrong, he knew, to wish for credit from anyone because after the nurturing stage came the warrior training stage; after the pattern, the pattern—and there was no praise for achievement. There was, in fact, only one achievement—the victory at the Trial of Position that waited for the few who survived the training to the end. By that time, praise was no longer necessary. Dermot had said that a kind word could alter the quickness of a warrior's response and that could mean the laser blast could catch you in the throat instead of your enemy.

A wave of surprise swept among the sibko, punctuated with gasps that were sudden enough to make Aidan finally look up.

Ellis now knelt on Joanna's chest. With terrific thrusts of her torso, Joanna was rocking Ellis while trying to squirm out from under him, but she could not dislodge him. A cruel look of triumph came into Ellis' eyes as he suddenly locked his hands together, shifted his body back along Joanna's legs. Bringing his hands down, he directed them at her head in what should have been a killing blow, or one that would at least have knocked Joanna out if it did not fracture her skull.

How she did it, Aidan was not sure, but instead of trying to avoid the blow, Joanna, whose arms were pinned, blocked it with the top of her head. In spite of the block, the force of impact of Ellis' hands against her head should have knocked her out and made it easy for him to dispose of her.

Joanna had always said she had the resources of the kind of mythic beast that, in Clan myths, came back to haunt heroes. Perhaps she did possess such power because, not only did she retain consciousness, but she took advantage of a slight shifting in Ellis' pressure on her torso to roll sideways and free one arm. She faked a backhanded punch toward his stomach, one whose weakness could not possibly have hurt Ellis. Nevertheless, in instinctive reflex, he moved to block it, and she opened her hands. Eluding his defense, and reaching above it, she grabbed the lower end of his leather tunic and pulled his close to her. In another situation, the move might have been that of a lover drawing to her the object of her sexual desire, but in this case it was the move Joanna needed to break Ellis' leverage. Artfully squirming through his legs as he struggled to regain equilibrium, she shot out the other side of his legs, rolled over, stirred up a lot of dust, and came up on the attack.

Ramming him from the rear, she knocked the already off-balance Ellis onto his face. He quickly curled up his body, however, and somersaulted to his feet, a maneuver at which Ellis had always been particularly adept. Unfortunately, Joanna anticipated it. She made no move to-

ward him and instead scooped up a rock from the ground
and hurled it at his head while she was still bent over.
To Aidan the rock seemed to sail slowly toward Ellis'
head, when in fact the missile was thrown with some
force and speed. Later, he would remember this as the
first of many moments in his life when movement around
him seemed to slow down, to occur at some different
speed from that of reality. There were times when he
doubted that any change had occurred and attributed it
to some dislocation of memory rather than time.

The rock caught Ellis, who was turning around at the
moment and consequently stepped right into its path, on
the side of his forehead, just above his temples. He
blinked hard a couple of times after the impact, looking
for a moment as though he might pass out, then he
growled fiercely and charged at Joanna.

Until his last step, Joanna stood her ground, a look of
arrogance on her face and a scornful smile on her lips.
In a sense, the fight was over. She had won. All she had
to do was finish Ellis off. She could have done that with
a well-timed jab at his stomach or a strike to the side of
his neck. Simple procedures would have done the job.

But Joanna eschewed simple procedures.

In a move that seemed to Aidan more dancelike than
warriorlike, Joanna deftly sidestepped, allowing Ellis,
who apparently expected some other response, to stumble his way past her. His attempts to regain his footing
would have been comic to Aidan if he had not seen, and
correctly interpreted, the killing look in Joanna's eyes.
Joanna had often told the sibko that feeling her own killing look, at the time when victory was certain and disposal of the defeated only a matter of routine, was the
greatest intoxication a warrior could know.

Aidan had wanted to ask her if she did not also feel
disgust at the results of carnage. But even if he had been
allowed to speak it would have been unnecessary. A Clan
warrior could not look back, could not care what thought
or feeling might preoccupy his or her victim. To be warriors, they must, in fact, stop thinking about such minor
details.

Joanna's killing look must have been obvious to Falconer Commander Ter Roshak, for he rushed forward

from his observing station toward the combatants. But his move came too late.

Joanna rushed at Ellis. Leaping feet-first, she kicked at his backside, sending him sprawling and sliding across the ground. Joanna came down on balance and ran to Ellis' now-crawling body. He was trying to get to the rim of the Circle, which meant capitulation. It was shameful, but sometimes worth the discredit. Warriors were more concerned with the art of victory than the shame of defeat, and a disgraced warrior could always erase the memory of a loss with a convincing victory the next time around.

If Ellis could pull himself across the rim, Joanna could no longer press the attack. His fingers were stretched out, the tip of his middle finger only a centimeter away from one of the stakes that formed the rim, when Joanna landed on him. Aidan's view of the kill was partially obscured as Rena, screaming with delight, slipped in front of him. As he maneuvered for a better view, he saw the result of Joanna's assault. Descending from what seemed a great height, she landed on Ellis' back, crushing Ellis' neck with her left knee. It was probably a broken neck that killed Ellis, though Aidan never learned. It could also have been another blow. Perhaps his back had been fractured. At any rate, Roshak ordered the body taken away, and after Ellis' death had been officially announced, the rumor mill furnished many causes of death, including the idea that Joanna had ripped out his heart. Some of the sibko even seemed to believe that absurdity, despite having been witness to the actual event. It was just that Falconer Joanna seemed capable of anything.

After ordering the disposal of the body, Ter Roshak wheeled on Joanna. The emotion in his angry face, the tension in his body, seemed a complete reversal of his normal demeanor. Aidan had never seen wrath erupt so suddenly or with such full involvement of every part of the body.

"Falconer Joanna, I cannot let this pass. Ellis was a fine warrior, a—"

"I am a warrior," Joanna said softly.

"Too much a warrior. There was no need to kill him."

"It would have been dishonorable not to."

"There is no dishonor in mercy."

"You would have had me maim him, paralyze him, disable—"

"You know what I mean! We have had this out before. We are not fighting a war. We do not have to—"

"How dare you criticize me publicly, old man? Here, in front of them!"

She gestured toward the cadets, all of whom were lined up and watching so intently that they seemed partially to form a second outer rim to the Circle. Taking quick glances to both sides, Aidan thought he could see in the stances of his sibkin a definite split between supporting Joanna and clear antagonism toward her. He tried to show neutrality. He was not sure why. He was clearly against Joanna, yet he did not want to join that faction, because a part of him considered any insubordination to be wrong for a warrior. For the first time, as he watched Joanna gather her resources and stand up to Ter Roshak, he realized that he had a grudging admiration of this officer who had provided such hell for him. But then he decided it must be one too many blows to the head, and that this feeling would pass.

Ter Roshak's anger had grown, apparently due to Joanna's defiance. He seemed to waver on his legs and his prosthetic arm gestured threateningly, as if he wished to dispatch Joanna with the same ruthlessness she had used for Ellis.

"I can say anything I want to you, *in public,* Falconer Joanna! The proper question should be how dare *you* speak to *me* that way in front of them?"

"Sir, you *claim* to allow us freedom."

"Yes. I did not interfere in your battle with Ellis."

"You are not allowed to. You are not allowed to cross into the Circle during a dispute, unless invited."

Ter Roshak seemed momentarily disconcerted.

"Of course you are right," he finally said. "But it is a rule I would willingly break if it meant saving a life. If I had had any idea that you would—"

"What hypocrisy is this? You heard our bids. The battle was to the death, we both said it."

"But in an honor duel, that is figurative."

"Not in my understanding."

"Damn it, Joanna, you should not have killed him."

"That is a moral decision. By my morality, I had no

choice. It is the way of the Clan. An honor duel must be fought by the arranged terms.''

''It is not the way of the Clan to pursue personal vengeance.''

Joanna looked ready to kill Roshak now.

''How dare you speak of personal vengeance? You, of all people? Did you not—''

Her words were stopped as Roshak hit her with the back of his false hand. The blow was hard and sent her reeling, a stream of blood coming out of the side of her mouth. She started to raise her hand, to touch the blood, then seemed to see that as a gesture of capitulation and dropped her hand abruptly. The blood reached the line of her chin and some drops fell onto her leather tunic.

For a moment, she stared at Ter Roshak, her body trembling with anger, then she composed herself and relaxed her body.

''Your orders, sir?''

''I would transfer you to another training unit, but we are already shorthanded. You are confined to your quarters until the start of the training day tomorrow. At that time, you will report to me.''

''As you wish, sir.''

Joanna strode right at the group of cadets, defying them to take any note of her. The sibko occupied itself with diversionary maneuvers, not one of them looking into Joanna's eyes as she passed through them.

Turning his back on the cadets, Ter Roshak loudly dismissed them. They returned to the barracks slowly, disconsolately, not speaking. In the barracks, the silence broke and most of them could not stop talking. Aidan did not join in but went to his cot instead. Looking at Marthe, his eyes invited her to join him. She shook her head no, with just the slightest, quickest movement.

Later, in the middle of the night, Aidan was summmoned to the quarters of Falconer Joanna. Others, Bret the most often, had received such a summoning, but it was the first time for Aidan. He had always felt that her distaste for him as a cadet was carried into her sexual life. In fact, she rarely needed the sexual attentions of any member of the sibko, but once in a while the summoning came and had to be obeyed. Bret and the others said she always made them maintain the vow of silence the whole time. When the order came for Aidan to report to her, he considered refusing, defying her once more, treating her quarters as another Circle of Equals. However, sex—unimportant as it was, annoying physical compulsion that it also was—never seemed vital enough to put one's life on the line for, and so Aidan went to her. The night was, as Bret and the others predicted, silent. The coupling was perfunctory, athletic and combative, like most Clan sex.

The entire night with Falconer Joanna was almost silent. She spoke only twice, both times after the sessions of coupling were ended. The first time she said, "I know your codex, and I know that, a few years ago, you killed a bandit, roughly and brutally. I was surprised by that, frankly, since I see in you a constitutional weakness, the seeds of failure. Maybe I have misjudged you. Time will tell, as the old saying goes. Until then, I will watch you, push you, punish you, have you close to me on nights like this. You will be with me like this often, until you do fail or you die or you choose to leave your sibko. Perhaps you will succeed." The second time she said, "I am the only warrior left from my sibko."

Even though, as a sexual partner, Aidan was allowed to speak freely with Joanna, he refused to say anything. He even suppressed sounds during the act. She did not seem to mind that.

Before leaving her quarters, standing in the doorway, looking back at the now strangely languid Joanna, he said, "I will not fail."

He may have been mistaken, but he thought he saw the hint of a smile prodding the corners of her mouth.

"You may not," she said. As he walked out the door, she added, "But I am afraid that you will."

If she had said that he definitely would fail, her words would not have bothered him. But she said, "I am afraid that you will," and he often stopped to wonder why she had used the word, afraid. Joanna showed no concern for anyone in the sibko, for anyone anywhere, for that matter. She could not possibly have concern for his success or failure.

Or could she?

## 7

Using a telescope that had been removed from some service battlefield weapon, Aidan had the freeborn in his sights. He could not kill him because the single weapon he had chosen for this exercise, a medium laser in the right arm, had been phased down and at best could only cause a mild stun, enough to make his opponent dizzy but not enough to render him or her unconscious. Perhaps choosing the single weapon had been a miscalculation, Aidan thought, especially since the others had made more conventional choices—machine guns and short range missiles.

The freebirth cadet he had centered on for his segment of the battle was a bland-looking boy, his hair cut so short that, except for the light gray stubble, he would have been taken for bald. Aidan had been told that his hairstyle was the current custom among freeborn cadets who defiantly wanted to distinguish themselves from trueborns as much as trueborns did not want any association with freeborns. Perhaps because of the grayness of the stubble, the boy's face seemed unnaturally red, giving him a demonic look in spite of his average features.

Anti-freebirth curses hissed through the staticky commlink. All the members of his sibko were contributing their own creative denunciations in deliberately chosen language. Because of the immobility of his 'Mech, he could not see any of his sibkin in their own reconstructed 'Mech shells, but his hearing perked up whenever Marthe's voice came online. He had not been able to adjust to her newfound reticence, and in the year it had taken them to get to this point in training, the distance between them seemed to have grown. Sometimes they still met in his or her bunk, but even the coupling now seemed to separate them. It had become no better, and no worse, than sex with anyone else in the sibko.

Aidan still had the boy in his sights, not that the calibration of the view was particularly accurate. He was sitting in the torso of a partially reconstructed *Wasp*, an obsolete pile of junk, but still suitable for exercises early in the cycle, as Joanna had told them. It was more or less complete from the head through the torso, but had no legs, and so was not maneuverable. Testing the right-arm medium laser, he had found its effective range to be about a third normal and the power turned down so that he could only stun rather than kill any target. He would have bid to equip the machine with an LRM rack instead of the medium-range laser, if Joanna had not discouraged him two nights ago, when he had last been with her, from adding too much weaponry to his proposed battle plan. The lowest bids got the most strategic positions on the training field, the most protection from the surrounding landscape, the better chance to win the points that would mean the awarding of a victory from the training officers from other units who were there to judge each cadet's performance.

The 'Mech also rested on an insecure foundation, a specific difficulty factor that was a part of the exercise. It was claimed that if a real 'Mech became immobile and lost its stabilizing gyros in the field, its pilot would have difficulty keeping it upright, so the swaying of this 'Mech was deliberate. If Aidan made any kind of extensive move, he felt his machine rock slightly under him.

It was frustrating not to be able to employ BattleMech maneuverability, but—according to the instructors—the sibko was a long way from stepping into genuine 'Mechs. About all the combat activity he could manage was to move the 'Mech's arms or manipulate the laser weapon. He had sent one beam that he thought was well-aimed past the boy. It sailed over his head by a few meters. Another had done no more than create an uneven singe line across the ground in front of his antagonist.

The freeborns participating in this exercise were told that they were getting anti-'Mech training, while the trueborns' purpose was anti-infantry. But it was clear to

Aidan that caste distinctions would never allow freeborns to have advantageous positions against trueborns, and so could not possibly be in BattleMechs against them. The freeborns, like Aidan's sibko, were allowed their own choices of weapons. This particular one had taken a couple of potshots in Aidan's direction with a conventional rifle, but had also missed completely. They had struck the lower part of the 'Mech torso but were not strong enough to do significant damage.

Inside the 'Mech, the cockpit was quite primitive, simplified for training purposes, as Joanna had told them. The nearly bare command console contained no monitors and not much in the way of recording devices, not even a minimal computer to go with the minimal 'Mech. All the recording of Aidan's performance was being done at command level, where the trainers were measuring and judging the performance of each individual sibko member.

The single cockpit device meant for his attention was a gauge that allegedly measured the heat level of the machine. Though most Clan 'Mechs were equipped with double heat sinks that virtually made overheating impossible, the training cadre wanted all cadets to be made conscious of the danger of rising heat in the event of a malfunction or of an overeager warrior putting his 'Mech in such jeopardy. The gauge was fake, controlled by those who were guiding the exercise. They could arbitrarily place any cadet in a dangerous situation and announce that the 'Mech had overheated. Then the cadet was declared "dead" in his seat (unless he or she had cleverly anticipated the event and scrambled out of the cockpit before the controller noticed), and his mock battle machine judged as defeated and taken out of the exercise.

Still, frustrating as the test conditions were, primitive as the partial 'Mech was, Aidan was exhilarated by the experience of finally being in a cockpit after all the verbal abuse from instructors and the endless classroom tests and the 'Mechless combat maneuvers the sibko had undergone. This exercise—at last—began the real training, the training that he and the sibko had been looking forward to so desperately. Instead of pretending to be a warrior while shooting imaginary weapons from his bed or in the midst of rare sibko recreation, now he had the chance to operate a genuine machine with real, if decrepit and barely loaded or charged, weapons.

It was time to dispose of the boy. Leaning toward the front viewing window, all the while longing for a holographic display of the whole battlefield, Aidan took a bead on the freeborn, then slowly pushed down the button on the arm of his command couch that would direct a laser beam at the target. He wanted to relish his first training kill.

He relished it for too long. Joanna had drummed into the minds of the sibko that timing was critical, and Aidan had forgotten the lesson.

The boy, standing between two tall trees whose bark shone wetly from a recent rain, fired a flare right at Aidan's 'Mech. Aidan had not even detected a flare gun among his enemy's weaponry. Its projectile exploded, apparently against the 'Mech's left arm, where the laser was mounted. There was a long moment of fierce blinding light. Aidan shut his eyes tightly and watched, on the inside of his eyelids, large, abstract, dark blobs that seemed to be engaged in their own personal combat. At the same time, he considered his second mistake, regarding the freeborn as subhuman. Sensing the light of the flare dying out, he opened his eyes. With that, the dark blobs turned into blinding light that, for a moment, prevented him from focusing. As clearer sight returned, he sensed a hard knock against the front of the cockpit. The 'Mech seemed to shake on its already shaky foundation.

When he could finally focus on what was happening, Aidan saw the freeborn boy clinging to the outside of the cockpit, staring in at its bewildered pilot. He grinned in a way that might have seemed friendly from a trueborn, but was spookily turned into a malicious smirk on the face of a freeborn. One of the boy's hands firmly grasped the rim of the viewport, while the other clutched to his chest what at first looked to Aidan like a bundle.

Before Aidan could adjust to the boy's presence on his 'Mech's surface, the freebirth suddenly disappeared from the viewing window, leaving a streak of dirt behind him as proof that he had not been Aidan's hallucination. The last thing Aidan saw was the bundle, now held downward away from the boy's body, reminding Aidan of a suitcase.

It was a moment before Aidan realized the significance of the object. It was neither bundle nor suitcase. The little bastard was carrying a satchel charge and he was going to attach it to Aidan's 'Mech.

In her weaponry briefing, Joanna had said nothing about satchel charges, though she had pointed out that no weapon would be life-threatening; this boy's was undoubtedly powered down, like all the rest of the weapons in the exercise. Aidan felt cheated. A satchel charge seemed like a violation of the rules, but of course, as Joanna had also pointed out, this exercise had no rules. As she had said, all was fair in love and war, and on the training ground, "what's unfair is even fairer." One had only to win.

And he could not win with the freeborn scrambling around the outside with a satchel charge in a suitcase. Aidan pushed himself out of the command couch and virtually leaped at the escape hatch, working it open rapidly. As he stepped out onto the 'Mech's shoulder, he felt, in a slight movement of the 'Mech on its shaky foundation, that the boy was somewhere on the back of the machine, behind the cockpit section. Looking there, he saw that the satchel charge was now secured by metal hooks to the back of the *Wasp's* head. The boy had positioned it so that it would blow through to the cockpit. If that happened, the judges would surely award victory to the other boy and declare Aidan dead in his pilot seat. Even if Aidan were to eject before the charge's mock explosion, the boy would win. Ejection meant capitulation, as Joanna had said.

A sickening feeling formed at the pit of Aidan's stomach. To be defeated by a lousy freebirth—it was too shameful, a stigma for any trueborn cadet.

Realizing that his main chance now was to do something about the bomb, then defeat the boy (where had he gone?), Aidan set his feet firm against the side of the 'Mech's head and reached toward the satchel. He could hear a faint humming sound. It was unlikely that the boy had set a long fuse, so Aidan was sure he had only a matter of seconds to get at the explosive device. It looked so innocent sitting there, like some bulky kit bag that had accidentally become stuck to the 'Mech's form. His fingers brushed against the satchel's leather surface, but

he could not get a good hold on it. Readjusting his body
to lean out further, Aidan tried again. The 'Mech, swaying slightly on its foundation, nearly made one of his feet
slip. That did not matter. His concentration was entirely
focused on the dark bag. Another rocking sensation and
he did lose his footing, but just as he managed to grip a
good handful of the satchel. His body slid sideways, then
toward the rear, right to the edge of the 'Mech shoulder,
but Aidan did not lose his hold on the satchel. The rocking stopped. Wrapping his leg around a mount intended
for a weapon he had rejected in his bid, he pulled at
the bag. It did not budge. When he tried again, one of the
far metal hooks came away. At the same moment, the
rocking of the 'Mech switched directions and Aidan began sliding backward, toward the gun mount. The rocking worked to his advantage, however, as the weight of
his body pulled more at the satchel. As he came to rest,
still wrapped around the gun mount, but leaning out near
the rear of the 'Mech, Aidan gave one last tug and the satchel
came away, the humming inside of it seeming louder than
before. Using his left hand to prop himself up on the
pitching 'Mech, he threw the satchel outward. It had
barely left his hand when it exploded. Whatever kind of
mild charge was in it, the explosion was loud. The bag
split apart, sending out growing plumes of smoke that
quickly enveloped Aidan and the 'Mech. It was like being in a dense fog, except that fog generally did not cause
such pain to the lungs. Even as he started coughing, Aidan noted with pleasure that he had at least evened the
contest. The satchel charge, if real, could have done scant
damage to the *Wasp*. The boy might be a little ahead on
points, but the battle was not over. Even as he continued
to cough, Aidan gained in confidence as he heard the boy
also coughing below him.

Using the gun mount for balance, Aidan struggled to
his feet, then nearly fell again as the 'Mech reached the
end of its rocking arc and started back again. Was he
mistaken or had there been an extra acceleration at
the start of the reverse movement? The initial swaying
had been scarcely noticeable, but Aidan detected a wider
arc now. Aidan suddenly realized that his enemy was attempting, through sheer physical force, to rock the 'Mech
until he could, with a final thrust, knock it over. Given

the usual tonnage of a real 'Mech, with all its machinery and materiel, such a maneuver would normally have been impossible. This 'Mech, however, was a mere shell with most of its equipment removed for the combat exercises. And the tactic might just work because the shell rested on an unsecured foundation so that it could be positioned easily in different sections of the training ground. It was a devious but legitimate tactic.

For once, Aidan cursed the Clan tendency to enforce every economy, any way of saving materiel. The Clans had a long history of scavenging, salvaging, reconstructions, improvisations, replacing metal parts with human bones, repairing apparently useless limbs carried in from battlefields and putting them back on any 'Mech that needed replacements, and all kinds of Tech miracles in deep, dark dungeons (warrior Tech shops were often called dungeons for the dirt, grease, disharmony, and mysteries that seemed to lurk there). It was second nature, too, for civilians to practice complicated economies, all for the good of the Clan. Aidan believed in the Kerensky traditions. The general had decreed that even though the Clan was a technically advanced society, the shortage of supplies and the harsh living conditions on their planets made it necessary for its people to conduct their lives in primitive ways, with primitive means. That way the future takeover of the Inner Sphere and the restoration of the Star League would be supported firmly and heavily. Nothing should be wasted to give any Clansperson a better life. None of the necessities of life in any caste should be used to excess or wasted. Battle materiel and supplies should be used wisely and, where possible, recycled—again, nothing wasted. Even lives displayed their own personal economies. No emotion should be wasted, with all feelings recycled into useful activity. Even play should contribute to the goals of the sibko and of the Clan. This time Aidan might have foregone the economy so that he could be tumbling around a better-budgeted training 'Mech.

He was glad for the obscurity the smoke caused. Nobody could see his foot slip and slide beneath him as he dejectedly held onto the gun mount. Finally regaining his balance, he used his natural agility to adjust to the side-to-side. As the smoke cleared and the 'Mech reached the end of its present motion, he quickly looked down and saw the boy, now so intent on toppling the 'Mech that he had not observed Aidan's current position. Stupid freebirth, he should have anticipated that.

Aidan nearly slid off the 'Mech's shoulder as the machine's rocking arc reached its limit and the boy pushed it back, the intensity of his effort forcing the sinews in his upper arms to bulge out. At the last second, Aidan grabbed the gun mount again. Holding on tightly, he rode on the shoulder to the end of its present rocking motion. At the point where the 'Mech again stopped, it seemed to teeter for a moment before halting, enough time to suggest it might crash before reaching its opposite point in the return arc, enough time for Aidan to see dew on a patch of grass just below him. Aidan realized that his presence on the 'Mech, clutching the mount, with his weight full against the weapon, might be just enough to precipitate the fall now. However, after leaning to its left for an astonishingly long time, the 'Mech began to rock back. Aidan let out the breath he had been holding for a long time. Had he even breathed at all since he had slipped out of the cockpit?

As the 'Mech slowly rocked back toward its right, Aidan was certain this would be the last arc. The machine would definitely crash to the ground. The freeborn had to realize this, too—or else be crushed in the fall. In spite of the boy's tainted birth, Aidan devoutly hoped his opponent would have the sense to get out of the way. Having him mangled under a training 'Mech would be a cheap, almost shameful way of winning. Aidan wanted a decisive win, one that Falconer Joanna could not question either publicly or in her bunk, where she often hurled insults these days while in the act of coupling.

Aidan planned his strategy quickly. During the brief moment when the 'Mech's shoulder was level, he released his grip on the mount and leaped over it. Now he exerted pressure, using the gun mount for leverage. He wanted to guarantee the 'Mech's fall. Over a loudspeaker mounted on a nearby tree, Falconer Joanna's voice screamed out. Fortunately, some static on the outdoor sound system, plus the loud sounds of the near-crashed 'Mech, drowned out her words. Aidan was sure he would hear them all later, anyway. He suspected that Joanna had never once in her life ever considered the possibility of verbal restraint.

He set his feet so that his body would be in balance at that moment the 'Mech wavered before it began its final descent. As the machine's right shoulder tilted once more and Aidan forced the motion further by leaning into the mounted gun, he scanned the terrain below, looking for the freeborn. There he was, backing away from the 'Mech, trying to get out of its way. As the other boy stared up at the 'Mech with wide fearful eyes, his feet suddenly slipped and slid across the wet grass. It was obvious that he had not yet seen Aidan.

Timing his move with the acceleration of the 'Mech's fall, Aidan leaped off the shoulder, sailing in what would have been a perfect dive during the excruciating swim-training that Joanna had supervised in her usual compassionate way. ("Drown, you repulsive slugs. You do the stroke my way or drown.") As Aidan zeroed in on the freeborn like an aerofighter in a suicide swoop, he had a sudden moment of doubt about the wisdom of his improvised strategy. The boy did not see him until the last moment, too late to put up any kind of defense. Aidan, just before impact, ducked his head and brought his arms down on the boy's shoulders. They collided with more impact than Aidan had expected, and even before they hit the ground, Aidan was momentarily dazed. Even with his head dazed, he managed to cushion his own fall with his enemy's body. The boy yelped in pain. Aidan was bounced off the boy's body as the 'Mech and the earth met with a tremendous thump. Light as the machine was, it still sent a minor earthquake of vibrations across the immediate landscape. The tremors sent Aidan sliding across damp ground like a child down an icy slope.

After he came to a stop, he maneuvered his body around to face the boy again. The freeborn, nearly as resilient, was struggling to his feet, too. Standing, Aidan detected movement out of the corner of his eye. Looking in that direction, he saw a long tube sailing toward him. He caught it just before it hit the ground. Jagged at each end, it looked like it must have been a section of the laser weapon's barrel.

He did not hesitate to use it. Joanna had screamed at them often enough that a warrior must use any material available to him or her to win a combat. Even the droning Dermot had pointed out that no warrior ever won an engagement by brooding over whether or not to use a particular weapon. Emitting the kind of falcon yelp that the trainers had drilled into them as the beginning and end of any calisthenic or marching drill, Aidan ran at the freeborn, the metal tube held over his head like a primitive club.

The freeborn, staring with surprise at Aidan's newfound weapon, had his own weapon ready, a short stub of a knife obviously carved out of some piece of scrap from the pile kept at the edge of the training ground. (Cadets were encouraged to scavenge from the scrap-pile for any need. Many made cups and utensils, tools, small artworks to decorate the single table allowed beside each bunk, and, although specifically forbidden, small weapons like the one the freeborn now held in his hand.)

In one part of his mind, Aidan almost admired the craftiness of his enemy in concealing a lethal weapon, getting it by the officers in charge, waiting for the right opportunity to use it. And that moment was now, with a trueborn rushing at him and ready to crush his skull with his own somewhat-less-lethal weapon.

But that was the only part of Aidan's mind that considered the situation coolly. The rest became instantly filled with rage. What right had this stupid freebirth to attempt to kill a natural warrior, a trueborn, in an ordinary training exercise? The bastard must die himself!

Aidan tried to be quicker than the boy. Switching the metal tube from his right to left hand, he brought it down toward the freeborn's forearm, hoping to dislodge the knife and hear the satisfying crack of a bone in the process.

But the boy anticipated Aidan's defense. He dodged to his right, and the tube just grazed his sleeve. Adjusting to Aidan's attack, he then quickly brought the knife up and forward, slashing the sleeveless cadet's forearm. Aidan's defensive move had not been as quick as the boy's because the momentum of his own thrust had set him off balance, with his feet stumbling on the wet soil beneath. Nevertheless, the blow was not as telling as the freeborn had intended and the knife blade just grazed Aidan's skin, barely drawing blood.

Now they were both off balance, their footing so insecure they looked like bad dancers in a village celebration. But Aidan still had one advantage—his rage. The boy, with the lack of involvement so characteristic of freeborns, merely wanted to win. Aidan wanted to kill.

Ignoring the pain from the knife slash, he stepped in toward the boy, and raising the metal tube fiercely, he caught him on the side of his forehead, enough to daze him. The boy stumbled backward, trying to return his weapon to the action but unable, it seemed, to coordinate the action. His arm flopped around like that of a rag doll. He looked foolish.

Aidan grabbed the boy's knife arm, and raising it to his mouth, bit fiercely, drawing blood and tearing some skin away. The tactic worked. The boy dropped the knife. For a brief moment, Aidan considered picking it up and stabbing the freeborn, but he did not favor knives, especially ones fashioned by the enemy. He also threw the tube away. He wanted to tear this freeborn apart with his bare hands, without weaponry. In his mind were visions of skeletons and gore.

He only got to the point of bashing the freeborn's head against the ground, over and over until no consciousness remained in the boy's open eyes. Training officers suddenly appeared from odd hiding places, from inside fake fortified trees and out of manmade hillocks. The analysts for the exercise descended to a clear patch of ground in a small helicopter. It took four of the officers to lift Aidan off the freeborn and another three to talk him out of his rage. By that time the boy was fully conscious again and staring at him with hatred in his eyes. Before they yanked him away, he had enough time to mutter, "You did not impress me one bit, trashborn." The savage insult was enough to revive Aidan's anger, but the officers restrained him again, as others dragged the freeborn away.

The anger returned again when the decisions of the evaluators was announced. Aidan was awarded the win all right, but only because he had nearly killed his enemy. The win was damaged because he lost points for not disposing of the enemy when he had a bead on him and for allowing the satchel bomb to be planted on the 'Mech's surface. He regained a few points back for his heroic way of removing and disposing of the satchel. He received even more deductions for allowing the 'Mech shell to crash, however. Indeed, Aidan scored lower than anyone else in the sibko. The officer who read the report in a scathing tone noted that the 'Mech shell was no longer repairable, except for a few parts. It would be added to the scrap pile. Perhaps the little freebirth bastard would fashion another knife out of a part of it, Aidan thought bitterly.

Joanna was not any easier on him than the evaluators had been. She said: "You are strong, you are agile, you are clever, you are even intelligent, but you are slow. The only praise I can give you is for defying me. I was just about to declare your 'Mech 'blown up' when you started your final strategy. I admired your anger, but your only real ruthlessness was at the end. You should have lost. Sometime you *will* lose. Prepare for a life as other than a warrior. I see in your eyes that you are full of rage now. Come to the bed. Take out your rage on me. I will take out mine on you."

"What rage do you have?" Aidan asked. (He talked to her when they were alone together, and had been doing so for some months now.) "You were just an observer today. What rage can you feel?"

"Eyas, I am never without it."

In a strange way, what she requested happened. The rage left him as he and Joanna coupled in ways that were more like combat. After, though, she held him in a manner that was new. Aidan did not understand why it comforted him, but it did.

# 8

Falconer Commander Ter Roshak had kept a journal ever since his cadet days on Ironhold.

There are times, he wrote, weary times when my mind stops working and the boredom of this training camp seeps in to fill the empty spaces. That is when I begin to think that growing old is the worst thing that can happen to a warrior. Being a survivor is, on one hand, a mark of honor—proof that one has been a fine warrior, winning his battles and protecting his command. On the other hand, it is a badge of futility, a tinny piece of metal to wear on your chest as a sign that your time has passed. Back on Terra, a millennium or so ago, they used to say that old soldiers never die. The Clan, however, has no use for its old soldiers, except as cannon fodder for assaults against a determined enemy.

Perhaps that is what I should have done instead of joining this training command. But there is a certain stubbornness within me, a pride at having succeeded as a warrior, that does not allow me to cast my life away like that—at least not yet. I can still guide others in acquiring the abilities to fight, even blundering cadets like the current crop. I do not think I ever made the mistakes these sibkin make. Then again, maybe I did. It is hard to judge them. This is only my second group of trainees and, I suppose, the first seemed just as wide-eyed and inept at this point in their training.

Guiding the fates of half a dozen sibkos is an awesome responsibility. Sometimes I would wish to be a simple training officer, a falconer concerned only with training the surviving members of a sibko. Three years is a long time to oversee the development of warriors. Some say it is too long, that we should just put the youngsters in BattleMechs from the outset, give them minimal training, and thus balloon our forces instead of leaving them perpetually understaffed. With this, I cannot agree. As Kerensky has instructed us, we must not be wasteful in war. Not because we lack the materiel or personnel but because the violence causing the waste will spill over into the very infrastructure of our society. It was the devastation of just such uncontrolled warfare that destroyed the Star League dream three hundred years ago, and forced the formation of the Clans. Adopting such wasteful practices would destroy our own spirits and permanently end the dream.

At any rate, I remain here with younger warriors, like that darned malcontent, Falconer Joanna. Her defiance, her glares, her innuendoes all mark me as an overaged warrior whose lines and wrinkles betoken uselessness and outdated knowledge instead of wisdom and experience. This Joanna questions everything, even when she utters not a word. In her anger and scornfulness, she is like no other warrior I have ever encountered, except perhaps Ramon Mattlov.

She will be reassigned to a combat unit. That should please her. She is so desperate to earn a Bloodname that she will do anything to get it. And get it she will. She only has to finish her penance on Ironhold, exonerate herself for whatever infraction or failure sent her here in the first place. I have never consulted her codex to find out what wrong she did, but her fine service here must certainly pay for it in full. I have never written such glowing reports for an officer. Except for her killing of Ellis, a foolish eruption of anger, her service here has no mark against it. Besides, the upper echelons tend to admire victory in any kind of conflict, even when unjustified. They prefer her kind of toughness, which wins battles, to interservice ethics.

It is a pity, really, that she will leave my command. Despite her unpitying ferocity and the way she treats the cadets, she is the best training officer I have seen. And she really does hate these hopefuls. It is not just a pose for the benefit of training, a faked hatred to stir up the sibko and turn its members into good soldiers. She cannot abide any less than high skill and is not content with mere potential among the members of the sibko. Worse, she hates being here and takes her resentment out on anyone in her way. She would even take it out on me if she knew how.

I have never been one to obey the custom of not discussing the sexual part of our lives. I agree that it is of little import, and if a drug were developed to suppress such urges, I would eagerly feed it to our warriors. What need have we to couple? Procreation is not a concern, and merely amounts to the occasional birth of worthy freeborn bastards for other castes. Worthy, but abandoned and forgotten. The genetic program that supports the warrior caste has much better results than the awkward contortions and inconvenience of the physical act.

Yet when I was young enough and combative enough, I could never free myself of the urge. Even now, at an age when such moments of desire come only rarely, I am tempted to employ command privilege and order one of the women in the training cadre to my quarters for some silent intimacy. When I am in a particularly foul mood, I am even tempted to summon Joanna. May that I never succumb to the temptation, for I would not want to couple with her.

The irony, of course, is that—in spite of her hatred of the cadets, in spite of the fact that her sexual appetite exceeds the usual lusty hunger of a Clan warrior (perhaps the reason for her exile here)—she would nevertheless choose a cadet for a bed partner over me. She would come to my bed begrudgingly if I were to order her, but she would never choose me on her own. Cadets are young and to be preferred because she hates age even more than she despises incompetence.

I have read that once was a time when my age—forty-two years—was not considered excessively old. Indeed, among other castes, it still is not. But here, among warriors, I might as well be roaming a pasture, fit only to supply fertilizer for growing fields.

I am meandering again. The privilege of age—to allow one's thoughts to wander, to bid erratically for the chance to keep living. I am still alive. In that respect at least, I have won the bid.

Let me continue to write so that I can continue to put off sleep and the dream that is the ultimate nightmare, the dream where I am no longer useful. It does not matter what the scene of the dream or what I am doing in it, the terror comes from waking up still in the grip of the dream's desolate feelings.

Besides Joanna, I am concerned for the cadet named Aidan. Of all the youngsters in his sibko, he is the one who most resembles his genefather, he and the young woman Marthe. But Marthe is no problem. She is highly skilled, the one member of this sibko whose success I believe to be assured. She has none of that dark look that the genefather Mattlov used to send my way when he was my superior officer.

Ramon Mattlov. He made my life hell and I loved him for it. Who knows how many times his meanness saved my life? I think of him, his 'Mech gracefully matching the heavy strides of mine as we crushed a wide path through some jungle or across desert dunes. When there was no fighting to be done, he kept up a steady commentary on life, crowding the commlink channels with gruff complaints and irritating pessimism.

In battle, however, he was usually silent. How many times did he rescue me from my own foolishness, for which I barely had a chance to pay him back? In my one opportunity to save his life, I failed. I can still see him, tangled irretrievably in the blackened and twisted wreckage of his 'Mech, the pulsing green light of a still-working Beagle Probe visible over his left shoulder, with me arriving only in time to see his chest let out its last breath.

I scrambled out of my own 'Mech after disposing of both the pilot and 'Mech that battered Mattlov, hoping to pull him out of the wreckage and resuscitate him. How could I have saved him? I had no medical skills, nor did my fingers burn with the warmth of healing powers. All I could do was stand by the destroyed 'Mech and its pilot, feeling the heat still rising powerfully from the shards of metal, cursing gods I did not believe in for taking the life of a warrior who had seemed destined to rise high, perhaps to become a Khan, even an ilKhan. But nobody guides armies from the grave, no matter what the grotesque legends of the mountain people say. I was not certain it would even be possible—once the wreckage was cool enough—to disentangle my commander, my friend, from the metal that seemed to have fused with his body. Yet, underneath the burns and the blood, Mattlov's face was peaceful, accepting. In death he had no more complaints.

I have written so often of my admiration, even affection, for Ramon Mattlov, and no doubt I will again. Now my concern is with his generational duplicate, the strange boy Aidan. Why I should focus on this one more than the others in his sibko, I do not know, but it has been so almost from the start. The facial resemblance, I suppose, along with the pride of his stance, a pride that surpasses even that of the other members of the sibko, all of whose cells also contain their halves of Mattlov's genetic blueprint. Yet this Aidan *is* the genetic reincarnation of Ramon Mattlov. Of this, I have no doubt. And he *must* be one of the cadets who prevails at the final Trial of Position. If he fails, then I fail, too.

Yesterday, I paid a surprise visit to the cadet quarters. They were engaged, as expected, in various studies. This Aidan was involved in assembling the various components of a *Kit Fox* in a holotank. That light 'Mech is extremely useful for recon duty yet laden with firepower. Having piloted a *Kit Fox* in my first days as a warrior, I have always been fond of its complex configuration of weaponry. Aidan was doing a good job of it, using his light pen to move the miniature pieces of a Streak short-range missile rack into place in the right arm.

In those eyes, so fiercely determined even in this small task, I caught a flash of his genefather. It recalled to me Ramon Mattlov analyzing the potential strategies of other officers in the hours before a bidding council. Better than any other Clan officer I have ever served or observed, better than me, Mattlov could foresee just how far an opponent would go, just what he might do to prod an opponent to do as *he* wanted, just when to deliver a carefully orchestrated finale to an apparently casual and even erratic series of bids. Even when he lost the bid, his loss would have so fired up the others, especially in their desire to win, that their use of deployed forces became sharpened. More often than not, they won the battle with the same combination of daring and skill that Mattlow always showed.

It is sad that the members of this sibko have no awareness of their genetic progenitor, other than that gleaned from their codex. Having one's genes selected for the gene pool is a wonderful honor, an extension of one's existence into the lives of others. It is like having one's name enshrined somewhere or a holiday dedicated in one's honor. But such acts always presume that we remember the person. When I question these sibbers, however, few of them have any knowledge of their father, just his victories. There is no Mattlov legacy. We fought in no great wars, he and I. We won only small skirmishes. With efficiency and style, to be sure, but the exploits were not quite in the grand manner of heroism.

Aidan's intensity in building his model was something to see. There was a sense of artistry in the way his delicate, spatulate fingers (the kind that can rack across a cockpit keyboard rapidly, guided by instinct rather than thought) held the light pen as it selected a piece and moved it into place on the construct. Ramon Mattlov would not have had this kind of patience. His hands would have crushed the model before finishing it, not because he could not build it, but because the task had no importance to him.

Remembering Mattlov and how he handled others, I shoved Aidan out of the holotank, deliberately found some flaws in the assembly, then—staring into his eyes— I wiped the program from the machine's memory. I tried to see in his expression any anger that I had just destroyed several man-hours of his work, but he remained impassive. The careful, studied look of a warrior-cadet was what he managed, and I felt good about that. When he first arrived here, we would have seen the fury. Now he has trained as a warrior for some time, and knows that unwritten rules specify with whom one may become angry and with whom one may not. And one must show no reaction to the unit commanding officer. "Build a better one," I said to him and walked away. He did. I was tempted to wipe out that one, too, but I do have perspective. I do have perspective.

He is not aware that I am keeping such a watch on him, for I find ways to intrude on the achievements and attempts of the other cadets also.

It is strange, the life of the commanding officer. Whatever I feel—and, more importantly, what I believe—must be hidden from all. There is only theory, there is only drill, there is only the final victory, there is only the Clan. I love the Clan. The others, the cadets and qualified warriors, even officers, they must love the Clan, too. I am not writing about glory and honor here. Not at all. The lowest caste member doing the most menial, odorous, filthy task must love the Clan as much as I do.

That is where the two Kerenskys, General Alexandr and Nicholas, were so visionary. A society whose goal is the restoration of the Star League cannot be tainted with self-doubt or criticism. Any deviation from the goal is waste; deviations are useful only if they can be remolded and refitted to the Clan ideals. Just as we collect our debris from the battlefield and refashion it into other useful materials, so must ideas be refashioned into utility. That is the way of the Clan. I have read that pacifism was once considered a sensible ideal, but to hate war should not be called pacifism. A warrior is not the opposite of a pacifist. A pacifist destroys his weapons and welcomes the nonpacifist into his home—to demolish it. A warrior deploys his weapons around his home but may never need to use them. Which person really desires peace? The man who dies because he will not use a weapon? The man who lives quietly on the other side of his weapons? Perhaps neither, but the man with the weapons at least has a chance when somebody attacks him. I desire peace and will fight to the death for it. The Star League is peace, or at least may be. The Clans will restore the Star League.

I must be tired. I am starting to sound like some rote repetition of some old, Kerensky-inspired text. Old warriors never die, they just ramble on.

I hope Aidan benefits from our harshness toward him. He seems strong, but has an edge of singularity about him. He is not like the others. There is a secret Aidan being held back from us, I am certain of that. Whether it will come out, I do not know. Whether it will bring him success or failure at the final Trial, I do not know.

I must make him succeed, for Ramon Mattlov's sake.

I know how difficult it is to be at this stage of training, where one is just learning the weaponry. Soon, they will begin to know the feel of a real, fully armed BattleMech, and then will begin the real tests.

How many of them will even reach the final test? This sibko started with twelve. Six cadets remain. I remember only slightly the ones who are gone. There was the one named Dav, who will succeed very well in the artisan caste to which he has been assigned. Also, the surprisingly athletic, stocky fellow, Endo. I cannot easily forget him, for I had to supervise the disposal of his body after he was run over by a light tank during field maneuvers. No one knew how he got in the path of the tank. The driver said the boy suddenly stumbled in front of the vehicle, then looked at it bearing down on him as if it were an apparition.

Others in the sibko have failed at different points of the training. I do not recalls any other names. Left are Aidan and his near-twin Marthe, a feisty scrapper named Bret, a skilled battler named Rena, and two others whose staying power seems unlikely: Tymm does not seem smart enough to handle a difficult fighting machine, while Peri is intelligent but only barely successful when manual skills are required. I would like to see her succeed in a BattleMech cockpit, but I suspect she will be out of her element. Though she would do well in any other caste, I notice in her codex that she scores well enough to go to the scientists.

Even if Peri could hold her own in all phases of the training, she will probably flush out in the next phase, when we accelerate the BattleMech exercises and set the survivors among this sibko against each other. Peri is not competitive enough.

This phase could eliminate Aidan, too. He is, in a way, too competitive. He needs too much to succeed.

I cannot write any more now. The joint of my shoulder, where my real bodily muscle is fused with the myomer muscular structure of my artificial arm, aches so much that I am unable to put further thoughts together.

Now I will just sit here in the darkness, trying to read the future in the carved lines of the palm of my prosthetic hand.

# 9

As she whispered instructions to Aidan, Joanna's voice was almost affectionate (but that was ridiculous, had to be just imagination). "Rotate torso back to center forward. Slowly. That is adequate. Not smooth but adequate, Cadet Aidan. Now you, Cadet Peri."

Aidan glanced down at the screen of his onboard computer monitor. It diagrammatically showed Peri's 'Mech, a stripped-down *Kit Fox* like his. The *Kit Fox* was a slower light 'Mech than some others, but at its best had reasonable versatility and firepower.

Observing from the control tower were Marthe, Bret, Rena, and Tymm, along with Falconer Joanna. Aidan was sure they were envious that he and Peri had been chosen for the shakedown runs in the first exercise with full-fledged 'Mechs. Of course, Joanna could override the controls at any time. No one was foolish enough to think a cadet could manipulate a 'Mech effectively the first time in its cockpit.

Joanna put Peri through the same maneuvers, simple movements of the 'Mech torso, that Aidan had just completed. He was pleased to see that Peri's control was not as sure as his. Her 'Mech seemed to rotate in quick, jerky moves, probably indicating nervousness in her pressing of control buttons (These *Kit Foxes* were being stabilized by the onboard computers rather than using the cadet's own sense of balance via a neurohelmet. This made the 'Mech's movements ungainly.)

On his screen the running score for Peri was accumulating slowly, and he could see that, at least in torso-operation, he would remain ahead of her in total points. She would not like that. Peri spent most of her off-time

WAY OF THE CLANS

worrying about how she could improve her initiatory and reactive functions in order to keep up with the physical side of training. She already scored second-highest, just behind Marthe, on the more academic challenges that training provided. Some thought that she had become Falconer Dermot's pet, which was the reason she was selected as one of the first two to actually get inside a 'Mech and operate it. Perhaps so, but Aidan wondered whether the two of them had been chosen not so much for their abilities but because Joanna perceived them as failures and wanted to display their ineptitude to the others. The more Joanna rode him about his mistakes, the more she searched for the psychological flaws in his makeup, the more she told him he would flush out of training—the more Aidan needed to succeed. Not only because he wanted to be a MechWarrior, had always wanted to be a MechWarrior, but because he was determined to draw a drop of approval from her. (He did not, of course, know that when that moment came, later that day, it would happen in the wrong place and be so damned disappointing.)

Peri finished the torso drill and Joanna addressed Aidan. "Cadet Aidan. Check your heat scale. Does it show up normal? Respond."

On the intercom, cadets always had to wait for Joanna's order to respond before they could press and hold down the blue button next to the 'Mech throttle and actually speak to her. He had expected the communication restrictions to be relaxed once in a 'Mech, and it surprised him to learn that he could still not speak to Joanna or any other officer without permission to respond.

"Heat scale normal," he said and released the button.

"As it should be. I tell you to check only to make sure you realize the most important cockpit rule. Never—not in the heat of battle or the excitement of fixing an enemy 'Mech in your sights, lining it up, and using your most skillful assault plan, your best array of weaponry in the fancy blasts and pulses that have become your battlefield specialty—never, *never* forget that you must be continually conscious of the ribbons of information revealed on the heat-scale gauge. A 'Mech is like a living being; it is like the horse of the cavalry, the camel of the desert warrior. You must continually care for it, not push it too much, not allow it to become overheated. Just as those animals speeded up the time, and in many ways, expanded the territory over which wars could be conducted, so the BattleMech—and especially the OmniMech—has quickened and enhanced the possibilities of ground warfare. But even with the improved heat-sink technology of the OmniMechs our scientists have provided us, we can still disable our own 'Mech, making it a sitting duck for others, or even get it blown up and ourselves with it, *because we get so caught up in being a hero that we forget the patterns of awareness that a 'Mech pilot must maintain at all times*. These patterns include the knowledge of your own 'Mech as well as the situation of the fellow warriors of your Star or Star Cluster. This warning is for all of you. Cadet Peri, you understand this, *quiaff?* Respond.''

''Aff.''

''Cadet Aidan? Respond.''

''Aff.''

''If you do, and if you have the stomach for combat, at the moment the special red light installed beside your primary screen begins to pulse, engage in battle.''

Engage in battle? Had he heard right? This was supposed to be a mere exercise in first-time awareness of being in a real 'Mech. Joanna had said nothing about battle in her instructions.

Aidan had no more time to ponder the question, nor was he allowed to question any order at this stage of training (a cadet could not address an officer without permission, even in a live-ammunition exercise like this), because the red light came on and Peri was wheeling her 'Mech around. Its right arm, the one with the autocannon clicking into readiness, was rising upward. Quickly, almost frantically, he began attending to the overhead controls. It seemed to him that to keep Peri from getting the upper hand right off, he had to make an anticipatory move. For a moment he panicked, briefly forgetting all the classroom and simulator training he had already endured.

Aidan maneuvered his 'Mech a step backward and to the right. His instinct proved correct, as Peri's first shots went wide to the left. He had no time to instruct his computer to calibrate, but he suspected those shots would have missed him even if he had kept his 'Mech standing still.

Crashing into his ears like an attack vehicle came Joanna's voice: "Poor start, the two of you. These are awesome machines, even ones as light and stripped-down as these. You can do better. Cadet Peri, use some sense. Do not shoot for the mere sake of shooting. Cadet Aidan, I do not want to see any strategic retreats. That is not the way of the Clan. Not until all aggressive tactics have been tried." For a moment, Aidan thought she had clicked off, then her voice came again, just as loud, just as angry: "And, by the way, my gentle eyasses, I hope you have taken note of the fact that none of your weapons are powered-down. We have detectors for everything you do, what you use and what you do not use. If you get nervous and soil your drawers, we will know it immediately. Now let me see at least the facsimile of a pair of warriors out there. No responses."

As she talked, Aidan was positioning the small pulse laser in his *Kit Fox's* left arm. Even before thumbing a shot, he felt unusually confident. He had scored well in weapons training. On every range, in every practice chamber, he had amassed amazing clusters of hits on any individual target. That was, of course, known-distance marksmanship training. Its fixed targets were a cinch compared to a moving 'Mech, as Joanna continually reminded them. In simulators, where computer versions of all types of 'Mechs came at the cadet suddenly, Aidan's scores were a bit less, but still second only to Marthe's, whom he beat on known-distance targets.

He checked the relevant conditions for battle on his computer screen. There was no wind, no weather factors to affect calculations. He noted good sight-alignment in the computer simulations of each weapon, and no reason to punch in any adjustment calibrations.

Before Joanna had finished speaking, he shot a series of pulses toward Peri's 'Mech, hitting it almost in the center of the torso, sending some large particles of armor flying. But she executed a rotation of the torso and his final salvos flew past the 'Mech. Then she swung the 'Mech's upper body back and began to charge at him.

He had to admire the maneuver. Desperate as Peri was, though, he knew she was the kind of pilot who would overheat faster than her machine. Joanna said often enough that too many warriors did not have enough heat sinks in their heads.

Aidan fired more bursts of his small pulse laser, not bothering to aim, just a little bravado to show the oncoming pilot that he could be just as aggressive and that employing peculiar strategies was not enough. Peri, halting her 'Mech a few meters away, quickly responded by raising her 'Mech's right arm straight into the air and shooting off some blasts of her own. In the boxy, long-legged 'Mech, the gesture had a distinctly human look, an annoying indifference to Aidan's skills, whatever they might prove to be. It made him want to finish this unexpected skirmish that much faster.

His laser fire had been a show of arrogance; now was the time to do some damage. Leveling his right arm, he fired a pair of missiles from his Streak 2-pack, hoping to catch Peri off-guard, but she was ready for the assault. An anti-missile machine gun in her 'Mech's left torso started firing. His missiles exploded before reaching a target, their flames and debris obscuring his view of the action for a moment. If any shred of doubt had remained about the reality of the battle, the shrapnel fragments flying by and bouncing off his *Kit Fox* would have convinced him.

His lapse at that moment could have been fatal. Peri used the temporary camouflage of missile destruction to move to her left and take up a different position. When the smoke cleared, Aidan was aiming at nothing in particular. She had, he realized, deliberately fired too many bursts to catch him napping and line up some new shots of her own. Her laser dispatched a steady beam that stitched a semicircular line in the armor of Aidan's 'Mech. As Peri's beams rocked his machine, he thought for a moment that he had lost control, that the *Kit Fox* would collapse, bend at the waist and fall forward and hit the ground. But he recovered quickly, his emotions rising into the dangerous regions of their heat scale.

He rotated his machine enough to face Peri again. Timing the shots precisely, he began firing his left-arm laser simultaneously with his right-arm LB 5-X autocannon. Peri responded sharply, revolving her 'Mech slightly and nearly avoiding Aidan's assault. Some shots grazed her chest armor, sending a few metal slivers sailing into the air but doing little damage otherwise.

Aidan tried to adjust to Peri's new move. Before he realized she had fired anything, his 'Mech was rocked by a direct hit on its left leg. A quick fall would have been the end of the match for him and his 'Mech, but this particular lucky shot was not enough to do more than rattle him momentarily.

Before Peri could inflict more injury, Aidan fired off a few more rounds from the autocannon. Dark smoke rose from the areas of armor where his shots had found targets, and Peri's 'Mech appeared to reel backward on its heels. Aidan recognized the move as a feint, designed to force his hand, fool him into launching an SRM or repeat the autocannon fusillade. He wished his 'Mech had jump capability, but this type of thirty-tonner was not equipped with that particular talent.

"What is this? Playground fun?" Joanna said in a voice that seemed to make the earphones of Aidan's headset tremble. "Have both of you planned what you will do with your future in another caste? No responses."

The words must have shaken up Peri, for her 'Mech regained its footing, and began running toward him with light, quick steps, all its weapons operating full-power and sending pieces of armor flying in all directions from various areas on Aidan's 'Mech. But her tactics were too showy and too desperate. At that moment, Aidan knew he had the battle won.

Staying calm, ignoring the light damage Peri's barrage was causing, he leveled his large laser and zeroed in on the joint linking her 'Mech's torso with its left arm. It was a bit of a crossfire, but it worked. His beam, steady and on target, burst through armor and disabled something in the link between the two sections. The 'Mech's left arm dropped suddenly, the two lasers operating there searing a deep line in the ground. The disabling sent Peri's 'Mech off balance and it began to teeter. Aidan did not know how he knew, but he sensed his opponent desperately struggling to set her machine aright. He knew she had lost control when the 'Mech began to bend forward at the waist.

"Cadet Peri!" Joanna shouted. "Check your heat scale. You are in danger of overheating."

"Not yet," came Peri's voice, sounding weak. "I have lost only 30 percent."

"No responses. That one will go on report, you can be sure. And you, Cadet Aidan. Have you become a statue? What of? The Bewildered Bystander? You have a chance to finish her. Do it!"

Finish her? Aidan thought. Any attack he mounted now, with him heavy with firepower and her nearly helpless, might kill her. Peri belonged to his sibko. He had known her all his life, had grown up with her. How could he be ordered to end that in a split second?

Yet, in every training session, the cadets had been inculcated with the necessity of obeying orders. And Joanna had ordered. Noting that his heat scale level was still in the normal range, he zeroed in both lasers and the autocannon on Peri's 'Mech, which was now beginning to right itself.

He set himself to observe his victory as he pressed the buttons controlling his weapons.

And nothing happened.

Peri's *Kit Fox* stood passively and no firepower was being emitted from Aidan's weapons. He began punching buttons so hard he felt his joystick slip and slide in its anchoring notch. No matter what button he pushed, there was no weapons response. The weapons display on his screen indicated complete shutdown.

When Joanna's voice came back online, she sounded quite pleased. "You might as well declare yourselves dead, the both of you. Cadet Peri, your actions looked suspiciously like cowardice. No response. Cadet Aidan, your hesitation would have set you up for the kill, had you faced an opponent skillful enough to see it and act on it. Do you understand this? Respond."

"I understand, Falconer Joanna. I should have reacted instinctively, taken advantage of the moment."

"At least you got something right, cadet. You had an entire second to react, and you did not. I shut off all of your 'Mech's functions by remote control. In that second of inaction, an enemy could have cut off your head, ripped the fusion engine out of its compartment, and eaten it for breakfast. Disembark from the training 'Mechs, both of you. Now!"

On the ground, as Techs checked out each 'Mech, Aidan felt humiliated. A look over at Peri showed she felt the same. Their sibko came out of the control tower. Instead of offering siblike consolation, their eyes were averted. They stood silently by, allowing Falconer Joanna to emerge from the facility. Her expression did not show the usual arrogance, however. Instead, it was impassive, glancing at Aidan and Peri as though they were from another caste. She ordered the Techs to inform her when the two 'Mechs were ready. One of them said it would be some time because Peri's 'Mech had heated up to low-dangerous levels.

"We will wait, cadets," she said, turning back to the sibko. "We have been allocated only these two light 'Mechs for our early training. A Clan economy, one that I question. However, we can use this intercession to consider the mistakes our less-than-valiant fellow sibkin have made. When you are in the cockpit, consider what you would have done, what you would do in other situations. Preparedness is the key to success in any warfare. Cadet Marthe and Cadet Tymm!"

Both cadets snapped to attention. Joanna walked over to them and stood very close when she spoke again: "You two will take the 'Mechs out next. This time I would like to see effort. Flash is useless. Shooting off your weapons like the heroes of village tales will get you nowhere."

Aidan wanted to shout at her. Preparedness? How did she dare utter the word, when she had sent him and Peri into a battle without a comfortable set of advance instructions like those she was now giving Marthe and Tymm? The moment the question entered his mind, he knew its answer. Joanna and the others had drilled it into them. There were no proper rules for the conduct of war, no instructions preceding an ambush. And that was what had happened to Aidan and Peri. They had been ambushed, set to fight without preparation just the way it could happen in the midst of a full-fledged engagement.

Joanna finished her speech to Marthe and Tymm, then went over to the Techs to berate them for their slowness. She never seemed satisfied unless she was complaining at someone. The Techs, as was their wont, looked respectful without allowing her words to interfere with their work.

As Aidan walked toward the others, each of his sibkin found a way to avoid his glance. Even Marthe.

Silently, he stood beside her. It seemed as if she had grown a bit faster and was now even taller than he. Or perhaps the trial he had just been through had taken something out of him, made him momentarily smaller. Perhaps a bad experience could do that, make your insides settle inside you so that you temporarily lost a couple of centimeters in height until you revived.

"Why are we no longer friends, Marthe?"

"We are friends. We are sibkin."

"And we have always been that. But it was once different between us. We were, well, close."

She seemed to shudder. "Perhaps. And I see now that it was wrong. It is wrong for two people in the same sibko to favor each other. The sibko is what is important, not its individual members."

He sighed. "Are you sure of that?"

"What do you mean?"

"Look around you and start praising the sibko. Once there were more than ninety of us. Now the others are gone, dead or assigned to nonwarrior castes."

"That is the way of the Clan for warriors."

"Marthe, only six of us are left. When it comes to the Trial of Position, even fewer will remain. There is no sibko anymore. There are only a half-dozen cadets ready to tear out each other's throats."

For a moment Marthe looked at him with some of the old concern in her eyes. "Be careful. If Falconer Joanna hears you talking such heresy . . ."

"Heresy? Is it that? She is one of those who have worked at setting us apart, all of us. It is calculated. That is the only thing I have figured out."

"Figured out? What right have you to—"

"Every right. I am just as concerned with my survival as you are with yours. And that, Marthe, is the difference."

Joanna had noticed them talking and was staring their way with suspicion in her eyes. He had never revealed his special affection for Marthe to Joanna, but he was sure she sensed it.

"Marthe, think of the history we have been taught. They tell us tales of armies shaped into fighting units, of

Stars whose warriors think each other's thoughts so closely that they are precisely aligned. But what do they do here? They find ways to separate us."

"I do not know what you mean."

"We come here as a unit, as a sibko that has grown up together, formed such an intimacy that we can almost read each other's minds. Frequently we do read each other's minds, to the point of saving lives. Now, after all this training, those of us who have survived hardly speak to one another. Bret and Rena have formed a kind of alliance, and the rest of us are on our own. They have split us up, the training officers."

"And I am certain, if you are right, that it is done with an excellent purpose."

"Then you admit that I am right."

"I admit nothing."

"And once you would have. Once we would have talked through the night if there was a problem."

"You spend your nights with—"

"Do you think I would if she did not order it?"

"I do not know what you would do."

"And once you would have known everything I would do. Do you not see? We are being trained to be isolated in the cockpit of a BattleMech, to be on our own, bid on our own, cheat each other if necessary, destroy each other if—"

"Is that why you hesitated when you had a chance at a clear victory today?"

"I might have killed Peri."

"And would that have mattered to you?"

"I do not know anymore. I think it would. Yes, damn it, I think it would. I remember playing at warrior with Peri when we were all children. That may have prevented me from taking the risk of killing her."

"Then you are a fool."

"Then I am a fool."

His response seemed to stop her for a moment, even to soften her hard gaze. It was only there for an instant, but he thought he saw the old kindness in her eyes, the old closeness that would have led at least to a brief touch. When was the last time they had touched like that?

"Look, Marthe, maybe there is some sense to what they are doing. Maybe we have to experience the, I do not know what to call it, the *isolation* of the pilot inside his cockpit—and from that we will learn the new closeness, not that of the sibko, but that of the warrior whose concern will be to an assigned unit. It almost makes sense to me—until I see that you are no longer—''

He stopped. He did not know how to say the words to her anymore. She was as remote to him as Falconer Joanna, but unlike Joanna, he was no longer able to embrace her.

"I am sure, Aidan, that even if you are right, everything is being done for our good. We should not question it, but merely, as ordered, become the best warriors we are capable . . ."

"Stop! That is what they want you to think. That is why we are not friends any longer."

"You are foolish to think of friendship now."

He wanted to say more to her, but Joanna was walking toward them, and he went past Marthe into the control tower. Glancing back, he saw that Joanna was speaking rather severely to Marthe, but he could not hear the words. In the old days Marthe would have repeated them to him later.

Perhaps Marthe was right. It was foolish to think of friendship now. He had to eliminate those traits that were interfering with his progress as a warrior. The next time he had anyone from his sibko in his sights, with live ammo in his weapon and the orders sanctioning the act, he should shoot, kill. Even if it was Marthe.

# 10

"You are angry with me for criticizing your performance in today's exercise." Joanna's voice was matter-of-fact, a tone unusual for her. "Go ahead. You need not wait for me to tell you to respond when we are alone together here."

He was acutely conscious of the stench in Joanna's quarters. Beneath the permeating scent of the sex act they had just completed were other odors, foul ones. Joanna, for all her discipline on the training fields, was not concerned with hygiene when she was alone. The debris she left on the floor might have remained there for days, had not Aidan regularly picked it up because he could not stand the disorder. The accumulated odors in her bedclothes, whose origins he could only guess at, were not pleasant to contemplate.

"You remain silent, eyas. Why?"

"You never call me by my name here."

"And that is why you are silent. How odd!"

"No, it is not why. I just noticed. You called me eyas, one of your nicer derisive terms."

She smiled. Like the matter-of-factness, another rarity.

"You are considering who you are. Let me tell you right now that you should not. Who you are is not important. You are a machine, just as much as the machine you will inhabit—if indeed you do succeed in becoming a warrior.

"The word is MechWarrior, correct? However you say it, the emphasis is on the first syllable, on the 'Mech. The warrior *of* the 'Mech, MechWarrior. The warrior who serves the 'Mech. The warrior who *is* the 'Mech.

Does that sound like someone who should worry about whether or not someone says his name?''

"I suppose not."

"That sounds suspiciously like sullenness, another trait unbecoming in a warrior. You have problems, eyas, *quiaff?*''

"Aff. As you continually remind me."

She sat up suddenly. The frayed old blanket she used as a bedcover fell away from her chest. Once he had viewed her small, well-shaped breasts with some interest, but too much time with her had removed any sensual reactions. Now he noticed more the sweat dripping from her chin onto her chest. There was a long scar running from just below her neckline to the side of her left breast. He had touched that scar so many times, but had never asked how it had come about.

"Sometimes," she said, her voice quiet, a third phenomenon of the night, "I question my choice to allow you to talk to me when you are here. In my room it might be better to continue the customs of the parade ground. What I am going to tell you now, I will tell you only once, and never again, not for the rest of time.''

She grimaced and reached for her tunic, which she had casually thrown onto a bedside table before getting into the bed. Pulling it over her head slowly, she began her little speech while clothing still hid her face.

"Eyas—*Aidan*, I chose you the very first day you arrived here. I saw in your eyes, in the way you held yourself, in the slight hint of defiance even when you thought your face was completely at rest, that the warrior's potential was in you. I was also intrigued by your seriousness, by the look of an adult in your face even when in the midst of that childish team tussle. You revealed an intensity that never let up. I liked that, was even attracted to it. That is why I tried to beat you to a bloody pulp that day. But you never lost the intensity, and you showed your defiance. I liked that, too."

The tunic on, she pulled on the partial jumpsuit that had become her trademark for the cadets. It was a faded silver garment with combat patches on pockets.

"In my own sibko I was the defiant individual, I think even more so than you. I never liked any of the others, while you show a certain vestigial loyalty to your sibkin, what is left of them. All I ever wanted was to become a warrior and get away from the others. I thought I would find genuine camaraderie in the ranks of real warriors, but all I found was even more people in the universe I could cheerfully hate. And I have accepted that, instead of wondering, as others might, if something was wrong with me rather than the others."

She smoothed out the wrinkles in her clothing with a device she had bought in a bazaar on some other planet. It was a round cylinder with a handle. It set off small electrical sparks when it touched the cloth, but she attacked each wrinkle methodically with smooth even strokes, and they smoothed out.

"I have used my hate well in my military career; it has given me a certain, well, impetus. And, frankly, I suspect it is easier for one to hate everyone rather than to struggle with the problems that other, kinder emotions can bring.

"But once in a while, I have a different feeling about someone. I suppose it is just a lesser form of my hate. Whatever it is, I have been cursed with you this time around. What this means is that I would favor one of two things happening: I would like to crush you, bash you into the ground so hard that your subsequent mental deficiencies allow you only the most menial, dirt-swallowing job when you leave here. *Or* I would like to see you become a warrior, fulfilling your potential instead of letting your personal defects conquer you.

"Oh, I recognize that you are different from the rest. And I know that you have formed an unnatural, shall we call it affection, for Cadet Marthe. I have, I think, ruined that, for her good as well as yours. She will become a warrior, and you will not stop that with your silly, romantic yearnings. And for you, she is no longer an obstacle.

"I saw the bond between you two immediately, and I struggled to break it. I am happy that I did. No, do not even comment. It is not for you to question what I do, even the secrets I reveal to you. I have gone out of my way to be cruel to you, to make the training hard for you, to *defeat* you. That is the only way you will succeed, and I know it. You think too much, Aidan, and that will be your downfall."

She stood up, finished with the dewrinkling device. Her long hair, as it usually did, miraculously fell into place, as if there had been some sort of device to iron out its irregularities.

"I see the hatred in your eyes. Good. I want that from you. This is the last time we will be together here. I will not summon you again. From now on, we will talk only under formal conditions. Leave now, without saying anything. I hope you fail. It would fulfill the curse I have put on you."

Aidan was happy to escape from her quarters. Her words had made him hate the place even more, hate her even more.

He spent the next few hours wondering why she had spoken to him in the way she did. Dawn came and went, but he still had no solution for it. All he knew was that he had to prove to Joanna that he could become a warrior. And on that day, the day he succeeded at the final trial, he would spit on her highly polished boots.

## 11

In rare, light-hearted moments, Aidan thought of the quickly passing days as so many fusillades from an autocannon, with him the target. They moved too fast for him to dodge the time-projectiles and they got him dead-center every time. Later, had he been challenged to write down an accurate time sequence of events, he would have failed.

From the day after Joanna had talked to him so openly, everything that happened seemed to separate him even further from others. From the sibko, from Marthe, even from himself. What Joanna had said about him needing to be a machine became true, at least partially. He deliberately concealed any feeling, performed training exercises by the book, snapped to when spoken to—in short, became the ideal cadet. The more he accomplished, the more Joanna berated him in front of the others. In the past her derisive criticisms might have angered him, because he had cared how the others in the sibko regarded him. Now that mattered no longer.

In his bunk at night, exhausted or not, he could not get much sleep. He almost welcomed guard duty, because it gave him something to do with his wakefulness.

One night on duty, he saw the rare sight: a figure out walking on the parade ground. As no one was allowed there overnight, he challenged the stroller.

Only then did Aidan recognize that he was questioning Falconer Commander Ter Roshak. He had heard that Ter Roshak often wandered around the facility at night. Briefly, Aidan wondered if he was making a mistake in confronting the commanding officer, but guard-duty rules stated that anyone, no matter what rank, must explain his presence to the guard if challenged.

Ter Roshak had been deep in thought. When he looked up, he squinted and said blearily, "Ramon? Is that you?"

Aidan challenged him again, and the commander appeared to clear his mind of whatever debris had made him speak so strangely.

"Falconer Commander Ter Roshak. Sibko training supervisor. Very good, cadet. I had forgotten the time. I have been out inspecting various sibkos. I was about to visit your barracks. Would you accompany me? Respond."

"Permission to leave my post, sir."

"Permission granted."

In the barracks, Roshak carried through one of his classic, surprise night inspections, and Aidan had to stand by and watch. The commander kicked Bret out of bed and gave him a hard knock to the side of his head with the artificial arm before telling him that his foot locker was scarred and needed repainting. He held Rena up in the air with the prosthetic limb while informing her that her last session in the training 'Mech was an embarrassment not just to her sibko but to his whole training Cluster. Tymm and Peri were treated similarly, one chewed out for his clothing deficiencies, the other for what Roshak called the set of her sullen mouth. Only Marthe was spared real punishment. Instead, he turned to the others and told them that they should emulate her. Aidan saw a glint in his eye that seemed to indicate a satiric element to his praise. Marthe was the highest scorer of the group, and by pointing this out, Roshak was planting the seeds of little jealousies and resentments into the psyches of the surviving members of the sibko.

Aidan vowed he would not react to Roshak's strategy. He would, instead, provide countermeasures to it, do everything he could to reunite the sibko.

Outside, after the commander ordered Aidan back to guard duty, he eyed him strangely, then said, "You. You are the worst in the bunch. You think too much of yourself, I can see that. You think you can beat the system. You cannot. Respond."

"I have no response, sir."

"I cannot fight you here, not while you are on duty.

Report to my quarters when you come off duty this morning. Respond.''

"Yes, sir.''

However, when Aidan arrived at the commander's quarters, the man was asleep. Without permission to address him, Aidan could not wake him. He waited at the entrance until reveille, but Roshak did not wake up. Nor did he mention the order again.

Aidan cornered Marthe after midday meal, backing her up against the barracks wall.

"The sibko is collapsing. We cannot allow it,'' he said.

For a moment the hint of derision in her eyes made her resemble Falconer Joanna, then she frowned. "Why are you saying this to me?''

"Because we were once . . . close.''

"You have listened too much to the myths. Our closeness, as you call it, was part of the play of children. We are not children now.''

"What are we then? Warriors?''

"You need not be sarcastic. It is a bad trait of yours. How often has Falconer Joanna said—''

"I do not give a damn what she has said. She wants the sibko destroyed.''

"If you are telling the truth, then no doubt the sibko should be destroyed.''

"Then what has it meant, all of our times together? I do not mean you and me, I mean all of us. Those who have survived and those who have died and those who have been reassigned to other castes.''

"It *means* that we have developed properly, that we have first joined together to find the warriors among us, that we have awaited our own fates, each of us, that we—''

"But that is only what they want us to think.''

"They?''

"Joanna. The others. Our sibparents. The training officers. All of them who have steered us, educated us, made us think the way they wanted us to think, influenced—''

"Really, Aidan, you have shut down mentally. You know the way of the Clan as well as any—''

"I am not speaking against the way of the Clan. I do

not know about the Clan. Neither do you. Our world has been circumscribed by our sibko ever since we—''

"And is not that an argument against what you originally said?''

"I do not understand.''

"You say the sibko must be preserved. Now you add that it is the sibko that has limited us. Therefore, the dissolution of the sibko is a necessary phase of our development as warriors. Therefore, the sibko is created so that it may be gradually phased out.''

Aidan wanted to shake her.

"That is nonsense, just recital of lessons. You sound like Falconer Dermot when you—''

"Not so. If I sounded like Dermot, then you would be asleep.''

The humor of the remark, plus the gentle way she spoke it, disconcerted Aidan. It reminded him of how she used to be, when they were still youths in the still-intact sibko. What bothered him even more was that he wanted her to speak to him like that all the time, and he knew that was not possible.

"Aidan,'' she said, the kindness still in her voice. "I miss those old days, too. Some of them, anyway. But I like now just as well. More. I *want* to be a warrior and I am willing to make any change, personal or otherwise, to achieve that.''

"Well, I want that, too.''

"Do you? Do you really?''

"Yes!''

His response sounded overdramatic, forced, even to him.

"I cannot believe you, Aidan. If you wished that, you would not be trying to convince me the sibko must be preserved.''

"But . . .''

"Please. There is no reason to continue this conversation.''

He tried to force her back, push her against the wall. She pushed back just as hard and knocked him off balance. In all their time in the sibko, they had never fought physically, except in the team tussle and other play. With her forearm, she hit him in the throat, just below his Adam's apple. He was angry enough to strike back at anyone else, but not Marthe. She waited for him to finish his coughing fit, then walked away.

In the ensuing week Aidan also tried to persuade the other members of the sibko that they should restore their former group feeling, that they should not let training officers divide them. Bret did not even understand Aidan's argument. He said he thought the sibko was as close as ever. Peri claimed there had never been a feeling of closeness in the sibko, not for her at least. She had, she said, always wanted something else. Rena would not even talk to Aidan, while Tymm merely looked as dazed about the subject of the sibko as he generally did during training.

Tymm, in fact flushed out a few days later. His scores had always been the lowest of the six survivors. Aidan never knew exactly why Tymm was found unworthy, but he suspected that Tymm's tendency to get his training 'Mech's feet entangled in undergrowth and his slowness in employing his weaponry must definitely have contributed to the young man's failure. Like many of the other sibko members who were gone, Tymm did not even say goodbye. One morning the sibko survivors awoke to find Tymm's bunk empty, its bedclothes properly rolled up and secured. That was always the sign. Soon a pair of orderlies entered the barracks and took the bunk and bedclothes away. Tymm's bunk had been at the end of a row, and now only a large gap remained.

The barracks, which had once seemed so crowded, suddenly seemed cavernous. The winds of Ironhold came through old cracks in the building and created uncomfortable draughts. Aidan caught another cold, as did Rena. Issued only a rough piece of gray cloth to handle such an illness, Rena annoyed Aidan by telling him not to steal her cloth to wipe his nose. That made him furious, because his own pronounced sense of personal hygiene made him careful to use only his own little gray swatch.

Marthe became more silent than ever. Two days after Tymm's departure, she moved her bed into the gap, thus isolating herself from the other four cadets. Bret, Rena, and Peri did not mind her withdrawal as much as Aidan did. After their last conversation, however, he could no longer find a reason to speak to her himself.

"We do not have enough people left to form a team tussle," Bret said out of the blue one night.

"You will always be a child, you stupid freebirth," Rena muttered.

Hearing the reviled epithet, Bret jumped on Rena and wrestled her to the barracks floor. His eyes seemed inflamed with anger. Aidan rushed to the grappling pair and tried to lift Bret off Rena's body. Peri, reacting just as quickly, pulled Aidan away.

"Let them fight. It is too exciting to miss."

"You call fighting among ourselves exciting?"

"The way things have been lately."

She nodded her head toward Marthe, who was merely sitting on her bunk and viewing the fight as if it were an entertainment.

"This is what I tried to tell you, Peri—about the sibko and—"

"Let it rest, Aidan. It is a lost cause. What we have to do is get through it."

Bret and Rena's brawl was getting vicious. She had poked him in the eye to get him off her, then kicked him between the legs. That would have finished off most persons, but Bret, his tenacity intact, managed to plunge forward and butt Rena hard in the abdomen. As headbutts go, it did not look like much, but it had its effect on Rena, whose face contorted in pain. She doubled over.

It was a ridiculous sight, each of them bent at the waist and trying to suppress moans of pain. (That was another contribution of Falconer Joanna, the requirement not to show pain. "Think of it, eyasses. You hurt and your enemy can see it. What confidence, what an edge you are giving away.") Peri put her arm around Bret, said some soothing words, while Aidan attended to Rena. Rena's eyes were glazed.

Glancing up, it seemed to Aidan that, for the first time in a long time, the four of them were grouped together in a way reminiscent of old sibko days. He reached out and took Peri's hand, thus linking the quartet together.

From the other side of the room came a loud laugh. Marthe was amused.

"Fools," she said, her intonation mimicking, it seemed, Joanna's.

Marthe walked to the group and knelt down across from Aidan. She put her hand on Bret's shoulder and gripped Rena's arm. She smiled at Aidan. Perhaps it was his imagination, but it seemed to him like the old smile. It certainly reminded him of the two of them together before warrior training began.

"Fools," she said again and shook her head slowly from side to side.

The sibko broke up in a few minutes, and the wounds of both battlers were attended to.

That night, another sleepless one for Aidan, he wondered if they had restored the sibko's old camaraderie. It would be miraculous if it were so.

The next day showed that was not to be. Bret went back to being argumentative, Rena sullen, Peri enigmatic. And Marthe stayed in her corner of the massive barracks, aloof, uninterested in anything her fellow sibkin might do.

There was never another moment when sibko feelings reemerged. They were separate forever. It did not matter. It was not long before only three of them were left, at the edge of a broad meadow, awaiting with cadets from other sibkos their opportunity to prove themselves in a Trial of Position and become warriors of the Jade Falcon Clan.

# 12

I earned my Bloodname more through staying power than actual acts of heroism, wrote Falconer Commander Ter Roshak. I participated in so many battles, racked up so many kills, led a Star that seemed blessed in rarely suffering even minor casualties—all minor achievements but they added up until I was worthy to contend for a Bloodname. I even won my Trial of Bloodright by being the last one standing, being the survivor, and not through any extraordinary skills.

Because I had studied Ramon Mattlov so thoroughly, I became good at bidding during my career, but that was my only talent related to strategy. In actual warfare, strategy was not my forte. Sometimes I was lucky enough to have an adjutant who covered my weakness in that area, but mostly I just blundered into the middle of dancing 'Mechs and flying projectiles and figured out how to get out of it. I suppose tactics were my specialty. Once in the middle of a conflict, I knew what to do, almost instinctively. I barked out orders to the rest of my Star, they carried them out, and we won. I saw the enemy's strategy and countered it. If five 'Mechs were converging on three of us, I knew how to deploy my forces, use surrounding terrain, feint and thrust, make surprise jumps, hide when necessary, tromp with my 'Mech's heavy feet on enemy pilots escaped from their cockpits, and whatever else was needed to extricate my command from an engagement successfully. I turned odds against into odds for.

But now I am in danger of becoming old, losing my edge, settling like fresh dirt into the grave of my memories.

Now that I think of it, my real talent was for logistics. I know of nobody who was better at arranging for the proper supplies, scavenging for food and shelter among hostile villages, transporting troops quickly and efficiently. The logistical mind sees what is needed most immediately, next-most immediately, and so on, then goes out and gets it. A logistical mind thrust into battle becomes, perhaps, a tactical one. In battle I would take stock of the dangers in exactly the same manner I planned logistics. I decided what was the most dangerous element or factor in the battle, the next-most, and so on. Once I had that set in my mind, I worked out the necessities coolly and calmly, and perhaps that accounts for my success record.

But I got away with it only so long. Superiors soon saw that I was a good warrior but not a hero. As they are prone to do, they got the best out of me, then consigned me to this duty of wet-nursing cadets. I will not say I am bitter about the assignment. I gain from it a certain amount of satisfaction. And it takes planning, too. I determine early on which cadets have the potential and which will undoubtedly be reassigned to the lesser castes. The warrior caste demands near-perfection, and the only way to obtain it is by winnowing down a sibko to its two, three, or four best cadets to compete in the final Trial of Position. Occasionally I have seen a sibko produce more than five—that is only logical, considering that the gene-pool contribution in some sibkos is nothing short of spectacular—but it is rare to see that many reach the last stage. It is estimated that half of the cadets fail this final trial, too. I am proud that none of the sibkos I have supervised has ever failed to produce at least one successful warrior.

There are those who criticize the warrior program as it is practiced here on Ironhold, those who have an economical turn to their minds. They say that we produce too few warriors, that our armies grow too slowly, and BattleMechs will be left gathering dust in underground caches. Their arguments become poignant when they discuss actual wars, where warriors may be killed at a faster rate than we are turning them out here. Yet we do produce many more warriors than anyone might expect, what with all the training units spread out over Ironhold. I am, after all, only one of more than a hundred falconer commanders in charge of training units, and each of our units processes at least twenty sibkos. I am overseeing twenty-six sibkos at present, ranging from newly arrived contingents to the sibkos whose members have been whittled down to their survivors. I believe we are, in fact, shipping out warriors at an astonishing rate, given the demanding, harrowing, and long training program they have to get through. Nicholas Kerensky would, I think, have been satisfied, and undoubtedly proud, of our accomplishments. The warriors we produce do tend to validate his genetic programs, starting with the gene pool from which most of us who qualify have emerged. His theories of eliminating the worst traits, those that interfered with the skills and thus the success of a warrior, and transmitting the best traits, those of our most skilled and wondrous warriors, to sibling companies have been proven over and over. And here on Ironhold, we carry on the theories by taking these products of the genetic program and doing our own eliminations. The end result is that we train the best warriors humanly possible. That is the way of the Clan and the wonder of the genetic program.

I am not prone to nostalgia (a negative trait if there ever was one), but I sometimes think of my own sibko and our days in training. We were a rough group, unlike some of the sibkos in training now, and at least half of us disposed of the other half before we got down to the serious business of molding ourselves into cadets worthy of testing. My first time out in a stripped-down 'Mech, I killed one of my sibkin. Looking down at his corpse, I wondered if we had ever been close. I walked away from the body with no regrets. And regret has not been a part of my arsenal since.

The Mattlov/Pryde sibko has reached its final stages. Five youngsters remain, including Cadet Aidan, whom I have observed carefully ever since noting such a strong Mattlov resemblance. They are nervous, eager, almost ready to attain that curious psychological blend of individual and machine that occurs when a warrior is at one with his 'Mech. I have tried to explain this feeling to many people over the years, but few non-warriors have even approached understanding. Even some warriors have claimed ignorance of this phenomenon, saying it is just the feedback from the neurohelmet that creates the illusion of oneness. But it could not be merely the neurohelmet. I fought countless battles with my headgear damaged and lost not an iota of my connection to the machine. I cannot imagine any warrior being successful in a 'Mech without having the sense of it as a living being for whom he or she is the driving force, the brain. But even that does not express it. The meld feels almost like a joining of metal and circuitry with the skin and innards of the pilot. Drivers of vehicles have told me they have often felt the same way about their machines.

Looking at the roster of Aidan's sibko, as I am doing now, I am impressed with the achievements of this quintet of survivors. Still, I suspect that one or two of them might not make it to the last test. Cadet Peri, whose intellect nearly matches that of the top student, Cadet Marthe, still lags appreciably in her mechanical skills. It may be dangerous to allow her to go much further. She will be useful in another caste. No sense wasting a life for purposes of bravado. I must speak with Falconer Joanna about Peri.

Of the rest, Marthe and Aidan have the superior skills, although only Marthe really knows it. I can see the doubts in Aidan's eyes, the residual effects of the riding that Joanna gives him. She has done everything to take away his confidence, to break him. But he keeps coming back, rising to his impressive full height as he did when she fought him so hard on that first day long ago when the sibko first arrived on Ironhold. Resilience seems to be his special talent. Yet, there is a weariness in him that worries me. I have told Joanna not to be so harsh with him, but she is adamant. She does not believe in the theory that says a training officer should go from being disciplinarian to mentor. Indeed, she insists that being kind to a cadet, even one who seems destined for success, gives him or her a certain slack that can affect everything from concentration to timing. Perhaps she is right. With my irritability and sudden temper, I would make a poor mentor. Yet, other officers who advocate the milder approach also turn out successful warriors with their methods.

It often seems strange that our training goes against the grain of military training as practiced in past eras. In earlier times, the idea was to take separate individuals and mold them into a unit that would work and fight efficiently together. As I understand it from some readings, the process consisted of conditioning the minds of the trainees. Any trace of individuality was removed in favor of group thinking so that the military unit would be united. In our approach, we travel an opposite route. We take a group that is united, a sibling company or sibko, and break down its unity. We even set them against each other, as we did with this particular sibko. And why? So that we can turn them into individuals, give them the singularity necessary to the character of a BattleMech pilot. Oh, we realize the necessity of unity in battle, but that comes later. Assigned to a Star, the individual relearns the unity of the sibko, this time with new companions. And, some say, it is a new and better unity, one that adapts to new warriors coming in to replace dead or departed ones, and to new units. The old team tussels of the sibko seem primitive when compared to the feisty concord and loose harmony of a genuine fighting unit.

It is hard to predict what will happen to the other two cadets in the Mattlov/Pryde sibko. The short one, Bret, is a battler, all right, and reasonably intelligent, but he is more bravado than skill. He might make it. He is certainly out to prove himself and will accept nothing less than victory, a quality we always say is necessary for a warrior.

The other one, Rena, does not quite seem like warrior material. She was once overweight and still moves with some of her former clumsiness and heaviness. Yet she has courage and a tenacity toward surmounting obstacles, so she may surprise us all.

I worry most about Aidan, not because he cannot succeed, but that he might not. Sometimes, when I dream of the dying Ramon Mattlov, the face of the corpse changes and becomes his near twin, Aidan. Interpreters would say that I fear something, something related to this stubborn cadet. I have seen many trainees who are too clever by half, and he leads them all in this respect. All I can do now is wish the best for him.

# =13=

Aidan woke up suddenly. Near his bunk a dark blur moved slowly, or else he was not really awake and this was a nightmare.

"Who is it?" he whispered.

The blur hesitated, as if it wanted neither to sleep nor to haunt.

"It is Peri, is it not?" he said.

Her shoulders sagged. She had not wanted to be recognized.

"I am leaving," she said. "Please do not speak louder. I do not want to display my humiliation to the others."

"It is not humiliation, it is—"

"I know. It is part of the whole damn noble goal we all seek. Only now I am out of it. Think of how it feels. All this time spent in training, only to be flushed out and told you now belong to another caste. Well, I do not *belong* to any other caste. Wherever I am, people will look at me and the thought will cross their minds that once I was in warrior training. It is like a brand mark on my forehead. I am a warrior and will remain so all my life. All my life."

Aidan sat up in his bunk and tried to make out her face in the dim light.

"Where are they sending you?"

"I am not told. Just that it will be in the scientist caste. I will be an apprentice, A Tech in training to be a scientist."

"That sounds good, Peri. Important."

"It is. As consolations go, it is acceptable. That is the way of the Clan, as they so often tell us. We accept what comes. Death or honor, success or failure. But I wanted to be a warrior, needed to be one. You knew that better than anybody. For some reason, I have never fathomed, you seem to perceive things the rest of us do not.''

"I used to think we all knew everything about each other, that such understanding was no special talent.''

"But we were each different. I always thought that was the interesting thing about our sibko—about most sibkos, I suspect.''

"What do you mean?''

"We come from the same gene pool. With the same genetic materials, we might have been identical in most ways. But, just as there is a great deal of physical variation among us, there are also differences of talent and ability. It says a lot for our genetic forebears, tends to confirm the superiority of successful Bloodnamed warriors and their achievements, that there are more than sufficient good traits in the two geneparents to be doled out among their sibspring. Validates the worthiness of the Kerensky program, in a way. Still, I wonder why so much variation in our sibko? Seems to me we should *all* have become warriors—or, conversely, all of us should have flushed out. But the differences in our performances have been phenomenal.''

She glanced around the room, where the others made various sleeping sounds. She seemed to be searching for answers to the questions she had posed.

"You know, now I think of it, I would like to study that. Certainly, if they choose to lock me up with a bunch of scientists, I stand a good chance of attempting such study.''

They fell into an uncomfortable silence. Aidan wondered if one should say something positive, thoughtful, comforting at a time like this. As Clansmen, it was so hard for any of them to come up with a pleasantry, a piece of well-considered counsel or even a polite farewell. If sibparent Glynn had not told them all those stories about heroes in other cultures, they might not even have been aware that there *were* alternate customs, alternate behaviors. Peri apparently had the same problems with saying goodbye, for she said, "Go back to sleep, Aidan. We do not know how to part from each other, even though we have grown up together and have rarely been apart until now. It was the same with all the others when they left. Maybe that is why most of us try to steal away instead of saying long goodbyes.''

Aidan nodded and lay back against his pillow. The dark blur disappeared, then returned.

''Aidan?''

''Yes?''

''You could have killed me that day. I was in your sights and nearly disabled. I could sense the moment when it should have happened. Why did you hesitate?''

''I am not certain. It did not seem right to kill you, so I did not.''

''You were wrong. You should not have hesitated.''

Then she disappeared again and did not return.

In the morning, with Peri's bunk in readiness for orderlies to transport it away, none of the other remaining members of the sibko mentioned her absence. Marthe did stare at the bunk for a brief time, but what she felt or thought was not evident on her face.

That same day Falconer Joanna flung open the barracks door, stood outlined in bright light, then announced with something distantly resembling cheerfulness that it was time to scrub down the entire building. Inside and out. At one time the sibkin might have exchanged wondering glances, the kind that clearly showed there was something strange about the order. Joanna had always left maintenance of the barracks to the sibko and had seemed satisfied with its performance. It seemed significant that she wanted a thoroughgoing cleaning now. Without the least non-verbal communication between them, the sibkin merely awaited their specific orders.

Holding the bucket and mop in front of her as if it were disease-ridden, Joanna handed them to Aidan and told him he was assigned the bathroom area, the ''Cave'' as it was called in Clan lore. And for good reason, Aidan thought as he entered it: it was like a cave, dark and damp. Turning on a lamp, Aidan worked hard at making the room not only clean but shiny. Every piece of offending matter, no matter what might have been its origin, was rubbed or scraped away until the room looked as it had the first day they had arrived at the barracks. Then it struck him. The first day. Which meant that some previous training unit had painstakingly scrubbed and cleaned it before his sibko had arrived. Which suggested that they were now leaving the barracks for the last time, preparing it for its next occupants. Which got Aidan so excited he could feel his heart beat fast and hard.

It was all he could do to remove the debris he had gathered up, so anxious was he to see if the others sensed what he had. Outside the Cave, he glanced at Marthe, who was shining the metal rim of a window.

"We are leaving here, *quiaff?*" he said.

She did not look up from her task. "Aff. Or, at least, that seems possible."

He tried not to notice the detachment in her voice, the indifference to what should have been an exciting moment. She just went on with her polishing. The surface already looked shiny enough.

"Where are we going, do you think?" Aidan asked her.

"There seems little doubt. The other side of Ironhold, where the heavy 'Mechs are."

"It is the final test, then?"

"The preliminary to it, I suspect. If you recall Falconer Joanna's instructions from last week, before we reach the Trial, we must complete our training using fully operational neurohelmets mated with actual 'Mechs, not just the usual simulators. Also, we will become familiar with the 'Mechs we will use in the Trial of Position."

"I can hardly believe the time has come."

She turned to him, frowning. "Why is it so hard to believe? It must come sooner or later, *quiaff?*"

"Well, aff. But are you not excited by its coming?"

"No more than I should be. It is, after all, just the next stage of the training."

"But it will decide our lives. Are you not worried about that?"

"Worried? Why should I be worried? Whoever succeeds will become a warrior. Whoever does not will be assigned another role to play, another caste to serve. I am satisfied with whatever comes."

"Are you? Truly, Marthe?"

"Of course. We do what we must to promote the goals of our society. That is the way of the Clan."

Aidan stared at her for a while, watching how calmly she finished up the job of polishing the metal.

"I do believe, Marthe, that you speak the truth. You will accept what comes."

"Of course I will. And so will you."

"I do not know you anymore."

"You never did. Nobody ever really knows anybody."

"I did know you. I did."

"You may think so."

"You will allow that, will you?"

"Yes."

Aidan nodded and walked away from her. He was afraid of what he might have said next. When the Trial was over and they were both warriors, they would have to have a good, long talk. He needed that almost as much as he needed to succeed in the Trial of Position.

Ter Roshak sat beside the pilot in the skimmer that took the sibko to its new training area. Aidan noticed that the commander never looked back at them, just as he had barely seemed to notice them when he boarded, just as he had always moved among them with supreme indifference except when he had a reason to inflict inexplicable punishment. It was said that he sometimes took out one of the 'Mechs in a Trial, just to mow down a specific cadet who had incurred his displeasure. In some stories he was a ghostlike or even godlike presence swooping down on an unsuspecting cadet and slicing his 'Mech into small pieces. Joanna said they were all lies, these stories, these myths, but—in the tradition of superstitions throughout the known universe—no sensible, forthright, unimaginative training officer could convince cadets of the foolishness of the stories surrounding Falconer Commander Ter Roshak.

On one side of the skimmer's interior, Bret and Rena pressed their faces against the skimmer's viewports, competing to spot bits of terrain or activity in the landscape. Their enthusiasm reminded Aidan that, after all, the four of them were still young, still barely out of childhood.

Occasionally Aidan looked out his window, noted that

most of the landscape resembled the area they left a couple of hours ago. For a while they passed over a large lake, where hundreds of fishermen were casting out nets or dangling complex networks of lines in the water.

Next to him, Marthe scarcely ever looked out. She stared forward or at the screen of a pocket computer, apparently considering something in her studies that she probably had already mastered. Perhaps her academic scores were consistently the best because she was continually verifying what she already knew better than anyone else in the sibko. What drove her to such perfectionism? Aidan wondered. He had a drive to succeed, as did Bret and Rena, but Marthe's was different. With Marthe the drive was obsession.

Marthe had changed physically over the last year or so, as had Aidan. He had grown thicker, putting on weight and girth along with the muscles that came to all cadets in their intense physical training. The training officers insisted that because they would spend so much time sitting in cockpits, they should continue calisthenics, running, marches all of their lives. A fat 'Mech pilot was a 'Mech pilot about to die, was one of Dermot's pithy sayings.

Marthe, while just as strong as Aidan, had become leaner, the physical training providing her a thin and wiry body. Her waist had become so small that he thought he could have encircled it with his hands only, had she ever allowed him near enough to try. (It was a long time since she had agreed to sex with Aidan, even longer since she had initiated the act. In fact, she seemed to have given up that part of her life altogether.) Her face had thinned out, too. Its cheekbones were more angular, looking knife-edged from certain angles. Her eyes had sunken a bit, and like the rest of her personality, seemed more guarded. There was a tightness to her lips and a new jut to her chin. Her skin, stimulated by the outdoor segments of their lives, had reddened. Her high forehead seemed higher, further emphasizing the triangular aspect of her face. All these changes had diminished the once-strong resemblance to Aidan. His face was less triangular, cheekbones more blunt, lips fuller. His skin did not reflect daytime exposure as much as hers did and, in fact, had a pale cast to it.

For him, the worst part of how she looked now came when he glanced toward the front of the skimmer and examined Falconer Joanna. Marthe now held her body in the same straightbacked way as Joanna did, tilted her head in the same just off-center manner, wore the same detached look. The look of disdain in Joanna's expression was only hinted at in Marthe's, but had become stronger as the days went by. He wondered if she would eventually attain Joanna's look and sound of mockery.

As he stared at Marthe in profile, wondering if he could use telepathy to make her turn and look at him, he realized that his feelings for her had undergone as much of a change as hers for him. He thought back to their childhood days, when she had helped him tend Warhawk or when they had shared sibko experiences. At that time, he had known a separate and special affection for her. He remembered the day when he had believed it might be the kind of love that sibparent Glynn had used to embellish her romances. He tried to shake off such thoughts, cursing himself now, as he had a thousand times in his life, for his tendency to dwell in reflection. None of the others in the sibko ever seemed to analyze events as lengthily or deeply as he did.

As he studied Marthe's stiffness, her detachment, her new resemblances to Joanna, he knew he did not love her now and probably never had. Like so many sibko experiences, what he had felt was merely enthusiasm derived from and enhanced by what, after all, was a closed environment. What he had thought was special was no doubt also experienced by the others. Perhaps they, too, had formed imaginary alliances of their own. Endo may have thought he loved Orilna, or Bret felt his attraction to Rena was unique. It was just another kind of childhood play. As Joanna and Dermot had both told the sibko, warriors did not love. Love was for other castes (and very little of it there, Joanna had mysteriously and sarcastically commented). Aidan no longer believed in such a thing as love. He vowed never to think of the subject again. Especially in regard to Marthe.

And yet, Aidan felt saddened by the knowledge that a part of their sibko childhood was gone. Looking away from Marthe, he turned back to the viewport. They were over an ocean now. There were no fishermen or boats or anything but distant agitated birds to draw his attention away from the water.

"I am Nomad," the short, bearded man said to Aidan. "I am to be your Tech."

"Nomad? A strange name."

"I have drifted from place to place. Techs usually stay put. Thus, they call me Nomad."

"And your real name?"

"I have forgotten it."

"That could not be."

"If you say so. Nevertheless, I am unable to bring it into mind."

"Or you will not, *quineg?*"

"As you say."

"I think I like you, Nomad."

"That is not a requirement, sir."

The meeting with Nomad was unexpected and disconcerting. A month had passed since the sibko, or the shreds of it, had arrived at Crash Camp, as it was affectionately known. Aidan was not sure it had any real name. It was probably, like most Clan sites, just a complicated identification number or symbol specified for mapping and filing purposes. In that time, they had not been near a single BattleMech, nor had they even seen one, except for one dark and cloudy day, when a final test was going on far away, beyond a thick woods. All they heard then was the distant sound of weaponry and a couple of heavy thuds that were probably 'Mechs falling; all they saw was smoke rising over the tops of the trees and one blown-off Gauss rifle that slowly spun and somersaulted as it flew up in the air until it reached its zenith and plunged abruptly back.

Instead of training in actual 'Mechs, they had been bombarded with more classroom lessons, more time in simulators that had become so unsatisfactory because they were not the real thing. At night the sibko's only topics of conversation were speculations about when the preliminaries to the tests would start and when would they get their first checkouts on neurohelmets.

Their days went from sunrise to sunset and sometimes

into the night. Joanna led them on midnight marches through swampy territory, making them perform calisthenics whenever a temporary break threatened to become too long. Sleep became something they did when there was just enough exhaustion, and little beyond, to overcome them. Joanna now employed a Medusa whip to reinforce her orders and even more frequent sarcasms. It was another of the electronically doctored whips, like the one she had used on Aidan in the Circle of Equals so long ago. She cracked it incessantly. She also flicked it at the sibko constantly but was careful never to actually touch anyone with it. Now that they were at Crash Camp, she was forbidden to punish her charges. If she should lose her temper and forget that, she would be brought before a Warrior Council and disciplined severely. But that did not make the whip any less frightening. The sibko's tension grew every time she raised the Medusa.

The sibko had now grown almost completely apart. They did not speak to one another except when necessary during a classroom or field exercise. This lack of communication made Nomad's arrival welcome to Aidan. Not that the man proved easy to talk to. More often than not, he responded in grunts or with the least amount of words possible.

"Nomad?"

Grunt.

"Are we getting our 'Mechs soon? I mean is that why you are here?"

"Could be."

"Well, what good is a Tech if he has nothing to . . . to do his Tech job on?"

Shrug. Grunt.

"Do you know when we will get our 'Mechs?"

"Mmmm."

Aidan was right. The arrival of the Techs, one to each cadet, did signal the assignment of BattleMechs. Without telling the sibko the purpose of the trip, Falconer Joanna took them to a tall building on the other side of the forest. After entering it through what seemed like a normal door, they emerged onto a walkway that stretched across a massive pit. Or at least it looked like a pit. They stood at a railing, and at Joanna's behest, gazed around them. The railing was hot from all the activity occurring in the mammoth chamber.

Way down below, jutting out through an opening in a tangled network of other walkways, machinery, complex repair devices, and hundreds of people, were a whole Trinary of BattleMechs, most of them standing tall with their heads a meter or so below the level of the walkway where the sibko stood. Techs swarmed all over the 'Mechs. Aidan recognized most of the machines as belonging to the *Summoner* Class, though a few medium and light 'Mechs were scattered among the huge heavies. His best view was to his left where he could see a *Summoner*-A turned toward him. It had the typical hunchback look common to all the models in the class. Its LRM-15 rested on its high shoulder like some cylindrical, many-eyed animal. Both arms seemed held at the ready, the right one threatening with its extended-range PPC, the left one functioning as a persuader with its deadly accurate LB 10-X autocannon. Both weapons had been praised often by their instructors for being controllable and energy-efficient. "In a *Summoner*, the heat sinks seem more like an afterthought," Dermot once said. "That is, if you have employed them properly all along."

"It is an impressive fighting machine," Aidan said to Nomad, who stood indolently at his side. "What do you think, Nomad?"

"It's a fine machine."

"Careful. You used a contraction there."

Nomad looked in no way concerned. "Always did have lowdown habits," he said.

Nomad used both contractions and slang mercilessly, as if to annoy Aidan. But Aidan was not easily annoyed, especially by Nomad. He liked the man. It struck him now that Nomad was the first person outside the sibko for whom he had ever felt that sentiment.

Joanna took them down to ground level on a large platform that served the installation at many levels. "We call this a howdah," she said, "based on an old Terran word for a basketlike device that allowed riders to be lifted onto elephants. Sometimes a smaller platform is used in battle situations and is called the field howdah."

Joanna conducted them on a tour of the installation, but Aidan later recalled little of what she told them, so rapt was he at the spectacle of the vast chamber. From this angle, looking up, he could see the 'Mechs swaying slightly as they were worked on. Techs stood, sat, crawled, hung, threw tools among each other, backed off from sudden sparks, rattled recalcitrant parts to make them work, climbed in and out of cockpits, cleaned the skin and innards of mighty weapons, ate food indifferently while continuing to stare at the various nuts and bolts that constituted their current challenge. The smell of the place was all oil and heat; its taste was bitter. The noise varied from spot to spot. In areas where Techs worked with power-driven tools, it could be deafening; in other areas, where Techs treated their jobs as a painter did his current masterpiece, Joanna's narrations seemed rude and intrusive.

Aidan could tell by the intense look in Marthe's eyes that she was as fascinated with the 'Mech installation as he was. Seeing how she clenched and unclenched her hands, he knew that she, too, was eager to get inside one of the *Summoners,* so much heavier and more battle-ready than the light machines in which they had been training, and show what she could do with it.

At the end of the tour, Joanna answered the question on all their minds: when would they operate one of these 'Mechs? "After you have been fitted with a fully operational neurohelmet, we will begin the final phase of your training. You will be operating fully functional BattleMechs and put through a course designed to prepare you to join an operational combat Star. After that, you will have one week to become familiar with the 'Mechs you will take onto the Trial terrain. At the end of the week, you and all the other eligible cadets will undergo the Trial of Position. If you are blessed, you will become a warrior of the Clan. If not, the honor of contributing to the Clan travels with you to some other caste.''

Aidan could see in the faces of his fellow sibkin that they, like him, had no intention of being relegated to any other caste. At the same time, the tension of anticipation threatened to envelop him completely.

# === 14 ===

At first the neurohelmet seemed heavier than it was. His neck muscles strained at its weight, and he felt an odd discomfort in the various places where the neurohelmet touched him. And so heavily did it make his scalp perspire that he wondered if it would soon cause a short circuit that would damage the functions of both his brain and the neurohelmet.

From the headgear's built-in commlink, he heard the voice of Falconer Alexander, the instructor for this particular phase of training. Alexander's voice was flat, uninvolved, with none of the clipped harshness so common to training officers. He was giving a rundown on the neurohelmet's capabilities, all of which had already been drummed into the cadets' minds ever since the early days of training.

Aidan glanced back at Nomad, who was slouched lazily in the other seat in the testing chamber. The Tech was there, Aidan knew, to disconnect the helmet quickly if he panicked or something went wrong with the equipment. He derived some confidence from the fact that Nomad appeared to think neither possibility was likely.

"Cadet Aidan," Alexander said, "your neurohelmet will now be activated. The first sensations may be a bit disconcerting, but as you know, these will diminish with further use of the equipment. Are you ready?"

"Ready, sir."

One of the pleasures of this phase of the training was that the regulation against cadets addressing officers was relaxed. They were, in fact, encouraged to speak freely. Aidan suspected that the practice was motivated as much by psychology as it was born of the necessity for instant communication between cadet and trainer. After all the repressiveness of their previous training, the cadets could now draw confidence from the fact that officers considered them worth listening to.

"Neurohelmet . . . *activated!*"

The moment Aidan heard the word, a sudden, almost deafening hum seemed to surround him. At the same moment, his head began to throb from a pain that felt like electric shock. His vision blurred. He felt like he was going to pass out.

"Easy, cadet," came Alexander's calm voice. "We all feel disoriented the first time. That is why we check you out on the neurohelmet in a test chamber. In a 'Mech, you would be too dizzy to control balance, and it would go kerplop, face-up in the mud."

There were several staticky sounds in his ear, which Aidan knew were Alexander making adjustments on the electronics of the neurohelmet. Momentarily Aidan felt downhearted. Until now, everything involved in running a 'Mech had seemed simple. It was as if the neurohelmet was being introduced at this time as a way of unnerving him and the other cadets. He had an urge to pull the thing off, cast it away from him as far as possible, and announce that he would run a 'Mech without using the contraption as a conduit for his brain waves.

"I can see that certain adjustments still need to be made," Alexander announced.

Great, Aidan thought, maybe you would like to reach in and rearrange my brain matter while you are at it.

"Shut your eyes," Alexander continued, "and concentrate on a world lovely in its colors in a slow orbit around a distant sun. See the rich hues almost in a pattern on the planet's surface, the suggestion of orange rivers and yellow mountains. A village, blue-skinned villagers going about daily routines amid rainbows of buildings, traveling on purple roads . . ."

Alexander went on in this vein, speaking very softly, and Aidan found he could visualize the scene the man was describing. It made him feel better. An odd pain was still in his head, but the hum was slowly weakening. He thought he could smell sea brine, but that must have been some effect of the neurohelmet on his brain.

"All right, now," Alexander said. "Concentrate again on the neurohelmet. Are you yet in pain, cadet?"

"It is fine now."

"No bravado here. The cockpit is the one place where you must maintain common sense. The bravery is what you do with the 'Mech, not some empty need to show others how courageous you are by not admitting discomfort. I know that the neurohelmet is not fully adjusted. It never is on my first try. Now, are you in pain?"

"Some. But it is better. And there is a hum, a . . ."

"Yes. We know about the hum. It has never been defined, but we can eliminate it. It will come back at times, and chances are you will not notice it. Some believe that a pilot may be harmed by it, gradually losing hearing. That I know nothing about. The half-deaf pilots I have seen are few. Techs more often suffer hearing loss in their jobs."

Inadvertently, Aidan glanced back at Nomad, who seemed drowsy. Of course, he was not wearing a headset and did not hear anything that Alexander said.

"Go back in your mind to that village. If you like, you might imagine a troop of young maidens all come to serve you, the heroic pilot who has come with his BattleMech to save them."

"Why should I think such outrageous thoughts?"

He heard a soft laugh from Alexander. "Oh, you are another of the unimaginative cadets? The Clan does not turn out romantics, does it? Do you not dream?"

"Well, yes, I do, sir."

"And do your dreams bear any relationship to your ordinary day?"

"They do not. They are filled with fantasies."

"And you are not comfortable with fantasies, I surmise."

"Well, yes, that is true."

"I have found great uses for imagination. It is even useful for battle strategies, even for unimaginative Clan warriors. Cultivate it, cadet. It may save you some day."

"Yes, sir."

"At any rate, I have made some more adjustments while we talked and the neurohelmet may be more comfortable now."

"Sir?"

"You may call me Falconer Alexander, or just Alexander."

"This is difficult when you are just a voice in my ear and I do not know you in any other way."

"And you never will. I never meet cadets of the Jade Falcon or any other Clan. I am an untouchable."

The man's words were as dizzying as the contact with the neurohelmet, especially as he followed them with a weird chuckle.

"I do not understand, Alexander."

"You were not meant to. You see, I am not of the Clan, or rather I am a Clansman from the other side of the bed."

In confusion Aidan shook his head, trying to clear it so that he could comprehend Alexander's words. But the action was a mistake. Something in the neurohelmet was affected by it. The hum increased and he felt a sudden twinge of mild pain in his head.

"Easy now, cadet. I can see you still need some fine-tuning in getting used to the helmet, *quiaff?*"

"Aff. Alexander, what did you mean about being an untouchable?"

"Just a fancy allusion, boy. What I mean is that I do not really belong. I was a bondsman, snatched off a Periphery vessel by Clan Jade Falcon. Through many misadventures, and some truly painful hard labor as the slave that a bondsman can be, my abilities were discovered and I was welcomed into the Tech caste. But somehow I remain close to my origins as a citizen of the Periphery, and you Clansmen will always be a mystery to me."

"Perhaps you are the mystery, Alexander."

Alexander's sigh was audible over the commlink. "That was impressive, cadet. Very unClanlike, that comment."

"I do not know what you mean."

"Of course you do not. You know nothing but the Clan, *quiaff?*"

"Aff. I think so, anyway. I know mostly the life of the sibko and the trainee."

"Well, there is much to come. I envy you."

"Why?"

Alexander's voice suddenly switched from soothing to irritable.

"Stop asking questions, boy. We have work to do."

During the course of a long morning, Alexander worked with Aidan and the neurohelmet, making—it seemed to Aidan—many adjustments. But soon it felt better. He felt no pain and the hum was barely noticeable.

After, he asked Nomad about Alexander.

"Heard of him," Nomad said. "Keeps to himself. Says things no one understands. Odd person. I do not like unusual people."

That seemed to close the discussion. After the introductory sessions with the neurohelmet, Aidan never heard of Alexander again.

All four remaining members of Aidan's sibko qualified on the neurohelmet during that day. Falconer Joanna remarked offhandedly that it was quite rare for an entire group to master the brain-wave headgear that quickly. "As a result we may have the initiatory ritual tonight," she said, and left before anyone could ask her what an initiatory ritual was.

Before nightfall, the sibko's clothing for the ritual arrived at the barracks in four large metal boxes. The four survivors gathered around the boxes, left neatly piled by the messengers, and did not know exactly what to do. Bret wondered if they should dance around them. Rena said maybe they should ignore them. Marthe, impatient, said just open them and get the job done.

Each opened the box with his or her name on it, and each found a different uniform. When they had donned them, Aidan noted that the clothing seemed to transform them from relatively drab-looking trainees into figures that bore at least a resemblance to actual warriors.

Bret wore a cape of falcon feathers dyed bright red, with a head drooping behind as a kind of unused hood. Underneath the cape was a dress uniform of Jade Falcon green with silver buttons, each delicately fashioned with a fighting BattleMech pictured on its surface. Red stripes went down the trousers of the outfit. He was particularly pleased with a dark leather belt with a massive Mech's-head belt buckle. Aidan's garments were similar, but his cape was black, and his jade green uniform was black-striped, while his buttons depicted a flying hawk in delicate, filigreed design. His belt buckle was a side view of a falcon going in for the kill (or at least that was how Aidan chose to interpret it.) Rena's cape was dyed a light green and her button-and-belt motif was a falcon with wings outstretched. For Marthe, the sender had chosen a deep purple cape. Her buttons and belt were decorated with various images of 'Mechs in ground combat. All of them were equipped with high black boots polished to a radiant sheen. The outfits had been precisely tailored to fit the cadets assigned to them. There was no way they could have exchanged uniforms.

They had dressed in some confusion, not knowing what to expect. What it turned out to be was Joanna leading two ranks of the camp personnel in a march. Directly behind her were four falconers from other training units. Joanna and the falconers were dressed similarly to the cadets, but with many medals and achievement patches on the basic uniform. Behind them was a line of orderlies and other support personnel, each in starched work uniforms. They walked in precise rhythm, reminding Aidan of what a band of 'Mechs might look like if they were to march in synchronous pattern. The idea was slightly ridiculous, but with Joanna and her cohorts, the march was impressive and even pleasing to look at because of its unified movements.

Joanna stopped at the door of the barracks, where the four resplendently dressed cadets stared out in disbelief. The buttons of her uniform depicted the stately Jade Falcon itself, perched apparently on an aerie, surveying for potential prey. With a gesture in which her hands seemed to revolve on her wrists like a 'Mech's arm rolling on its torso, she bid the cadets to come forward. They walked uncertainly to her.

Without speaking she gestured the cadets to line up in much the same way they would on the parade ground. Going from trainee to trainee, she inspected their clothing, managing to find something to adjust in each outfit. She straightened Aidan's collar, wiped a smudge off Rena's top button, adjusted Bret's belt buckle, and retied Marthe's cape. When satisfied, she backed away from them and rejoined the others, who had remained at stiff attention the whole time.

Joanna's voice broke the silence. "I am the Oathmaster! All are bound by this conclave, until they are dust and memories, and then beyond that time until the end of all that is.''

"Seyla," whispered the gathered throng.

Her next words Aidan recognized as spoken in a Clan dialect of mountain tribes, but he could not make out the sense. As part of a ritual, perhaps the words signified something about origins. It was said that Nicholas Kerensky retired to a mountainside cache where Battle-Mechs and other war weapons were hidden, and there the concept of the Clans came to him. It was also said that he conceived the idea from watching several 'Mechs lined up in what seemed to him like a fighting attitude. He had been brooding about how to unify his dispersed and combative people so that one day they could return to the Inner Sphere and restore the Star League to its wayward worlds; a more immediate problem was how to do it while adhering to his father's fiercely austere theories about the need for the people to sacrifice on altars of Spartan necessity. While considering all this, he either fell asleep or had the vision. Whichever it was, he saw the 'Mechs of the cache transformed into a fighting horde, exhilarated by the blood and glory of warfare. When the dream or vision was over, he saw that he could organize his warriors in a new way, eliminate the Regular Army, with all its unfortunate sympathies to Inner Sphere political divisions, and reform it into separate clans that would compete with each other while devoting their energies to preparing for the return to the Inner Sphere. Each clan would have its own allegiances, its own particular beliefs. These would replace the old alliances and sympathies.

Whether she chanted of the Kerensky vision or of something else, Joanna's voice built to a deafening crescendo. Then she stopped suddenly, saying: "You are no longer cadets. Whether or not you succeed in becoming warriors, you have left the sibko and will be on your own in whatever caste to which you are assigned. Tonight we initiate you into your future, while you give up the ties to your past. Come with us.''

Signaling to the others, she marched them away, gesturing for the four cadets to take up the rear and follow.

They came to a clearing lit by many fires. The group

gathered around the flames of various fires, apparently taking up already chosen positions. Joanna stood alone by the largest blaze, in the center of the clearing. The firelight illuminated the Jade Falcon figure on her belt, making it seem alive and fierce. Its flickering was also reflected in her eyes, whose own natural flames had always been powerful enough. Now her eyes seemed those of some mythic demon or dragon, glowing with a mystery that Aidan knew could probably never be comprehended. It occurred to him that Joanna was certainly beyond his ken and always would be.

Joanna raised her arms above her head. Again the firelight changed her aspect. Something shiny in the sleeve of her dress uniform caught the light and sent it rocketing outward. Blinding flashes swept by the cadets' eyes briefly. For a moment Aidan was gripped by a fear that the fire would grow and envelop them all.

Then Joanna walked through the fire, actually took a step into it, then another, then was on the other side of it, walking toward them, no hint of pain in her glowing eyes or even the knowledge that she had passed through the fire.

Taking Marthe's hand, she told the other cadets to also link hands. Aidan grasped Marthe's other hand, and also took Rena's. Bret, looking frightened, followed Rena. Joanna led them forward toward the fire. It was a moment before Aidan realized that they, too, would walk through the flames. He had a sudden urge to release the hands of both women and bolt this clearing. But such timidity was, he knew, unClanlike. He felt all his muscles tighten as he continued forward.

Joanna again stepped into the fire without looking back. Marthe followed her without the slight hesitation that Aidan felt. But he was pulled forward by Marthe as he, in turn, drew Rena toward the fire. He wanted to close his eyes as he stepped into the flame, but his fascination with his own possible demise kept them open. Though he was only within the flames briefly, it seemed long enough to burn him to a shriveled darkness. The heat was tremendous, but he felt none of it within his high boots. It was then he realized that the footwear must have been treated beforehand to resist the flames. Still, as the flames warmed the rest of his clothing, he did not feel at all safe and was glad when he had stepped onto the ground on the other side of the fire.

After Bret had cleared the fire, Joanna lined them up and gestured toward the path they had just taken. "On the other side of the flames is your old life, the life of the child, the mistakes and the foolishness, successes and failures . . . the members of your sibko who have not reached this point. On the other side are the useless fantasies and unClanlike ambitions. Your life is no longer your own. It is ours. We are all connected in a vast network. Your 'Mech cannot move without you, just as you are guided by your superiors. We all are controlled by the rules of our individual Clan, and the Clans must work together for our common goal, the restoration of the Star League. Complex as these links are, each is crucial to the others. When one is broken, others along its line are weakened. If you fail in a battle, others may be killed. If you bid ineffectively, you may be taking away the futures of others. If you show traits that are weak or even evil, others may copy them, transmitting the weakness or evil in rays throughout your part of the network. So you are more than an individual, you are many individuals with each act you perform, each word you say, each gesture you make. You must think of this with each act, word, and gesture. If you are a Clan warrior, you are not like the effete warriors of the Inner Sphere, with their showy displays of empty valor. You are strategist when you bid, tactician when you fight, warrior when you return with your unit intact. Cadets, you are on the verge of becoming Clan warriors. Think on what I have told you."

Joanna had barked out this speech in the same manner she gave orders during training. Now her voice lowered and she spoke quietly and precisely: "It is time for the trial by sword."

The cadets exchanged puzzled glances. None of them had ever heard of anything called a trial by sword.

Joanna clapped her hands and an orderly brought forth four swords on a dark blue cloth. She lay them at Joanna's feet. Joanna clapped her hands again and the four falconers joined her by the fire. Their faces were grim as each picked up a sword and took up a position in a semi-

circle. Each crouched and held his or her sword in a battle position, pointing outward.

"In a battle, trust is important. If we, as Clan warriors, do not trust the others above and under us, then he must fail. Cadets, each of you must now face one of these swordsmen."

Still mystified, the four cadets arranged themselves so that each faced a different swordsman. Joanna walked to a point directly in back on the sword-wielding foursome. Holding her arms out, she addressed the cadets: "Each Clan warrior must trust all others. An untrustworthy warrior would also break the links. You, my cadets, must trust these four swordsmen. At my signal you must run toward the warrior in front of you, right at his sword. You will trust him or her not to kill you. This ritual goes back many generations of Clan warriors. When my arms come down, run. More, you must run as fast as you can. I can tell if you shirk. I know each of you as well as I ever knew any warrior with whom I served, any member of my own sibko. I can read your faces as well as your actions. For the time being, as has been true since I first encountered you, I am your god."

She stared at the cadets for what seemed to Aidan like an eternity. He set his feet for the run, wondering if he should just turn his back on this ritual and walk out of the clearing. He had an urge to defy Joanna, but looking into the face of the swordsman in front of him, her face dour but firm, he knew he was not afraid of the woman or her sword.

Joanna's arms came down slowly. When they reached her side, Aidan and the others broke into a sprint. He bore down on the swordsman, focusing on the sword itself. There was no wavering. The swordsman held it firmly. Was it possible this was a suicide ritual because Joanna or Ter Roshak had decided none of the four were worthy of becoming warriors, so they must be killed? No, Joanna had said they must trust. He must trust this woman, even though he had never seen her before. And only because she was a warrior of the Jade Falcon Clan. At his last free step, with the sword still pointed at his chest, he leaped at it.

And landed at the woman's feet, on his face. As he learned later, all four swordsmen had whipped their swords out of the way at the last possible instant. It was, as Joanna had said, merely a ritual.

As Aidan and the others stood up, Joanna walked around the line of swordsmen. "You see," she said, "the act of running at the sword required trust. You had to know deep down that you can trust your comrades—that is the way of the Clan. It is essential to know that completely. If you doubt us, then we doubt you."

She walked slowly among the group of cadets. Aidan and Bret were brushing dirt off their clothing. Marthe apparently had run at her sword without falling to the ground as a consequence.

Joanna stopped by Rena, who stood quite still. Without warning, the falconer, with a clean swift stroke, drew her sword across Rena's cheek. Rena backed away two steps but did not bring her hand up to her face. A line of blood appeared at the cut and began to drip down the side of her face in several thin lines. Aidan noted that the blood seemed dark, almost black, but perhaps that was a trick of the firelight.

Joanna peered into Rena's eyes. "You hesitated," she said. "It was perhaps only half a second and you did not quite stumble, but I saw clearly that you nearly dodged sideways, that your step slowed before you completed your run. For an instant in time, your trust deserted you. Perhaps you are not ready to be a warrior, *quineg?*"

"Not so," Rena said. "I am ready. But you are correct, Falconer Joanna, I did—I do not know how to describe it—I did flinch, nearly hesitate, had a moment where I did not expect the sword to move. I deserve the punishment you gave me."

"Of course you deserve it. You have no reason even to hint at a doubt. The hint is like the flinch before the sword. Yet let me say your honesty is to be praised. Do you wish to continue your warrior training?"

"Yes!"

Joanna nodded her head. "Then you will. Everyone, form a circle and link hands."

The training officer who had held the sword for Rena gave her a med-cloth, treated to staunch blood at a touch. Rena held it on her cut for a short time. When it came away, the bleeding had stopped, although the cut itself was red-rimmed and appalling to look at.

In the circle Aidan linked hands with Marthe and an orderly. Joanna stood in the center of the circle, by the fire again, now holding one of the swords. New wood had been heaped on the fire and the flames burned high. When Joanna began to speak again, she swept the sword through the highest flames at her words' many points of emphasis.

"Hail the Jade Falcon as it swoops down on its prey!"

"Seyla," came the response of all.

The Clansmen in the circle, including the cadets, affirmed in the same ancient way each of her bellowed statements. They were all used to the ceremonial forms. Most of her words described the greatness of the Jade Falcon Clan. There were praises of heroism, war, the proper behavior of warriors, the values of all the Clans, the greatness of the Kerenskys. The ceremony lasted for more than an hour, at the end of which Joanna's voice had become hoarse. She ended by yelling, "Thus is the way of the Clan!" She attacked the flames with her sword as if they were the souls of her enemies.

"Seyla," the circle breathed as one.

Then Joanna repeated the phrase, her sword working at a feverish pace now.

And again did they affirm, "Seyla." Several times more did Joanna bellow, "Thus is the way of the Clans!" Each time there followed the chorus of voices, "Seyla!"

Then Joanna held her sword pointed high above her head. *"The Clan will prevail!"* she shouted.

"Seyla," came the answering, massive shout to the heavens.

Aidan was exhilarated, adrenaline rushing through his veins as the fever pitch of the ceremony combined with the way he had risked his life at swordpoint. He had always wanted to be a warrior, but sometimes had doubted his own worth. Tonight there were no doubts. He *would* be a warrior of the Clans. He had to be.

# 15

How well I remember the first time in a heavy BattleMech, Ter Roshak wrote. It is a sensation I recall so vividly, though it happened so long ago. I envy our current cadets this unforgettable moment. There is something different about getting into the cockpit of one of the big ones. After all the training in the lighter models, where you get used to a certain ease of movement, the heavier 'Mechs at first seem graceless and hard to maneuver. All that tonnage underneath their feet gives the neophyte pilots some qualms. They wonder how something as fragile as a neurohelmet working off one's brain waves is able to keep an unwieldy monster like a 'Mech in balance, keep it from falling flat on its angular face. And more than the balance, how can they trust the neurohelmet to make the 'Mech take its steps efficiently and naturally?

If we were not of the Clan, the first time in a 'Mech would perhaps be a worrisome experience. But the Clan blood charging like cavalry through the intricate pathways of our bodies tells us that no large conglomeration of metal and other materials is beyond our capabilities. The basic sensory difference between piloting a smaller 'Mech and guiding one of the big ones is only a temporary setback, a fear that comes only once. We gain control, and from then on are either warriors or failures. No other outcome is possible in the Trial of Position. The failures either survive and go to another caste, or they die. Here in Crash Camp we have swept countless corpses off the battlefield.

People I meet from outside the Clan, Periphery bondsmen and the like, often question the harshness of such trials, which, like so many of our customs, they find somewhat pitiless. They especially center on the Warrior Caste. They do not understand that the trials *must* be almost insurmountable; it is the only way to turn out exemplary warriors. Anything less, any cadet passed along and given the name of warrior while retaining flaws, renders the training meaningless.

We are not here, after all, to churn out the kind of dispensable soldier that in the past was called cannon fodder. Such warriors were the products of a certain democratization on Terra, when mass man was recruited to fight battles by power-hungry leaders or zealous rebels. It was considered glorious to charge an entrenched enemy, leaving behind many dead heroes in a triumph that gained perhaps two centimeters of the battleground. If one side had significantly more personnel than the other, that side could win a battle—not through strategy or tactics but through attrition of the other side. Such situations were not war, but rather mere organized slaughter. Personal sacrifice was an ideal that sounded better than it ever was in practice.

I do not criticize here the individual heroic act, which is admirable. In any kind of warfare soldiers who give up their lives to save others or whose acts of bravery damage or destroy enemy facilities to settle a battle that might have been costlier are examples of heroic deeds that stand apart from the issues of the war at hand. Victory or defeat, right or wrong, absurdity or glory—those concepts do not apply even to such deeds. The act justifies itself without benefit of doctrines.

The war that wastes lives disgusts me. Unnecessary personal sacrifice is a waste; the heroic act that saves no one is a waste. General Kerensky was right when he proclaimed that war and preparation for war must be accomplished with a sense of economy. The minimum number of warriors necessary for the battle is the only number that should be sent to it. Anything else is wasteful.

The bidding system is the Clan's greatest contribution to the actual conduct of war. We declare to our opponent what the prize of the battle should be—factory, genetic material, whatever we think necessary for the advancement of our Clan. The defender responds by naming the forces he will use in defense. We then bid among ourselves for the right to fight the battle and then engage in combat. Only the warriors and materiel bid by the individual commander are allowed to engage in the contest. Reinforcements can be called only up to the point of the second-best bid.

As a result, our warfare style saves lives as well as treasure. There are no crowds of noncombatants on the battlefield to be blown up by an errant missile. We do not engage in barbarous attacks against our opponent's industries or lower castes. We understand the necessities of war better than any force previously engaged in one because we so meticulously analyze how much of our own people and supplies to put at risk.

The principle of economy works for the other castes, too. Few citizens live in anything approaching luxury, except those who have clearly earned it. Even those in the merchant caste, famous for its shrewd dealings and carefully calculated profits, do not often seek what they do not deserve. It has often been said that our major blemish, the bandit caste, are people who could not grasp the wisdom of this system, and they are all the more detestable for that. Most Clan castes are, however, devoted to our major goal, the return to the Inner Sphere and restoration of the Star League. The lives of our people are dedicated to making the overall machine of society function.

I have prided myself on maintaining all my own commands well within the concepts of Clan utility and economy. Every usable piece of material is as strictly maintained as the 'Mechs themselves. I demand proper polish and the control of waste. Nothing is discarded without the approval of several of my subordinates. Anything that might be used again in any way gets a second, third, or fourth life. I know what they sometimes say about me and do not mind at all being described as the man who would rework garbage into gyros, crumbs into ammo, zombies into warriors if I could find ways.

Do I digress again? That at least seems to be one skill of mine that seems to increase with age. It is easy to see why the Clan removes aging warriors from active service, why it shunts them off to rear-guard support positions or assigns them to training units. Again it is a question of husbanding one's resources. When instinctive reactions come slower and the eyes can not focus as easily on the monitors or the targets and the body takes longer to perform any action, it is only logical that the warrior be removed from active service; he has become a detriment to the others in his unit. Waste creates waste. A mistake by an aging warrior can kill a younger one. Though age, and the experience that accompanies it, may bring some valuable wisdom, it is also true that too much detritus collects in the mind as the years pass. When something is no longer useful at or near the front lines, it must be utilized in other ways. So the aged and injured, both categories to which I now belong, are salvaged in order to perform other roles in the warrior caste. Nothing should be wasted that is in any way still usable.

Still, as in any cycle of waste and salvage, something is lost inevitably. I miss active service, and if ordered, would return to a combat unit without a second thought. Peripheral duties—no matter how important—offer no real satisfaction. Like any warrior, I still crave the pleasure of watching an enemy go down in flames or feeling a jaw crack underneath my fist or accurately slicing armor off the 'Mech in my sights.

I miss war and I do not mind admitting it, in the privacy of this journal.

But my fighting days are over and I have to live vicariously through these cadets. I am hard on them because my orders so require; I am even more rigorous because they are my enemy now. An odd thought, that. I had never perceived the cadets in that way before. With their innocent ways and their frequent ineptitude, they constitute all the obstacles to be overcome. I hate all their failures, want more from them when they succeed.

When the sibkos have been winnowed down, I then focus on the useful material—that is, the cadets who definitely could become warriors. Potential waste (in terms of warrior potential) has been eliminated and reassigned to worthwhile roles in the society.

Digression. Digression. Looking back over what I have just written, I seem to subscribe to what might be called an excremental view of history. Nevertheless, a control of human and nonhuman assets is essential to a successful military operation of any kind.

Which is not to say that I am overwhelmingly dedicated to saving everything. I will dispose of even human lives if the objective is reasonable. I will sacrifice a 'Mech if it means demolishing other 'Mechs. In the battle that cost me my arm, I had to send one Star on a suicide mission, and I still remember every single one of its members.

I pile digression upon digression. It is time for me to try to sleep, though I will probably be unable to. In three days the present sibko will fight its Trial of Position, and I think about that constantly. For the three who remain, I have ordered that they undergo the Trial together. I prefer that only two go out at a time, as is the declared custom, but when the number is odd, I reluctantly order three out against nine. Joanna is excited by the prospect, seeing the Trial as a kind of battle royal. She is a bit bloodthirsty, that woman. I think she would not mind if all the cadets were defeated. She has no sense of economy.

It is a pity that we lost one cadet so close to the Trial. When that happens, it is always a minor tragedy, not so much for the cadet who is killed, but for the loss of a warrior at a time when more warriors are needed.

# ═══ 16 ═══

It might have been better, more meaningful, if Rena's corpse were not so twisted and bloody. Aidan definitely wished her eyes were closed, and would have closed them himself if Falconer Joanna did not stand between him and Rena's body. Joanna's face was emotionless, looking at Rena as if she had not known her for so long, taken her through so much training. Aidan edged closer, sensing Marthe and Bret also moving in a step or two behind him. He had seen Rena fall, seen the dark spots appear on her fatigues before he realized that she had been hit.

"She was aware this was a live-ammunition exercise, *quiaff?*" Joanna asked.

"Aff," Bret replied.

"And she stood up suddenly, *quiaff?*"

"Aff."

"And there was no reason for her to stand up, *quineg?*"

"Neg. No reason."

"Then it is clear she was not meant to be a warrior. She was, like all cadets who do not succeed, a fool. She should have died that first day, sparing me the time I spent training her. Dispose of the body, the three of you."

Joanna walked away without looking back. None of the cadets made a move to obey her directive.

As Aidan looked down at Rena, he wondered if he should remember something significant about her, perhaps make some sort of valedictory before she was carted off to the medical facility, where her usable organs would be extracted and stored, and the rest of her cremated. The leftovers. That was what faced most of them, unless they were lucky enough to be disintegrated in battle and rendered not worth dissecting or burning.

In idle moments, in classrooms or alone in bed at night, he had been able to call up all kinds of childhood memories, but now with the sibko itself almost a memory, he could think of nothing specific about Rena. No immediate image of her alive in pre-cadet days came to him. For that matter, he could remember nothing about any of them. All those memories he used to cherish about him and Marthe were, for the moment, denied recall. (Later, in his bunk, looking ahead to the Trail and back to the sibko, such incidents flooded his mind.)

Marthe touched his arm. At first he thought it was a renewal of the old friendship, but then it was obvious she was pushing him aside.

"We have a job to do. Bret, you take her feet. I will carry her by the shoulders. Aidan, you go ahead and make the arrangements."

Aidan took a step in the direction of the medical facility, then he turned back and addressed Marthe: "What happened? Why did she die?"

"It is beyond us as warriors to consider weighty abstractions, unless required for strategy."

"I did not mean that! I mean what *specifically* happened? How did she come to stand up? All of us knew better. *She* knew better."

"I suppose she could not have, considering that she did what she did."

With Bret positioned at the body's feet and Marthe at its head, they picked Rena up at Marthe's signal. As strong as they were, the carrying of a body required no strong effort.

"Unless she killed herself intentionally," Aidan commented.

"That is not possible. Rena was a warrior. Warriors do not kill themselves. Go on to the medical facility, Aidan."

"Are you sure? That is only classroom talk, as far as we know."

"You doubt what we are told?"

"No it is not that, it is just—I do not know what I mean. Forget I spoke."

"That would be easy."

"You sound more like Falconer Joanna every day, Marthe."

She turned and glared at him.

"And you sound like one of your hawks, squawking and growling at every chance. You complain too much, Aidan."

"I speak my mind."

"Whatever you call it, it is a bad habit."

He started again on the path toward the medical center. Marthe called after him: "You say I sound like Falconer Joanna. That is a compliment, Aidan. A compliment."

Then why, he wondered, had she been so angry when first he said it?

After they had delivered Rena and her body was on its way toward eventual dissolution in flames, the three remaining cadets returned to the exercise in which they had been engaged when Rena was killed. All passed the test with high scores.

In the midst of the maneuvers, with the heat of the fusillades descending on them like quick storms, Aidan did not think again of Rena. For him and his fellow cadets, her passing was like the departures of their fellow sibkin, sharply noted but easily forgotten. That night Aidan had his few moments of memories, but then he turned his attention to the important time ahead, when he would finally fight a real battle with a real 'Mech against real opponents. In spite of the Clan idea of utility, he itched to turn an attacking 'Mech into useless scrap.

# ═══17═══

The site of the test was kept secret from the cadets until the actual day of the Trial. In a rare speech, Falconer Commander Ter Roshak explained that the Jade Falcon Trial differed from simpler Trials used by other Clans such as the Clan Wolf. In contrast to those, he said, the Jade Falcon Trial of Position intended to recreate actual battle conditions, where warriors had to fight in unfamiliar terrain and with looser rules of engagement. All the cadets would know beforehand was contained in a map of the terrain and a brief "recon report," both documents issued an hour before the Trial.

"This duplicates battle conditions," Ter Roshak said in his loud but unemotional voice, the voice of a warrior who had gone half-deaf from too many combat engagements. "Prior to an action, a military unit often has little or no data to go by. Sometimes it has even less. This Trial will assume that you have been separated from your unit in enemy territory. You have had to leave your BattleMech for reconnaissance purposes. Your recon has discovered traces of the enemy's presence, so you are alert to potential danger. The Trial begins as you are making your way back to your 'Mech. Remember, you are in hostile terrain. You may be attacked anytime during the initial part of your trek. At this point, the training in hand-to-hand combat may come into play, so be prepared for anything."

The camp pipeline had it that a small contingent of freebirths had been shipped in during the night to portray enemy footsoldiers. Even Ter Roshak knew that the cadets had probably heard about the importation of the freebirth squad. Though he had no intention of informing the cadets of the freebirth presence during his talk, he thought it appropriate to hint at it. The danger the "secret" squad posed was, after all, no different from what might occur in a similar wartime situation. In many of the battle situations the commander had experienced, even when his unit landed in known terrain (*especially* in known terrain), there had been unexpected surprises.

"Once in your 'Mechs, you will have to mobilize them from an inactive state. That is when your cockpit training will come into play. Check everything rapidly but meticulously. Then you must start your search for the enemy."

Aidan felt a little dizzy, not from Roshak's words or his warnings about the Trial, but from the realization that, after all this time and all this effort, it was about to take place. Everything they had known and lived since their earliest childhoods had been leading up to this, focused on this, and now the moment was at hand. In his mind seemed to congregate all the members of the sibko who were not here, in this room, listening to the pre-Trial indoctrination. There were those who did not make it to warrior training in the first place, those who flushed out from training, and those who were dead. Dead and alive, they were all like ghosts, vaguely outlined, appearing momentarily in memory, then vanishing like wraiths.

"During the search for the enemy, the three of you must operate as a unit, even though eventually you will have to split off to fight your preselected opponents. Consider at this point the lesson I gave you not long ago. The camaraderie of your sibko is behind you; it is the stuff of childhood now. Your loyalty will be to whatever unit you are assigned. Sometimes that unity is quickly established on a battlefield. Fortunately for the three of you, you do know each other and I think, have reunited as a fighting unit, much like a Star and unlike a sibko. This is good and should serve you well in the first phase of the Trial.

"Discovering the enemy will depend on your individual abilities and the skill with which you use your sensors. But make no mistake: if you do not find them, they will find you. As you know, in the trio of 'Mechs lined up against you, the lightest will engage you first, according to custom."

Yes, Aidan thought, unless you engage first. A strategy

had formed in his mind, and he intended to act on it. He had awakened one morning with the firm realization that it would be better to do more than just succeed in the Trial; he would attempt to defeat two, and perhaps all three, of his opponents. Achieving a double "kill" meant entering active service with the rank of Star Commander, while a triple would immediately earn him the rank of Star Captain. Not only did he desire the power of a higher rank, but it seemed to him that the better rank he could achieve, the closer to a Bloodname he would be. And that was the point of it all, was it not? Becoming qualified to compete for a Bloodname, then going on to have your genes included in the gene pool.

"The opposing 'Mechs will engage you one after another. However, engaging any 'Mech other than the one you are fighting will open up the battle to general melee. This includes the 'Mechs that are opposing your sibkin. In such a case, any 'Mech that you kill will count for a score. Remember that your opponents are all experienced pilots who have served the Clan for some time, so never lose the watchfulness we have inculcated within you."

Perhaps they *are* experienced, Aidan thought, but they are also prepared for certain strategies, certain modes of attack. Which made it all the harder for the cadets, who had been taught conventional assault against conventional defense. The best route to a super-kill would be the unconventional one. And Aidan was surer than ever what his route would be—what, in fact, it *should* be.

"Each of you starts with a *Summoner,* whose weapons are fully charged and supplied with the ammunition loads you have selected for your configurations. Your survival will depend on how you use the skills we have trained into you, plus your natural aptitudes and instincts. If you are alive when the Trial is over, you will be warriors or . . . something else. The Clan can open its ranks only to the best, so that is what you must be, only the best. In fifteen minutes, you will be transported to the battle site. When this session is ended, Falconer Joanna will distribute your maps and recon surveys. Study them well, now and on the way to the site. Intelligence is just as much a key to success as battle skills."

\* \* \*

The map and supporting material in their hands, the cadets went about their study in different ways. Marthe read coolly and methodically, while Bret seemed to race through the material, then went back to a section, then on to another one, and so on. Aidan at first had difficulty in focusing on the diagrams, drawings, and words, the whole packet seeming to have been written in some alien language. All he could think of was the Trial itself. He was so eager to get to it that in his fingertips he already felt the tension of maneuvering the *Summoner* and firing its weapons. He saw himself mowing down not only his own opponents, but Marthe's as well. Helping her would perhaps thaw the coldness of their relationship.

Then the pages of the survey and the details of the map finally came into focus. First, Aidan saw that the terrain was mixed. The stretch through which they would have to pass to reach their 'Mechs was relatively flat, but with plenty of greenery, including a wide, thick stretch of woods that obscured any view they might have had of their 'Mechs. The 'Mechs themselves were cached near a row of hills that hid them from enemy view. On the other side of the hills was a wide meadow crossed by a stream running down from the hills. The stream widened and deepened at several places. At the meadow's far end, just before a forest, the flatland became more hilly, with many militarily advantageous mounds and knolls. On the left, the stream emptied into a small lake.

Switching to the recon report, Aidan saw that it postulated a Trial of Possession for an armor-producing plant. The enemy had chosen to defend with a Cluster-sized unit of 'Mechs and Elementals in a sector of terrain that was mixed with woods and rolling hills. The enemy was also reported to be using unarmored garrison infantry. Aidan grinned, thinking that those irregular infantry would be the freebirths. Approximately two Stars of heavy 'Mechs were known to be operating in the immediate area.

The recon report indicated that the infantry strength in the immediate area was not known, nor was its available weaponry. Aidan knew that they were not skilled fighters, however, or else they would not have been assigned Trial-site duty. They were no better and no worse than the obstacle courses through which the cadets had been put in recent weeks. If he could climb a wall with a rope, then rappel down its other side, he could outsmart any freebirth obstacles they put in his way.

The weather projection was unsettling. Strong winds were projected and it had rained overnight. That meant the ground might be muddy, creating the risk of an accidental fall. Aidan had had some difficulty piloting the lighter 'Mechs in heavy winds, but the heavier *Summoner* should, in that respect at least, be easier to maneuver.

Would the skimmer ever reach the Trial site, he wondered as the itch to get to battle seemed to travel all through his body.

Reaching the general area of the Trial site, the cadets were given a choice of personal weapons for the first phase of the Trial. While Marthe chose a pulse laser-rifle and Bret a submachine gun, Aidan decided on a laser pistol. Bret questioned his decision and Aidan replied that he wanted to travel light, so he was willing to sacrifice range for the one-gram comfort of the pistol. He did not say it, but he also intended to use survival techniques instead of artillery power should any freebirth opponent get in his way.

Then they boarded a personnel carrier, which would take them to the actual starting point. Joanna and Roshak rode with them inside the dark, expansive carrier, whose window slits had been filled in so that the cadets could obtain no advance views of their destination.

When the carrier doors opened and the cadets climbed out, Aidan saw that clouds had gathered but there was no rain. Ahead of them was the Trial site. Although it no doubt conformed to the coordinates of the map they had been issued, it still seemed a long way from their starting point to the hills where their 'Mechs were. As they started on their way, the flatland ahead of them was not as flat as it had seemed on the map. There were numerous trees and rocks, large stretches of tall grass, all good ambush points.

As the trio stood at the line from which, in half a minute, they would be ordered forward, they visually scanned the terrain just ahead of them, searching for any sign of a freebirth out to improve his lot by hitting a trueborn with a lucky shot. Aidan wondered if he should have chosen a weapon with heavier firepower and range. But he did not have time to decide, for the half-minute was up and Joanna ordered that the Trial now begin.

# 18

Within the first minute of the Trial, the muddiness of
the ground hidden by tall grass tripped up Aidan. When
he scrambled to to his feet, the front of his jumpsuit was
spotted with mud. Glancing back, he saw Joanna glaring
at him. He would rather have seen her laughing, for that
would have marked him as clumsy rather than inept.
Marthe and Bret had gotten ahead of him, and he rushed
to catch up.

"We should not stay so close together," Marthe said.
"Spread out."

Bret and Aidan each moved away from Marthe, in separate directions. There were no paths in the high grass,
no indications that any other cadets had ever passed this
way before. Aidan guessed that Techs went over the site
after each Trial, scouring and smoothing away any signs
of the combat just past. Greenery was probably trans-
planted to hide scars not so easily removed.

Why was his mind occupied with irrelevant detail? he
scolded himself. Must concentrate. Must be alert.

Grass and leaves were stirred up by a slight breeze,
which was much less strong than the weather details of
the recon survey had indicated. Perhaps that was why
Aidan thought he detected suspicious movement in a high
tree on his right, a slight twitching of some branches.
Whirling, he brought his pistol up and fired where a
branch still vibrated. A crashing sound and more activity
of the branches followed his shot, but no one fell out of
the tree. Then, when the branches stopped moving, they
became utterly still. Although Aidan was sure he had
disposed of one ambusher, he had no time to verify the
kill. Continuing on, it occurred to him that he might have

just wasted some of his laser pistol's charge on a large bird. He shoved the weapon back into his belt.

Suddenly he realized that both Bret and Marthe were far away across the field, leaving him alone and vulnerable. Suppressing an urge to run toward them, he decided instead to go on as he was, depending on himself. He rejected Ter Roshak's warning that cadets should cooperate at this stage of the trial. After all, the action of any one of them could get the others killed.

Better to rely on his own instincts and abilities. Aidan felt comforted by his aloneness and wanted no help from Marthe or Bret. His training seemed to have proceeded on a direct line from his sibko dependence to this sense of isolation at the Trial grounds. Having decided to reach for a significant triumph, what would be the point of letting Marthe and Bret get in his way?

As he ran forward toward the thick woods, he thought he saw figures lying in the grass, weapons held at ready, pointed at him. But he soon realized he was dodging shadows, flinching at animals. Taking deep breaths, a difficult process when running at a fairly high speed, he struggled to clear his mind, to force his eyes to see only what was there. Fantasies were of no use to a warrior—a thought he should offer to Dermot for use in one of his sententious lectures.

Aidan had almost reached the rim of the woods. Looking to his left, he saw that Bret was just entering the woods, while Marthe was nowhere to be seen, having no doubt already crossed the line. Aidan did not like being last, and he pushed forward all the harder, passing into the woods quickly enough to just miss being hit by a rifle shot. The shot took away some bark from a tree next to Aidan's shoulder.

Hitting the ground, then drawing the pistol from his belt, he crawled forward in the direction from which the shot had come. The forest floor was damper than the field had been, and it was suffused with peculiar odors. These puzzled Aidan at first, then he guessed that they were oil and burn smells, the residue of old Trials, the kind of battle traces that no sanitation and clearance squad could scrub away.

The sniper—obviously a freebirth for no trueborn would be so stupid as to fire so soon—shot again. He or she could not have known Aidan's location, so the shot was more nerves than sense. And it gave away the sniper's position. Again, the shooter was in a tree. Aidan wondered if that confirmed his suspicion about the first possible sniper.

Angling to his right, Aidan crept toward the sniper. Using techniques he had learned in hand-to-hand combat training, he stirred little greenery, rattled few fallen branches. The darkness of the woods would hide any small disturbances that were unavoidable. The sniper, apparently getting edgy, rocked the branch where he or she sat.

As Aidan came near the sniper's tree, he saw that it was a young woman dressed in camouflage fatigues. Seeing the back of her hand was against her mouth, he realized she was gnawing on her knuckles. And for good reason: she was looking for him and pointing her automatic weapon in the wrong direction.

Aidan took a bead on her, surprised that his hand was shaking enough that he had to steady the laser pistol with his other hand. He had not felt any agitation, but the shaking did not worry him. Joanna had once said that, in a warrior, nerves that were too cool often meant too much numbing of the brain. What he did ponder briefly as he observed the unsteady movement of the pistol's barrel was the wisdom of choosing such a light personal weapon. The range he was sacrificing would be canceled out if his hand shook too much when he was close enough for a good shot. Getting the pistol under control, he gently squeezed the trigger, feeling in his hand the slight vibration of the weapon firing.

The sniper pitched forward. As far as Aidan could tell, he had hit her just behind the ear. She dropped onto the branch, setting it bobbing up and down, then fell to the ground with a quiet thud. Aidan stayed still for a minute, waiting to be sure that no members of the freebirth squad came to investigate the fall of a compatriot. When he was sure that all was clear, he crawled toward the fallen sniper, his pistol held steady now in case she was faking.

She was not faking. She was dead. Looking down on the slightly worried expression that remained on her narrow, birdlike face, he wondered why Ter Roshak, always so concerned with conserving and recycling materials, would put personnel at risk in the Trial. Perhaps it served to sharpen the warriors he turned out in successful trials, justifying the life lost. Still, was it worth this young woman's death?

Aidan had to work at it, but he knew he had to make his mind a blank. This tendency to reflect on events was useless to him, especially at such an important time, at the time of the Trial. The dead sniper was a freebirth, after all. Why should he care about what happened to a freebirth?

Searching her body, he found nothing he could use. He was tempted to take her rifle, but it might be cumbersome, so he decided against it. He would stick with the pistol. It had served him well, so far at least.

Having lost his sense of direction by now, Aidan had to use his compass to start back through the woods again. He moved slowly, prepared for another attack. Seeing some light ahead, he thought perhaps it was the end of the woods.

Off to his right he heard a barely discernible sound of laser firing. Going toward the sound, he came suddenly upon three freebirths, all turned away from him, shooting wildly. Looking beyond them, he saw that they had Marthe pinned down. She crouched behind a tree next to the clearing that would lead to the 'Mechs, not firing, obviously waiting for her attackers to expend their fire.

He could have left her there, getting a head start in his 'Mech and increasing his chances of winning. But this was Marthe, and they had grown up together, and there were still residual (if dormant) loyalties. Besides, Ter Roshak had emphasized that they should function as a unit.

So, with three quick shots, he killed the three freebirths. They fell almost simultaneously. He came out from cover and stood over them, then looked toward Marthe. She had walked out a couple of steps into the clearing. They stared at one another wordlessly for a moment, and all Aidan saw on her face was bitter resentment.

# 19

Most Trial participants are not as efficient as Cadet Aidan in disposing of freebirth opponents during first-stage maneuvers, wrote Ter Roshak. He totaled five kills, the most freebirths ever lost to a single cadet in this ordeal. His shooting was, in fact, better than any of his target-range scores. But that can happen. Many a 'Mech-Warrior's abilities are best tested in actual combat, and no amount of organized measures will predict them.

I am sometimes accused of waste, perhaps the worst blemish on a Clan training commander's records, because I approve risking freebirths in Trial maneuvers. Why not just put in realistic targets, my accusers say, as we do? A target popping abruptly out of the ground has just as much effect against a cadet's alertness as a living freeborn leaping out from underbrush. I believe, however, that I have always been able to successfully defend my position. Once a cadet knows he is being attacked by metal-and-cardboard constructions, it is no longer a true challenge, but a game, a joke, every time he encounters another ridiculous manmade obstacle. It is these constructions that are the real waste—a waste of useful materials for a useless purpose. Yet if cadets defeat, even kill, freeborn trainees in the course of their runs to their Trial 'Mechs, they are honing their own skills and, as a bonus, raising their own adrenaline levels for the important battle to come. Facing a bit of danger helps one to face even more dangers. The cadets do not realize, of course that the game is slanted in their favor. Freeborn weapons have been doctored to make them unable to kill. At worst, stunning the cadet for a few seconds. Even with those odds, I rarely lose a freeborn with real promise in this part of the Trial and I have never lost a cadet. I say that the results support my methods.

As far as waste is concerned, the opposite is true. The Trial is better, its participants perform more skillfully, the training command turns out better and more aggressive MechWarriors. I am satisfied. And so are others, for I am grateful to note that more and more of my colleagues are adopting my methods.

It is also significant that my command has the highest rate of success in training freeborns, which makes the occasional loss of a few in a valuable test situation logistically acceptable. Whether in war or peace, the strategy and tactics that result in either victory or the kind of loss that exhausts the enemy are all that count. Results justify, complaints obstruct. And I am successful enough to turn my head away from obstructions. I have heard that, historically, massacres and slaughters were condemned by people who thought of themselves as "right-thinking." I agree, but I believe that the Clan has countered the blame that such people imposed on events with a control of life as well as death. The number of warriors who fall is calculated precisely. No one should be killed *unnecessarily,* and that is the key word. There are necessary deaths, necessary massacres, necessary slaughters. That is what the right-thinkers did not realize. If the deaths of a thousand people further the scope and goals of the mission, those deaths are glorious. But one man's unnecessary death is the atrocity. We Clansmen have redefined such words as atrocity and glory.

Even the freeborns perform better knowing that they are part of the Trials of trueborns. Most of them are eager to attack a trueborn, even though they know that Clan society views freeborns as the more expendable of the two genetic categories.

No, I see no waste. None at all.

Nevertheless, Cadet Aidan's killing of five of the freeborns shocked even me. Then, when he was down temporarily, with a vengeful freeborn standing over him, representing the sixth potential slaying, I was tempted to abort the whole exercise. . . .

# =20=

Afterward, long afterward when he had time to reflect upon the entire experience, Aidan decided that it must have been a minor explosion that knocked him off his feet, perhaps from the kind of training grenade used on an obstacle course. Though its charge was light, it could have done some actual physical damage if it had landed closer to him, and it was strong enough to make him unconscious for perhaps one or two minutes. He came to with the sun, newly arrived in the sky, shining behind the towering figure of one of the freeborn ambushers. Even though the figure was in shadow, Aidan could tell that he held a pistol in his hand and was pointing it at Aidan's head. Whether or not the freebirth squeezed the trigger, Aidan was never certain. There was a possibly false memory of a whooshing sound by his ear as he rolled sideways and sprang rapidly to his feet. For once, all those sibko acrobatics, practiced endlessly in calisthenics and team tussles, stood him in good stead. He had not been the most adept at such exercises, but his talents were enough to catch this freeborn off guard before he could shoot again.

Not even trying to steady his own balance, Aidan thrust himself on his attacker, pushing him backward a few stumbling steps, then onto his back with Aidan on top of him. Aidan spotted a hand-sized rock next to his enemy's head and grabbed it. Just before he slammed it against the freeborn's forehead and knocked him cold, he was chilled by the look of icy hatred in the young man's eyes. He read it as the same kind of hatred that trueborns felt for this inferior class. It had not occurred to him that the hatred's intensity could be returned just as strongly, if not more so.

The look enraged Aidan. By what right did free-borns feel scornful of their obvious superiors, even if this one had been chosen to train as a warrior and was thus a cut above his own kind? As if bouncing the ha-tred back onto the freeborn, Aidan gave the uncon-scious man an extra blow against the side of his head. His body jerked abruptly and went still. Aidan thought he might be dead, but did not have time to verify the kill.

Standing up, he scrutinized the immediate vicinity, saw no potential danger. Without looking back at his latest victim, he started running toward the 'Mechs again. As he came to a slight rise, he saw Bret already lifting on a field howdah to his *Summoner*'s cockpit. An arm of Marthe's 'Mech was already moving, indicating she was in her pilot seat and ready to engage.

Damn! If that stinking freeborn had not interfered with his progress, he would be piloting his own 'Mech right this moment. Now he was going to be the last to start off.

Lowering his head, Aidan began to run as fast as he could. His head was down because he did not want to watch the others get the jump on him, but he could not keep out the sounds. First came the rhythmic pulse of one fusion engine starting up, then the other, the clomp of one of the pilots testing out the footing of his or her 'Mech, the slight whir of the weapon system being po-sitioned. He knew his ears were deceiving him, but he could have sworn he heard Marthe's muttered curses as she tested out her commlink.

Suddenly he was there, at the foot of his *Summoner*. Looking around, he saw that Marthe's 'Mech was already heading up the slight hill beyond which the enemy waited. Bret's was just taking its first step.

And his 'Mech, as if rudely signifying his single op-portunity to be a Clan warrior, stood uninhabited. To Aidan, the *Summoner*'s face glared down at him, as though condemning him for slackness. Aidan stepped into the field howdah, which sensed his weight and immedi-ately and smoothly rose to cockpit-level of the 'Mech. The cockpit hatchway was open, and Aidan virtually dived through it in his haste. He bumped his head lightly against the side of the hatchway. The bump hurt, but he ignored it as he stumbled over his own feet and nearly fell into the command couch.

## 21

**A**idan could never have explained how or why, but he seemed to hear an eerie silence beneath the ever-present noise within the cockpit. All sensors were operational, and he only had to find his way into the command couch, don the neurohelmet, make the proper quick checks, and get the 'Mech itself moving.

A note was taped to a secondary screen. It read: "Welcome to your Trial. Now your real mettle is revealed. No matter that I despise every one of you, I wish you success. [signed] Falconer Joanna." Grunting, Aidan tore the paper off the screen, crumpled it up, and tossed it over his shoulder, where eventually it would be sucked into the waste system and cast out of the 'Mech in tiny shredded pieces. On the screen itself was the set of commands that would activate the 'Mech, a substitute for the checklist that a pilot would normally perform with his chief Tech. Aidan went through the steps rapidly, seeing on the primary screen that Marthe had already reached the crest of the hill and Bret was not far behind. He *had* to catch up with them before they disappeared over the hill. It was a matter of honor. Nobody liked to bring up the rear, even less when you were so behind you looked like a straggler. During the forced marches of training, a straggler was ostracized by the rest of a sibko.

In the early training days of Aidan's sibko, the cadet named Dav, whose talent was artistic rather than physical, always had difficulty keeping up with the others. Although the sibkin revered Dav's gentleness and affability, they made his life a living hell until finally he kept up with them on the marches. (Dav never knew that Aidan and Marthe had secretly lightened his backpack before these marches, and was thrilled at what he perceived as his own achievement.) For a time, Dav had actually become a promising cadet, then the training became too severe for him and he flushed out. Like most of the other cadet washouts, he crept silently out of the barracks one night, but, unlike the others, he left behind a well-executed drawing of each of the survivors.

Satisfied that his neurohelmet guidance system was in sync with him, Aidan started his 'Mech on its first step without first testing the legs. It nearly became a costly mistake as the 'Mech wavered from side to side. Concentrating, Aidan executed a perfect second step, and the 'Mech regained balance. To an observer, the *Summoner* would have seemed to stride surely and confidently up the hill, reaching the crest much faster than the other two 'Mechs had done.

On his primary monitor, Aidan surveyed the valley, pictorially divided into lines and grids, in front of him. Up ahead, Marthe and her *Summoner* walked cautiously, the 'Mech's head moving slightly from side to side as she searched the terrain for her opponents. Bret's 'Mech was lumbering sideways, apparently having detected something.

From his high vantage point, Aidan saw activity beyond a clump of trees. Apparently Marthe had discovered it, too, for her 'Mech started moving quickly toward it, feet crushing greenery into flat, scarred swaths. Switching from grid picture to natural picture, Aidan saw a trio of 'Mechs, Marthe's three test opponents, emerge from cover behind a thick clump of trees. At the same time, Bret's opposing 'Mechs seemed to come out of the ground, though actually they were cresting a hill to Bret's left. And further away than this six, the three that Aidan knew were destined to be his adversaries burst out of a camouflage cover that had looked like a group of high rocks, but that his computer's secondary monitor analyzed structurally as merely a construction. One of them, a *Hellbringer,* lifted its left arm and pointed it straight at Aidan, a gesture indicating that this was Aidan's first opponent.

He cursed the distance between him and his Trial antagonist, who was too far away for Aidan to initiate his strategy. He could shoot off an LRM salvo, but it would either be blown out of the air or just pass over the *Hell-bringer*'s head like a harmless balloon. He had to get closer, so he shifted his 'Mech to face the other 'Mechs directly, and took the first step toward engagement.

When Marthe fired the first shot of the contest, a cannonade of energy blasts from her right-arm PPC, the vibration rocked Aidan's cockpit. The shots were true, right on line with the torso of one of her opponents. Armor flew off in all directions, some of it as far as the feet of Marthe's *Summoner,* where it set off isolated fires that quickly burned out.

Starting out aggressively seemed to be Marthe's choice of strategy, for she immediately shot off another volley, hitting the same spot and enlarging the hole she had already opened up in her opponent's armor. Aidan, impressed by her offensive, wanted to shout encouragement to her. The other pilot countered her attack by launching a short-range missile from the left side of his 'Mech's torso, near where Marthe's shots had hit so truly.

Bret was already on the defensive. With a kind of sixth-sense reaction, he expertly leaned his 'Mech's torso to the left so that a fusillade of PPC bolts flew past him. If Bret's *Summoner* had had hair, it would have been trimmed a bit, a centimeter or two off the side. Bret fired a cluster round at his rival. Aidan, who could keep track of the others on a side screen, noted that the cluster round was reasonably effective, a real gyro shaker that missed much of the torso, but ripped off a section of the opponent's right knee joint.

Well, he wished Bret luck, but there was no point in keeping track of his battle when Aidan had one of his own to contend with. His foe, the *Hellbringer,* fired a PPC burst that fell short. Aidan launched a long-range missile salvo, but it was only a feint to lull the pilot of the *Hellbringer* into expecting a conventional attack. The full flight of fifteen missiles at the very edge of their effective range, sailed over the 'Mech, which did not even bother to utilize its anti-missile system.

Aidan pressed his *Summoner* forward and kept his weaponry silent for a few steps. To his right Marthe's 'Mech was rocked by a hit to the center torso. He caught his breath, fearing that she might be toppled, but Marthe regained balance expertly, at the same time chipping the

armor of her opponent, also in a *Hellbringer,* with a short-range missile attack launched from her left shoulder. She had reconfigured her 'Mech to replace its primary LRM-15 system with a heavy Streak SRM-6 mount. Quickly following up on her assault, she set her 'Mech into a run, going straight at the enemy, firing a medium laser that she had installed in the torso. The laser fire seemed to cut a smooth line across the chest of the *Hellbringer,* sending it rocking backward. Switching to her LB-10X autocannon, she lay down a barrage that caused a series of explosions in the foe's torso. The explosions sent up clouds of smoke. The smoke momentarily obscured Aidan's opponents, too, a stroke of luck that he had not bargained for. He was sure the cheer he let out would have confused any commlink listeners.

He used the smokescreen to help him execute his primary maneuver. As he fired his jump jets, he rose above the smoke, flying over the terrain between him and his trio of rivals. Doing so, he noted that the 'Mech Marthe had attacked was falling, apparently onto its back. Aidan felt his own energy surge with the certainty that Marthe was about to make her first "kill," qualifying her as a MechWarrior who, if she could now finish off a second one, could enter the command structure at a higher level. Her success heightened his own confidence. They had been so close for most of their lives. They looked alike, had the same skills and talents. Whatever one did, the other could surely do, too.

Pushing his 'Mech's jumping capability to the maximum, Aidan flew over his trio of Trial opponents, each of whom was now beginning to turn his 'Mech's torso to follow his flight. As he rose to zenith, Aidan realized he was momentarily vulnerable, but he counted on the factor of surprise to protect him. The last thing expected of him at this point was to try to get *behind* his antagonists. He felt the usual wave of dizziness at the high point of the jump, just as his 'Mech started to come down, but not so much that he could not get his weapons ready for the assault that would come as soon as his 'Mech's feet touched ground. Diving down, his 'Mech straining a bit from the drag and weight of all its armament, Aidan verified that the large pulse laser he had configured as an additional right-arm weapon was still at full charge.

He brought his *Summoner* to a smooth landing on both feet, scattering a number of small animals in all directions, and quickly angled its torso so that it faced the *Hellbringer* directly. Bringing both arms up to a level parallel to the ground, he began firing rapidly at the other 'Mech with everything he had. A surge of heat assailed him in the cockpit, but he had figured he could endure the excess without risking dangerous levels. Everything depended on how quickly he finished off the *Hellbringer*.

A quick check of his short-range scanner showed that the *Hellbringer* was just standing its ground, less than three hundred meters away, as Aidan's *Summoner* closed in. The barrage from all Aidan's weapons except the LRM had created many charred and smoking areas in his foe's armor. Glancing at his long-range scanner, he saw that Marthe had indeed beaten one of her opponents, and that Bret, whose battle was going on nearby, was holding his own.

"Cadet Aidan!"

It was Falconer Joanna's voice. He should have known she would interfere. There was supposed to be no communication until the Trial was over, except where Trial rules came into effect.

"You have violated the enemy line. The judges consider it a brave but foolhardy move, and you should know that all three of your rivals may now engage you—that, in fact, all 'Mechs in the field are now eligible to fire. According to Trial rules, you have initiated a melee. I hope you knew that risk when you took the chance, for it may now decide the fate of your fellow sibkin as well as yours."

Of course he had known, but he would not give her the satisfaction of revealing his strategy. An unexpected melee was designed to throw off everybody in the field, including his cadet allies, who would not like the change in situation any more than the MechWarriors assigned to the opposing 'Mechs. He would show her.

After checking his heat scale to be sure he did not risk sudden overheating, he fired one last shot at the *Hellbringer*, then suddenly rotated his 'Mech's torso abruptly to face an enormous *Warhawk* that was just completing its turn to join the skirmish. Next to it, the third and largest of his opponents, a massive *Dire Wolf*, with its apparent crouching stance and sizeable weaponry, was still in the process of turning. He would try for the *Warhawk* first.

With his pulse laser, Aidan aimed for the joint that connected the *Warhawk*'s right arm to its torso. Disabling the arm would rob the 'Mech of nearly half its weaponry. He knew from study that a *Warhawk,* in its primary configuration, concentrated too much of its armament in its arms. Aidan yelled as his shots rang true. The enemy 'Mech's right arm suddenly dropped, still connected but rendered inoperative.

As he had hoped, the *Hellbringer* closed ranks, edging in toward the *Warhawk.* Between them was a large rock. It was time for his calculated risk. Using the left-leg jump jets for a quick leap backward and sideways, Aidan simultaneously released a long-range missile barrage, aimed downward so that it would land between the two enemies, impacting against the rock and sending enough shreds and shrapnel against the two 'Mechs to send them both to the ground.

Even with the jump, his 'Mech was still rocked by the explosion. The *Summoner* came down on one foot and toppled sideways. It was all he could do to keep his 'Mech upright. Checking his sensors, Aidan learned something about the experienced pilots in the pair of 'Mechs. They, too, had each jumped sideways, away from the impact. The explosion had riven a great hole in the right side of the *Warhawk,* but it remained upright and functional, despite the extensive torso damage and its disabled right arm. The *Hellbringer,* however, had fallen onto a patch of trees, which held it over the ground at an oblique angle.

All right, Aidan thought, now it is time to finish off the *Hellbringer.* Then, with any luck, he would whirl around and get the *Warhawk.* The latter 'Mech had jumped far enough out of the way to be effectively out of the action for at least a few seconds, especially as it was now showing Aidan its already-damaged right-arm side. The *Dire Wolf* was still positioned poorly for encounter.

Any hope that the *Hellbringer*'s pilot was hurt or unconscious because of the fall was dashed when Aidan saw the 'Mech's knees bend into a kneeling position to push itself away from the top of the clump of trees. Its torso rotated ominously toward Aidan's charging 'Mech. Despite the extensive torso damage, verified by the way armor pieces littered the countryside around the *Hellbringer,* all its weaponry appeared to be functional. PPCs in both arms were blasting at Aidan.

With the 'Mech kneeling, however, Aidan still had the tactical advantage. He managed to maneuver out of the way of some bursts aimed at his 'Mech's right knee. Bringing his own weaponry to bear on the ill-positioned *Hellbringer,* he rocked it with another salvo of coherent light and elementary particles.

He moved in for the kill. Every one of his senses seemed heightened, almost as though he had developed another two or three. His damage-control screen showed only a few ineffective hits from his adversaries. With a sense of victory expanding his chest, he looked at his heat scale and saw there was no time to lose. He had to act now, or else find a quick retreat to cool down and recharge, giving the second and third opponents a chance at him. He saw that the *Warhawk* was, in fact, already getting into position for a good shot at him.

He figured two bursts from his right-arm pulse laser should be the fusillade that earned him qualification as a MechWarrior, and he lined up the *Hellbringer* in his sights.

Keeping track of his proper trio of opponents, Aidan had not seen the fourth 'Mech that came toward him, running. It was a legal Trial move, for he had opened up the combat into a melee. But with all the others so actively engaged, he had not expected a move toward him.

His hoped-for finishing shots at the *Hellbringer* went wide as the intruding 'Mech made a direct hit against the cockpit of Aidan's *Summoner.* He could feel the heat of fire rushing at him as the computer announced the beginning of the automatic eject sequence. Desperately, he wanted to get off another barrage, hoping for a lucky shot before his 'Mech expelled him.

He flew high into the air as the cockpit area of his *Summoner* exploded behind him. His consciousness left him just as he realized that he had been beaten by Marthe. She had not only shot him down in the Trial a moment before he would have qualified, she had obtained her own second Trial victory, earning her the right to enter the

Jade Falcon Clan as a Star Commander, the very rank for which he had been aiming. Now there would be no rank for him, no chance to become a MechWarrior. Marthe had destroyed those chances for him. Marthe, to whom he had been devoted from the earliest days of the sibko. Marthe, who had once thought she might love him. How could she have double-crossed him just as he was about to qualify? Was this the true way of the Clan? It was with these last thoughts that Aidan hit the ground in his ejection seat, immediately passing out from the excruciating pain in his left arm.

# 22

"I saw my chance and I took it," was Marthe's succinct explanation as she stood by his hospital bed, casually holding her brand new Star Commander's field cap in one hand. Aidan wondered if the cap was meant as a further insult as he gingerly touched his legacy from the battle, a broken left arm.

"But the sibko, Marthe, what about the sibko?"

"What about it? There is no sibko any longer. We outgrow the sibko. That is the way."

"We were once so close."

"As children. We are not . . ."

"I know, I know. We are not children now."

"Do not be bitter."

"What do you expect me to be? I *needed* to be a warrior."

"Need is not a good warrior trait, I suspect. We are trained, we succeed or fail, we find our place in the Clan. Those who succeed at *being* warriors earn their Bloodnames and find their place in the gene pool. That is all that happens, or should happen. You nearly succeeded in becoming a warrior. So few get even that far. Now you are assigned to the technician caste. You will be a good Tech. The Clan has found the proper place for you, and you accept that, *quiaff?*"

He wanted to deny it, but he said, "Aff."

She turned to go.

"Marthe?"

"Yes?"

"You had already made your first kill, and you had a fine chance at a second among the opponents selected for you."

"I remind you that one of them did defeat me finally, stopping me from achieving a third triumph."

"All right. But you might have won, without turning on me, without—"

"Do not say more. I did what was proper. The rules provide that, in a melee, any 'Mech on the field is a fair target in a Trial. You were a fair target."

"But what of all the time we spent together, all the feelings, all the—"

"Do not talk to me of feelings. Such things are illusions for which we have no time—"

"But once you said perhaps you loved me."

"A child's game. It was only the foolish stories Glynn told us that led to such statements, not any so-called feelings. I was merely a child imitating what happened to be in my environment. We grow up. Or, at least, I grew up."

He could not mistake the sarcasm in her last statement. Not only did she place herself above him, but in terms of Clan castes, she now occupied a higher social position. He would never persuade her of the unfairness of her tactic—nor, deep down, did he actually believe it was unfair. It was unfortunate, yes, and he was bitter about it, but he could not call it unfair. No matter that he had formed an excellent strategy. He had not been able to achieve it because, like a failed commander in a battle, he had not anticipated something in the forces aligned against him.

"It makes no sense for us to talk together any further," Marthe said. "I came, obeying the customs of politeness. Defeated and hospitalized enemies must be visited once. So I have done. If we meet again, it will be as members of different castes, and caste rules will apply. Goodbye."

"Wait."

She turned wearily. "Another question?"

"One more."

She spoke like a queen bestowing a favor. Her tone made him feel helpless, inferior. This must be what it was like, he thought, to realize for the first time, the caste difference.

"Do you know," he said, "that had I been in your

position, seeing you vulnerable in the melee, I would never have attacked you?''

She sighed.

''I thought you might say that. And I admit having given the matter some thought. Aidan, I know you would not have . . . not have attacked me in such a circumstance. But perhaps that shows the essential difference between us, the one that made me a MechWarrior and you a Tech. I took the opportunity that you would have refused. Perhaps you were not destined to be a warrior.''

''Marthe, you have become so—''

''I have not become anything. I am a warrior, and that is everything. You have had your question. Now I must leave.''

He let her go. What more could he say to her? All he could do was lie in bed, refighting the Trial over and over in his head, wondering if he—had he seen Marthe coming—would have shot her down in self-defense. He was not sure he could have, although in his thoughts he killed her over and over.

Was she right? he wondered. Was it destined that he not succeed in the Trial to become a Mechwarrior? Yet he had come so close. If Marthe had not intervened, he would have defeated the *Hellbringer,* he knew it! He could probably also have taken out the already-wounded *Warhawk.* Even if the *Dire Wolf* had lumbered into the battle, he would have had a chance at it, too. Well, that was perhaps getting too carried away. The one victory was certain, the others he could fight in his mind for the rest of his life laboring away as a Tech.

Aidan shuddered at the thought. He had never even considered being assigned to a subcaste. Marthe might have been able to accept whatever came, but Aidan was not so comfortable with that attitude. He had to accept it, yes. It was, after all, the way of the Clan. But he did not have to like it. He did not.

As he eased into sleep, a new thought came to him: Did he have to accept it? It was the way of the Clan, yes, to fulfill the proper role. But people walked away, did they not? If he could get help, or learn schedules, or *something,* he could hitch a ride on some ship going away from Ironhold, pursue life in some other place, find new uses for whatever skills he proved he did have. Clan society held wanderers in almost as much contempt as bandits, but what had he to lose anymore? So far, he had known only the sibko and then the life of a cadet. Perhaps there was another life out there for him among other parts of the Clan, among other Clan worlds.

Did he think these thoughts or were they just figments on the threshold between waking and sleep? As Aidan drifted off, the questions dissolved into dreams where he fought mighty battles—sometimes in BattleMechs, sometimes on his own, sometimes in bizarre vehicles or on fantasy animals. He kept winning. Nothing or no one could defeat him.

# ═══ 23 ═══

**D**amn, wrote Falconer Commander Ter Roshak. Damn it to some appalling Inner Sphere hell! Warriors are warriors and the Clan is the Clan, but sometimes the rules do not fit the game; the standards do not apply to the particular social action or even the individual experience. As I watched the risk-taking cadet fall to a barrage that was more luck than skill, thoughts raced through my brain and I felt an uncharacteristic frustration, even a sadness for a fate I did not believe in. It was all I could do to keep a tight rein on my emotions before Falconer Joanna and the other training officers in the control room.

We all know the necessity for luck in warfare, yet I do not like to see a cadet defeated by shots fired from virtual ambush, especially when it is another cadet rather than one of our Trial cadre doing the shooting.

Yet, Cadet Marthe is to be praised. Her improvisation was brilliant. She will become a fine MechWarrior, a fine officer. Aside from the personal interest I have taken in Cadet Aidan, I have other reasons for regretting that the incident occurred. Aidan's strategy was clever, too. Indeed, he accomplished something that had never been done before. He threw the whole Trial into disarray, and then would have won it with actions that would have been heroic in a real battle, but for Cadet Marthe's tactical quickness. As a good tactician myself, I appreciate her skill, but it is not pleasing to see it used against another candidate who was equally deserving of success.

At one time, I used to believe that exceptional cadets should have a second chance at the Trial, but I was voted down by chiefs of staff. Eventually, they won me to their point of view, which faithfully adheres to Clan military beliefs.

But any rule has its exception, and I believe Aidan should be one of these. If I had it in my power to reinstate him, I would.

But there is no way.

Or is there?

I know I am not through with this Aidan, this generational twin of my old comrade, Ramon Mattlov. The first thing I will arrange is to keep him within my command. That strategical maneuver is, at least, within my power.

And then—

And then—

Who can say what will happen then?

# 24

After his first week as a Tech, Aidan knew he could not stand the life, especially not here, in the same place where he had failed, where hopeful cadets, confident in their abilities, were still in training and reminding him of what he had been. When he chanced to pass by Falconer Joanna on several occasions, she had looked right through him. That, more than the hard work and the certainty that being a Tech was a demotion in caste, discouraged him. He could not abide being continually reminded of his failure in the Trial, but neither could he avoid the constant reminders.

Nomad, for whom he now worked as an apprentice, perceived Aidan's problem from the first day. "Take the work as it comes," he advised. "Work is the best cure for anything. It numbs the feelings."

"What makes you think I am feeling anything, Nomad?"

"If you say you're not, you're not. I don't argue what's in somebody else's head and body. That's a problem for them and any doctors whose scrutiny they have the misfortune to come under."

"Do you have to use so many contractions when you speak? It sounds coarse."

"Away from your old friends, the cadets and warriors, we are by their standards—coarse. We use contractions, we use ancient cursing styles. The lesser castes do; the freeborns have made a ritual of it. We chat about forbidden subjects. You'll have to learn all this. You're a Tech now, Friend Aidan."

"Do not call me friend either. I will work with you but . . ."

"With us, Friend is just another title. Like Cadet or Falconer or Commander. You'll get used to it."

"Never."

"Techs are not petulant either, Friend Aidan."

Now that they were Tech to Tech, Nomad was more talkative than when he had been Aidan's virtual servant. The outcome of the Trial had dissolved the class barrier, Aidan realized, and Nomad had dissolved the emotional distance between them almost immediately. Cheerful when away from warriors, he had done much to ease Aidan's immediate transition into a new caste. Aidan's chiding of Nomad's speech flaws was done with a similar affability. Indeed, he experienced an almost sibko-like friendship with the other man now. Perhaps, after all, Aidan *would* someday fit in as a Tech.

But he could not accept Nomad's counsel, could not lose himself in work. The work was not a cure. If anything, it depressed him more. So much of it was meaningless. Awaiting their assignment to a 'Mech, they were doing futile mechanical tests on transport vehicles, repainting surfaces, adding plates of new armor, adjusting weapon calibrations, learning to reconfigure 'Mechs in the field, all dull work from which Aidan could not find the sense of accomplishment that it seemed to provide Nomad continually.

From the first day, Aidan realized that he would have to find some way to numb his mind in order to perform the monotonous tasks that were now his lot. Not that Nomad's mind was at all diminished by it. He seemed to relish the least task, taking a high degree of satisfaction from transforming something that was not working right into an efficient component.

One day, after finding that a chest-mounted medium laser was jamming because of a structural flaw in the surrounding casing, Nomad sang while tearing one section out and welding in a new one. Except for the chanted, almost monotonous tunes of the warrior rituals, Aidan had never heard much music. Nomad's song was lively and melodic. Some of the words, too, were unfamiliar.

"They're farmer's words," the Tech said. "Rural language. All the castes have some music. But we don't all have to warble that dry stuff that cadets are stuck with in their stiff and stuffy rituals.''

"You find our—*their* rituals unappealing.''

Nomad looked all around him before speaking, then he kept his voice low: "I never said that. I meant that their songs or chants or whatever are not as lively as the music in the lower and freer castes.''

"Free? What does that mean? You work all day, lead a subservient existence, are dominated by routines and restricted by laws, follow caste customs—how is that free?''

"We don't have to jump into magnificent dustbins and risk our lives at the command of others.''

"But that is honor, glory, hero . . .''

"That is just so much of what the bull leaves behind him on the road.''

"Sometimes I do not grasp your slang, but it is as repellent as your overuse of contractions.''

"You make too much out of contractions and slang. You're headstrong but a bit dim, Friend Aidan. Contractions, slang, they're just words, words like your honor and glory and such. Just words.''

"That sounds like treason to me.''

"In a cockpit, maybe, but down here, among the Techs, it's just chatter. Do you seriously think a warrior is going to hang a Tech for treason? They need us. There are not enough Techs to go around. Nobody ever gets hanged who's indispensable.''

"You pretend to a wisdom beyond your station, Nomad.''

"Who's pretendin'? And it's your station now, too, Friend Aidan. If you want to keep from steppin' into the pile of wisdom that's available to you, that's your business. In the meantime, hand me that wrench.''

Every morning, Aidan found it more difficult to roll out of his bunk. He dreaded facing another day of tinkering with some piece of machinery while cadets and training officers passed him by, oblivious to him. Their snobbery enraged him. What right had they to ignore the people who maintained the essential vehicles, the buildings they lived in, the 'Mechs they might fight in? Now they cut him dead, but a few weeks ago, he had been one of them. (And, Aidan realized suddenly, he had ignored Techs just as blithely.)

It especially bothered him to have been assigned to remain at Crash Camp, when most failed cadets were sent away to more geographically distant positions. Was someone trying to punish him? Perhaps so. Perhaps he deserved further punishment for overstepping his boundaries in the Trial, for defying the rules. If so, it was all the more reason to want to escape the camp.

Though Aidan felt trapped, his urge to get away might have agitated him for some time, left him smoldering in his bunk with plans unacted on, had a particular incident not prodded him. That day he had been on a real garbage job, hauling new coolant containers to a freight skimmer that was to take them to a 'Mech repair facility on the other side of Crash Camp. Nomad had said that they were scheduled for permanent assignment to that very facility fairly soon. They were only on the Trial site until after a new crop of cadets arrived.

Aidan was thinking of the new crop as he drove a fork-lift loaded with coolant tanks to the skimmer. In his mind, he saw the cadets arriving nervously, then going through all the tests that Aidan and his sibkin had endured, finally facing the Trial itself. Nomad told him that all this would become just so much routine. All the new cadet sibkos would start to look alike, their experiences so repetitious that eventually Aidan would forget he had ever been one of them. Aidan doubted that, but he would have to wait and see, see if he would, after all, adjust.

As cargo Techs unloaded the forklift at the skimmer, he strolled around the general area, noting that there were three freight skimmers being dealt with in various ways. One was obviously being repaired, another was unloading food supplies.

Suddenly he saw Marthe walking toward him, a clipboard in her hand. She was dressed in her crisp new warrior fatigues, a slate gray jumpsuit with dark blue piping. On her chest was the medal given to cadets who had succeeded in their trials. She wore her cloth cap, also gray with blue piping, at a jaunty angle. Whatever was on the clipboard, she was studying it.

As she passed near him, he called: "Marthe!"

She stopped for a moment without looking at him. The

way she held her body, the indifference in it, reminded him of the snubs he'd already endured from Falconer Joanna. Then she resumed her walk, her eyes ever intent on her clipboard.

Rage hit him like a cluster round, expanding within him just as quickly. He whirled around and chased after her.

"Marthe!"

She picked up her pace, but that was her only reaction.

"Marthe! Talk to me!"

He started running toward her. She hesitated, then resumed walking at normal pace and did not even look back.

The indifferent set of her shoulders and the fact that she would not look at him enraged Aidan even more. For the last few steps between him and Marthe, he ran even faster. When he reached her, she turned around suddenly and brought up her clipboard. With a backhanded blow, she struck him just in front of his temple. The blow diverted his attack just enough so that he missed grabbing her and fell to the ground next to her, landing on his back.

For a brief moment, he saw her looking down at him, a benign and inscrutable look on her face. The pain in the side of his head made him blink several times. She nodded once, then turned to walk away. Turning over and crawling forward, he seized her ankles and pulled at them. She fell forward, onto her knees. The clipboard dropped out of her hand, its papers curling up beneath it as it skidded along a patch of ground.

He waited for a counterblow of some kind, but she merely stayed on her knees, with his hands around her ankles. She stared forward. Scrambling to his own kneeling position, he released her ankles and quickly grabbed her around the shoulders. He pulled her slightly toward him, realizing that the movement placed her in an extremely uncomfortable position, her legs bent backward, her back curved painfully. For the first few seconds, she made no move to resist his hold. Aidan meanwhile tried to get to his feet without freeing her, but the attempt loosened his grip. She responded almost automatically, thrusting her arms outward and breaking the hold. Putting her hands on the ground, Marthe pushed herself to her feet in one smooth and graceful movement. When he came toward her, she elbowed him in the chest without turning around, then spun about and gave him a high kick to the jaw. Aidan reeled backward, as Marthe merely leaned down to brush dirt from the legs of her jumpsuit, then calmly retrieved her clipboard. With quick but unhurried steps, she walked away. The set of her shoulders was tense now, anticipating another attack, but Aidan merely watched her go.

A resolution to their skirmish no longer mattered. Somewhere between her first and last blows, Aidan had suddenly known he had no other choice but to get away from Crash Camp and even from Ironhold. Marthe had decided that for him.

As he walked back to the skimmer to reclaim his forklift, it was not the result of her blows that hurt him. What pained him was that she had not uttered a word, nor even a sound of any kind, neither before, during, nor after the fight.

# === 25 ===

I could not believe my ears, wrote Falconer Commander Ter Roshak, and so I asked Falconer Joanna to say it again. "Astech Aidan is gone," she repeated. "He did not report to duty yesterday morning, but Tech Nomad, who supervises him, said that Aidan had been sick the day before. Having assumed that Aidan had reported to sick bay, he was not worried until Aidan did not show up for duty again today, Nomad checked and found his sleeping cubicle empty. Most of his possessions were missing, too."

I did not look at her, but I sensed Joanna staring at me, incredulous that I could react at all to the desertion of a minor individual, an astech, as I paced, rather nervously I am afraid, around my office.

"There is not trace of him anywhere?"

"My preliminary investigation indicates that he probably took one of the three freight skimmers away from here, though none of them reports a passenger or a discovered stowaway. I suspect that he took the one to Winson Station. A DropShip left there this morning. He could have concealed himself or been engaged as crew, though he would have had to act fast to come up with credentials, forged or real. Then he—"

"Yes, yes, Falconer," I said, agitated by her meticulous report. I expect my officers to confine themselves to the facts, leaving speculations to me. "What do you expect we should do about Astech Aidan?"

"Do, sir? Why do anything? We never usually—"

"I want him back here."

Falconer Joanna looked puzzled, but she had enough acuity not to question a superior officer's decision.

"Do you wish, sir, to go through channels to locate him?"

From the question, I saw that she apprehended more than I would have given her credit for. She knew that, whatever my reason for wanting the return of this particular Clansman, it was a devious one.

"You may use channels cautiously, but, no, Falconer Joanna, I want this Aidan actively pursued and then returned here."

"I will assign some—"

"You will assign no one. You will do the job yourself. I will detach you from your duties and get you interworld travel credentials, with freedom to go anywhere."

"You want me to undertake this mission alone, *quiaff*?"

"Neg. You may choose an aide."

"I choose Aidan's superior, this Tech Nomad."

I am sure my eyebrows rose. All the way to my hairline, it felt like. "You wish a Tech as your companion?"

"Yes. He seems competent. And he knows this Aidan as well, and perhaps better, than I do. They were more closely associated, if only for a short time."

"Why not take someone from his sibko then?"

"Marthe? No, he would run at the sight of her. And the other survivor from that sibko, this Bret, has left camp on assignment."

"Very well then. Tech Nomad it is."

She started toward the door.

"Falconer Joanna?"

She turned. "Yes?"

"Do not come back without him. If you do not find him, I will cut orders isolating you to a border planet, chasing bandit scum."

She smiled. "I am not sure I would dislike that as much as you think, Commander Ter Roshak."

"I want Astech Aidan back, Joanna!"

That I did not use her title registered immediately. Her eyes narrowed. I drop titles only for emphasis, and she got the message. She gave a rapid, old-fashioned salute, the kind that mocked the Inner Sphere military, and left my office.

Of all the persons I might have sent in pursuit of this young man, Falconer Joanna is the only one who might actually find him. She is the kind of determined warrior who would not slack or give up on any assignment.

I am certain she would like to know why I am sending her to chase him down, and I almost wanted to tell her. But my pleasure at watching her astonishment would have been only temporary. She would not approve my intention. She is one of those who believes a cadet has the right to only one chance at the Trial. She would balk at the second chance I plan for Aidan. Unprecedented as it is, as it must be.

Of course I cannot just decree a second chance. I will have to plan another identity for him, one he can use in the Trial. We cannot just manufacture one. We will have to take it from someone already here. A few people will have to die. I will have to arrange an incident. The concept appeals to me. An accident, a few secret little murders, a new identity, a second chance. If he succeeds the next time, there is no waste. If he does not, I will have no choice but to kill him, too.

# === 26 ===

More than a year passed before Joanna and Nomad found Aidan. The search had been long and laborious, consisting mostly of interviews with people who had either seen Aidan or who sent the investigators off on false trails. Along the way, the two worked together efficiently, while making life hell for one another.

Their reports, transmitted back to Ter Roshak at regular intervals, showed that Aidan set a fast pace, world-hopping almost frantically, as if no individual place could hold him. (At least, that was Joanna's repeatedly stated conclusion.) Roshak, on reading such comments, was reminded of the peripatetic Ramon Mattlov, who—never satisfied with anything in his life—was happiest when traveling.

Aidan had left Ironhold on a freighter, posing as a member of the laborer caste. Being in desperate need of a cargo-hauler, the bosun—like most merchant mariners on all planets—took the easy way out when Aidan claimed to have misplaced his papers. Aidan's Tech experience at Crash Camp served him well in the hold, and the bosun came to trust him.

When the bosun offered to sign him on for a tour of duty, Aidan pretended that he might accept the job, then he disappeared into the teeming city of Katyusha on the planet Strana Mechty. It had always been said of Katyusha that it was a city where anything and everything was for sale.

"I knew there was something odd about that kid," the bosun told Joanna and Nomad. "He did his job too well. But he did not steal anything. I can vouch for that. It is the rare cargo stiff who is not tempted by one of those capsules that break open, you know, *accidentally?* But Aidan, he was honest.''

Joanna was not sure of the value of this information, but she was happy to get away from this DropShip officer, whose breath stank of offworld dream herbs.

Aidan evidently spent little time in Katyusha. From there, he took a short hop to Marshall, where he got into some trouble. They heard of this from a restaurant laborer they met in an eating establishment in the tough outskirts of an otherwise quiet city called Custer. From her, they learned that Aidan had picked a fight with a trio of Elementals who were in the restaurant imbibing a bucket of some local concoction. ''The one you seek was taking his meal at a corner table,'' she said. ''The Elementals were across the room. I was engaged in duties away from the main room when the Elementals finished their drinks and wanted another round. Not seeing me, they simply ordered the one you seek to get up and serve them.

''Well, this—you say his name is Aidan—this Aidan stood up and confronted the Elementals, looking ready to explode. By now I had finished with my chores out back and had entered the room in time to see what was coming, but not in time to stop it.

''One of the Elementals—a man called Stong—rose from his seat to chastise Aidan.'' The woman broke off her tale suddenly and, unable to continue, looked at the floor.

''Go on, Leonor.''

''I do not know how to continue except to tell the simple, honest truth. I could not hear what words they spoke, but suddenly this Aidan marched over to the table of Elementals and stood toe-to-toe with Stong.

''Everyone of those fellows was a good head and a half taller than your young man, but he did not even wait for the dare that surely would have been the next thing out of Stong's mouth. Those Elementals were, of course, even more enraged that he had insulted their ritual.''

''Of course,'' Joanna said.

''It was a surprising fight. He tried to take on all three Elementals at once.''

Nomad raised his eyebrows appreciatively, but Joanna gave him a baleful glare.

"For a while, I almost thought this Aidan was going to be able to floor all those giants lined up against him. But they were, after all, Elementals, and nobody could take on all three. They dealt him quite a beating, but still he would not satisfy their ritual.''

"Now, what ritual was that?''Joanna asked.

"That he kneel before them and beg forgiveness, as befitting a member of the laborer caste.''

"No,'' Joanna said reflectively. "He would not likely have done that.''

"A wonder they did not kill him,'' Nomad commented matter-of-factly. "Elementals are not known for leaving survivors in close engagements.''

"They might have,'' Leonor said. "I have seen warriors do so after such an insult even when the laborer performed the necessary ritual of forgiveness. It may be that the Elementals let him live in admiration of his defiance.''

Continuing their search on Marshall, Joanna and Nomad turned up no further clues for awhile. Then Nomad, whose specialty was wandering into places where even warriors might fear to tread, learned from some dockworkers that someone fitting Aidan's description, but calling himself Damon, had left on a shuttle to Grant's Station only a few days before. When Joanna questioned Nomad about why he thought this particular person might be Aidan, Nomad pointed out that Damon was Nomad spelled backward.

Grant's Station was a Wolf Clan planet. There were times, those periods when relations between the Jade Falcon and Wolf Clans were strained, that a Jade Falcon warrior might have had difficulty gaining entrance to the planet. But this was a calm period, politically and socially, and Joanna, as a Jade Falcon officer, was actually welcomed. Perhaps too welcome, for Joanna's acquaintanceship with a 'Mech pilot named Alexey temporarily diverted her from duty. Nomad kept his own counsel, but her actions set him to wondering if this might have been the flaw that had exiled her to Ironhold in the first place. Left on his own, Nomad conducted his own investigations. Though he located several people who remembered Aidan, he uncovered nothing that would further their search.

\* \* \*

One night, when Alexey was off somewhere on duty, No-mad reported to Joanna what he had found.

"Not much," she said.

"My apologies, Falconer, but can you say that your association with Alexey has turned up more?"

"You really despise him, do you not? *Quiaff?* Answer."

"No, I wouldn't say I despise Alexey. For a fellow whose mustache threatens to make his upper lip sag to his jawline and whose brow cannot be found, he is a wonderful specimen of a warrior."

Joanna bristled, but dropped the subject. Yet, Alexey proved a revelation even to Nomad. The Wolf Clan warrior nearly found Aidan for them. One day, he led them to the edge of a forest, where they awaited a rendezvous.

"What is this place?" Nomad asked.

"You do not care, so do not ask," said Alexey, who tended toward brusque speech and behavior. "This is just the place where they will hand over to us the young man you seek."

"Will it offend you, Alexey, if I ask just who it is that is supposed to give us Aidan?"

"I am not offended. This is bandit territory. The young man you seek has been with a tribe of them for the last month. He went through their punishing rites and, I am told, performed impressively."

"You mean he was accepted into a bandit tribe?"

"Yes."

"And the tribe will turn him over to us?"

"Yes."

"Do they have no loyalty, these bandits?"

"Not when you can pay them generously for what you want."

Nomad turned to Joanna, who was uncharacteristically silent. She had been staring at Alexey, a strange look in her eyes. Nomad thought the look might be her version of regret. Having located Aidan, they would leave Grant's Station. If ever there was an ideal mate for Joanna, No-mad thought, he would look, sound, and behave much like this Alexey.

Alexey straightened into alertness, hearing some forest

sound that Nomad must have missed. When Nomad did catch the sound, he identified it immediately as horses racing toward them. Alexey's hand rested lightly on a laser pistol holstered at his side. Joanna, too, crouched in readiness. Nomad, never a fighter, looked for a place to dive to if danger arose.

Five people on horseback emerged abruptly from the edge of the forest. One of them, just before he might have trampled Alexey, reined in and spoke to him. It seemed to Nomad that sweat from the horses and their riders splashed the air all around him, while aromas he could not identify clogged his nasal passages.

Alexey suddenly grabbed the reins of the bandit speaking to him, his expression indicating he would have liked to topple both horse and rider.

"What do you mean, escaped?" he shouted.

The bandit, thick in body but unusually short for a Clansman, replied: "It was not even an escape, warrior. When we went to fetch him, he was gone. As soon as you and I had concluded our deal, I had a sensor device planted in his clothing, and we thought we had tracked him to a spot not far from here. But all we found were the clothes. He had no other garments. He is running naked somewhere, but we do not know where."

"I think I know," Alexey said.

Methodically, he went among the bandits, pulled three of them from their horses, throwing them roughly to the ground. Then he ordered Joanna and Nomad onto two of the horses, while he swung his bulky body onto a third magnificent steed.

Once settled onto the smooth unsaddled back of the horse, Alexey lost no time urging the animal forward, Joanna and the remaining bandits close on his heels. Nomad was not so quick to respond. Timidly, he suggested to the oversized beast he rode that it might be suitable if it followed the others. The horse, apparently used to keeping with the pack, took up a position at the rear. The two of them bounced along after the others for what seemed to Nomad an uncomfortably long distance, during which he periodically had to resist the urge to deposit some of his last meal along the roadside.

Alexey led them to a small outpost at one end of the forest, a garrison composed of warriors whose main task was to keep the bandits in check. As the group came through the outpost gates, they heard a sudden roar as a small hovershuttle quickly rose above the outpost, and with a rush of power, flew away. Alexey cursed, knowing the story that the freebirth captain of the garrison would tell even before he heard it.

The captain reported that, indeed, a naked bandit had climbed the walls, disarmed a sentry, forced her to give him her uniform, knocked her out, descended from the guard post, ambushed the warriors guarding the shuttle, and then ambushed the craft—taking the shuttle pilot with him. Alexey said that of course that was the outpost's only shuttle. The captain replied that it was, and Alexey rendered him unconscious with a single, hard, abrupt left jab.

These warriors have rather limited responses to crises, Nomad thought, but was careful to keep it to himself. Joanna would not be shy about raining some of her best blows on him.

Though they sent a message to the spaceport that Aidan be taken prisoner if he showed up there, the message was garbled by a sleepy comm specialist. Aidan, posing as a personnel evaluator on a tour of military encampments, had hooked a ride on a ship just before it lifted off.

"Damn!"

"What is it, Falconer?"

"Nomad, I am beginning to admire our quarry. And now our search is going to get even tougher."

Nomad cocked his head inquiringly.

"Because now he knows we are looking for him."

"I'm not sure that's a problem."

Joanna shuddered at Nomad's continuing use of contractions, but she had stopped cautioning against such vulgarity. "Yes?"

"Aidan still has the instincts of a warrior, Falconer. He will try to flee, but he'll always be willing to meet us on the field of battle. He'll get showy. Just you watch."

"I do not know why I talk to you, Nomad. You are clearly mad."

"True, but that doesn't impair my judgment."

"Go to bed."

"Will you join me? I am not Alexey, but—"

''You are *not* Alexey. And I do not, as you know, believe in intercaste relationships. So, good night.''

Joanna decided there might be some validity to Nomad's logic when they easily traced Aidan to the planet Barcella, where he joined another bandit group. They expected to corner their quarry there, and would have— except the report they received upon arrival on Barcella was that Aidan, disguised as the commander of the local battalion, had been found out and executed.

# ═══ 27 ═══

**W**hen I first read Falconer Joanna's dispatch from Barcella, it astonished me, wrote Falconer Commander Ter Roshak. I could not believe that the chief participant of my master plan would ruin it by getting himself killed in some foolish local politics. Despite my Clan blood and upbringing, which teaches us to accept necessity, I still could not allow that I had put my faith in the wrong person, that in fact, no destiny marked Aidan, no special aura because he was the reincarnation of his genetic father.

At the very least, I was disappointed. Not merely because I would not be able to put my plan into practice, but because I was being deprived of the opportunity to see if it would work or not. I have always felt cheated by lost opportunities. The battle for which I was outbid, the campaign from which I was excluded, the return to the Inner Sphere which I will miss if it does not occur soon—all these make me feel as though I have trained to run a race that, at the last minute, has been switched to another universe.

In reply to Joanna's dispatch, I sent back one of my own telling her to verify Aidan's demise. I could envision her, bureaucracy-hater to the core, despising the performance of that order. But it turned out to be an order worth sending.

Came the reply from Barcella:

"Corpse in question not that of Astech Aidan. I am told it was not even a member of the bandit group, nor was it the man they thought they had executed. Some grand strategy was involved. Aidan tricked them, perhaps to mislead us. We have no present indication of his whereabouts, but Tech Nomad is certain we will find him. I have learned to respect Nomad's instincts. We carry on. Falconer Joanna."

I was as elated now as I had been downcast before. The master plan was still in operation.

There is still time. I have selected the unit to be destroyed, and can do so at any time. We will lose one warrior training officer, which is unfortunate. But I purposely selected a unit whose officers include some with questionable service evaluations. None would be missed, least of all the one who will die.

Aidan's physical specifications, and for that matter, his general abilities, match up with one Jorge. They say Jorge has shown some pronounced anti-social traits, which could link his behavior type with Aidan's occasional rebelliousness. The main difference is that Aidan's streak may translate into admirable officer traits, while Jorge—being a freebirth—would have to suppress his rage, a dangerous quality out in the field. Jorge might have some potential for piloting a 'Mech—and is, in fact, at the top of his group in that department—but he would not make a good officer. And, besides, he is only a freeborn.

## 28

She had changed a bit in the short time since he had last seen her. Her face had grown older in some indefinable way, her eyes more serious. Her eyebrows also seemed to have been reconstructed into a permanent scowl. She had become thinner, but her body had lost some of its cadet tautness. In the intense sunlight of Tokasha, she had developed a permanent tan that also aged her. He wondered how she could stand the odd, decaying smells of the laboratory where she now worked so determinedly.

On the pocket of her lab coat was a Jade Falcon warrior patch, which former cadets, even those who had flushed out, were allowed to wear in whatever caste they served. The patch showed a Jade Falcon in flight, magnificent wings outspread, keen, small black eyes searching for prey. The Jade Falcon was native only to the planets of Ironhold and Strana Mechty, and then it was seen only rarely. Legend had it that Jade Falcons disappeared from nature for precise periods, hibernating or perhaps hiding in some spirit world until it was time to fly again. Aidan had never seen one.

The patch was also intended to remind people in other castes that sibkin, even those who had not qualified as warriors, were among them. Their genetic origins were respected—and frequently resented—all over the Clan worlds.

"Peri," he whispered.

Startled, she looked up suddenly. From the look on her face, she might have been staring at a ghost. Then again, he probably did look phantasmal.

"Aidan? Is it you?"

"Yes," he said, and fell unconscious.

He did not come fully awake for several days. In that time, he would stir a bit, and it seemed that Peri was always at his bedside. Once he said blearily, "I am keeping you from your work, Peri."

"Not as much as you think. Are you . . ."

But he was asleep again.

Another time he was conscious of someone dabbing at his head with a damp cloth. Opening his eyes, he saw Peri again.

"You are looking better," she said quickly, as if she had been waiting for him to waken so she could. "You looked so awful when you came into the lab. You looked like—"

"I had been in the jungle. There were . . . terrible things there."

"That is Tokasha for you. This part of Tokasha, anyway. Yesterday I saw—"

He passed out again.

The next time: "Peri, I failed."

"Hush, let the medicine work."

"I was in the Trial and Marthe—"

"No. Do not tell me. When I left Crash Camp, I put all that behind me. I do not want to hear."

"But—"

"Do not excite yourself. This fever is still dangerous, especially when you involve—"

Another time. Maybe not the next one, maybe it actually came before. Later he could not be sure of what he remembered and what he might only have dreamed.

"Do not scratch your arm, Aidan. That rash can become permanent. A never-ending itch, and you do not want that, do you?"

"Peri, I think Joanna is after me."

"Oh? What makes you think so?"

"I was escaping in a shuttle. On . . . on Grant's Station, I think."

"I have been there. A true hellhole."

"And there was a port in the shuttle. When I looked out, I saw people who were pursuing me, bandits and others on horses. They came into the camp. The bandits were the ones I had been with."

"Bandits? You have led an odd life since last I saw you."

"No, listen. It was Joanna on one of the horses, I am sure of it. How can you miss that—"

"Hush. You are getting too excited."

"And Nomad, I think, too."

"Nomad?"

"My Tech. I was his assistant, his Astech."

"This sounds too fantastic to me. Calm down."

She smoothed his forehead with her fingertips until he fell asleep again.

When he was better, Peri fed him soup.

"This is delicious. Did you make it in your lab?"

"No. There is a cook in the village. He is teaching me some of his simpler concoctions."

"Village?"

"It has no name, but it is nearby, on the other side of the small forest that helps to isolate our scientific community. The village is where the service personnel for this facility are housed. I think they have some vulgar terms for it."

"And this is an experimental station?"

"Yes. But you knew that. How could you have found me otherwise?"

"Luck, for one thing. But, yes, I intended to come here, find you. You are right about that."

"I am a scientist. On the way to becoming one, at any rate. I do not accept coincidence until all the chance factors have been analyzed. I have the impression you did not come here by, shall we say, the main routes?"

"No, I was running away. They saw through my fake credentials at the spaceport, tried to detain me. It took only a few of the fighting tactics we learned back on Ironhold to lay my captors out. Warrior training does have its advantages, *quiaff?*"

"I do not know. I have not had as many opportunities to test them as you apparently have. My life is relatively quiet."

"It will not be if I stay here."

"I have thought of that. Stay. I accept the risk. So far everyone in the facility thinks you are a stray citizen who got lost in the jungle. I told them you were with a geological team, but that you got separated from them and have been wandering for days."

"The wandering for days is the truth. What with that and my sickness, I have lost all sense of time."

"You have been out for about nine days. And now your voice is weakening again. Eat some more soup and then hush for a while. We will have much time to talk later. I intend to keep you around for a while."

"But Peri—"

"Hush. I have saved your life—more or less—and you are obligated to serve me. Here, let me wipe that dribble off your chin."

In a few days, Aidan felt normal again. Peri had arranged with someone in the village to not only launder his clothing but to restore it to a tensile strength duplicating brand-new garments. It was the first time he had encountered the procedure, and he marveled at how fresh the clothing felt.

Apprenticed to Genetic Officer Watson, Peri often had to leave Aidan on his own. When Watson made his suspicion of Peri's story obvious, Peri had taken a chance on telling him the truth. Apparently the tall portly scientist was pragmatic enough to respect their secret in the interests of keeping his prize apprentice content.

Peri was engaged in a project devoted to the improvement of genetic procedures. The scientists were attempting to isolate all the traits in DNA and RNA in the hopes of extracting any small bit to combine it with the best traits from other genetic sources.

"Sounds horrible!" was Aidan's first reaction when Peri explained the work.

"Why do you say that? Is it not a Clan goal to breed the best warriors available in gene pools?"

"Well, yes, but—"

"Think of how many recessive traits come though in sibkos, even though the genes of the best warriors have been combined to form them. If we can isolate—"

"No. It is precisely because the genes come from the best *warriors* that we should continue the present methods. It is not just an assortment of traits that we want, but all those that go into the makeup of a—"

"Easy, easy. I know all those arguments. We all do. But, as things stand, neither view is *proven* at the present time, and you cannot begrudge our efforts to find a better way. Perhaps our work will merely lead to the elimination of the lesser traits of a chosen warrior from the gene pool.''

Aidan sulked. "I do not know. Something about that does not sound quite right, either. Take away a single trait and you are no longer transmitting the genetic material of the individual warrior.''

Peri laughed suddenly.

"What amuses you? Do I seem so much a fool?''

"Oh, no. No, not that at all. The laugh comes from pleasure. It reminds me of when we were all young and together in the sibko, before so many of us were reassigned. Remember all the bedtime chats when Glynn and Gonn and the others were trying to force us to sleep?''

"Yes. Yes, I do. I think of such things often. Too often, Marthe told me. She calls it nostalgia, says it is a sickness.''

"She is probably right. But, frankly, I enjoy the memories.'' Peri touched his arm. "At any rate, Aidan, let us do our research. It may simply end up forgotten on a shelf somewhere, like so many files and reports of scientific studies. But should the Clans approve the results and put them into practice, then we will know all is for the best.''

"What difference does it make what I think? I have failed, I will never—''

"Hush. You pity yourself too much. You are human and you are Clan, that is enough, *quiaff?*''

He nodded. "Aff. I am glad to be with you again, Peri, even if only for this short time.''

"Oh? Are you leaving so soon?''

"No. But they will find me, and I will have to—''

She put her hand on his lips. "Hush. If it is true that you are glad to be with me, then hold me. Touch me. I have not . . . not been touched in that way since I left the sibko. The people here do not have much interest in coupling, and I have discouraged those few who show inclinations. But you are sibko, Aidan. I do, against my better judgment, long for you.''

"Peri, I—''

"I know I am not Marthe. But that made no difference when we were younger. I remember what your body feels like next to mine, Aidan, and I do not mind the thought of it.''

"Marthe has nothing to—"

"Quiet now. I am giving the orders here," Peri said, laughing as she slipped the lab coat off over her head. "I have a staff meeting in an hour. That is more than enough time."

## 29

Nomad felt as if he were being pulled in two directions. On the one hand, he wanted this mission to end so he could return to Ironhold and continue doing what he loved, tinkering and fixing. On the other, his respect had grown each time the young man wriggled out of their imminent grasp, and he began secretly to wish Aidan would succeed. But with someone as tenacious as Joanna under the orders of someone as stubborn as Roshak, this mission threatened to go on forever. Roshak had said they could not return until they had found Aidan, and only universal catastrophe or Roshak's death could change that.

Joanna was positive that Aidan was somewhere on Tokasha. He had, after all, been identified at the spaceport, and all departing ships and shuttles since then had been searched thoroughly. The worldwide surveillance network indicated that no prohibited vehicles had been spotted anywhere on Tokasha. Unfortunately, Aidan's trail had grown cold. Nobody seemed to have seen him after he had subdued his captors and fled the spaceport.

"It is as if he vanished into thin air," Joanna said. She and Nomad were in the spaceport's officer's lounge, filled with oversized chairs and long tables. Joanna relaxed in one chair, her head nearly buried in the long, dark fur of her dress cape. They had just finished interviewing the base commander.

"Perhaps he did vanish. He is, as you have said so often, resourceful."

"I am never sure what your sarcasm means, Nomad."

"Are you sure it's sarcasm?"

She suddenly gave him a backhanded slap against the

side of his head. His vision blurred. It was the first time she had struck him, though she had previously not hidden the fact that she wanted to.

Joanna made no explanations or apologies. All she said was: "I think we have been on this mission for too long. If it goes on longer, I may have to kill you."

"Just to relieve tension, Falconer?"

She stiffened as she mentally examined the remark for its implications, then replied, "Something like that."

"So what do we do next?"

"I suppose we could travel around, ask questions."

"Tokasha's a large planet. It could take a few days."

Clearly disturbed by his continued sarcasm, she tightened her fists. But it was not in Nomad's nature to retreat, even if it meant suffering another slap from Falconer Joanna.

"I know the planet's large and, for that matter, heavily populated."

"Have you made a computer search?"

"I tried. But Aidan's name would not be on record, nor is it likely he will identify himself truthfully anywhere on Tokasha."

"What about the name of someone else?"

"Who else?"

"This is a Jade Falcon planet. Other members of his sibko may have been assigned here."

Joanna stared at Nomad for a long while, then she relaxed her body, opened up her hands, and smiled. "You may have something there," she said. "I will get Ironhold's Personnel Depot to send us the complete sibko roster, including those who failed before they came to us. In the meantime, I still recall a few cadet names. Let us try them."

Nomad rubbed the side of his face as they left the lounge. His skin still smarted from her blow, but he was happy to see that her hands were unclasped and swinging unthreateningly at her sides.

# ====30====

"Why do all the scientists have last names?" Aidan asked Peri. "They are not Bloodnames, are they?"

"No, they are not. I am told the custom is in use only within the scientific communities themselves. Outside, even in the smallest Clan group, they are not allowed to use them."

"But why have them at all?"

"That I do not know. Aidan, I have only been here a short time and I—"

"The names give us an identity that we deserve but are not allowed to earn," Genetic Officer Watson said. He was standing at the doorway to the lab, his stomach—it seemed—halfway into the room in front of him. It was unusual to see an overweight person anywhere in Clan society, so severe were the conditions of life, so austere and controlled. Watson, and for that matter, a few of his colleagues, were pronounced exceptions to the rule. Their lives were sedentary, these obese people might have said, but Aidan knew it was because they had ways of obtaining food not available to other castes. The genetic program was considered so valuable to the Clan that the Councils allowed scientists many privileges, one of which was the apportionment of extra rations. Several of the scientists also maintained a hothouse where they grew various fruits and vegetables. In the few days since Aidan had been hiding here, Watson and the other scientists had encouraged him to eat well. Now even he was beginning to feel a bit flabby around the middle.

Watson ambled easily into the lab, twisting his body adroitly to avoid disturbing or dislodging any lab furniture or equipment. Despite his bulk, the man always seemed graceful to Aidan, who figured the agility came from the continual need to maneuver among typically narrow work spaces. "Our names are not Bloodnames, nor have we earned them according to the rites and customs of the Clans. They are like open secrets. In our own environment, we use them to remind ourselves of our own importance. Perhaps it seems foolish, but in a corner of the universe where warriors reign supreme, where they are the only ones who merit the surnames originally held by those who followed the great General Kerensky in the Exodus, other persons also have the need to feel that their contributions represent another brand of heroism, if you will—are also worthy of some honor. Thus, we award ourselves names, and make no mistake, we fight for them just as fiercely as do warriors. Our melees are not violent, but they draw blood nevertheless, maiming egos rather than limbs."

Aidan's brow furrowed. "I do not understand, sir."

"Those of us with surnames have achieved something, have shown skill in scientific study or observation. We do not fight in a field, but rather vote in our own small councils at to whether an individual deserves to have a labname, as we call it. We cannot call it a Bloodname, in spite of the blood we metaphorically spill in order to achieve one. Perhaps this mimicry of warrior customs seems absurd, but I do believe that we carry our labnames with a pride that is near the equal of a warrior with his or her Bloodname. I can see that you are still puzzled, Aidan."

"I do not understand all your words."

Watson laughed, a good, hearty bellow that threatened to dislodge solutions from Petri dishes. "I suppose we like to flaunt our vocabularies around here, as well as our achievements. Let me just say that the labnames help us psychologically as well as giving what you warriors call a command structure to our organization."

"What I have wondered," Peri said, "is where the names come from. None exist among the Bloodnames."

"No, they do not. The names are those of past scientists who have contributed throughout history. Thus, I am Watson, after the man who discovered DNA. Newton is Newton and Tesla is Tesla because of certain contributions those scientists made to the evolution of science itself. Sometimes, if we transfer to another lab and discover an already-entrenched Watson or Newton, we have to petition for a new labname. It is a complicated life, my children, a complicated life.''

The phrase *my children* had an almost vulgar sound to both Aidan and Peri. Though neither was born of natural parents, neither would have been willing to give this imposing scientist lectures on Clan prurience.

''Why I am here,'' Watson said, ''is to tell you of a general communique that specifically mentions you, Aidan. It included a clear description, plus the information that you are being sought because of your criminal activities.''

''That is a lie! How could they—''

''No doubt a design to force anyone who has seen you to turn you in. I sent back the routine sort of message, that no one of that description has been seen in this region.''

''Thank you, sir.''

''But I must warn you, I cannot vouch for others here. If any of them come upon the communique and decide to win a few points with the planetary council, then the game is up.''

''You should go, Aidan,'' Peri said after Watson had left them. ''This place may be too dangerous for you now.''

''It is the only place on Tokasha where I have friends. And, Peri, all Tokasha is dangerous for me. I am tired of traveling from place to place. I like it here, here with you. I will stay.''

''I do not know whether to be pleased or angry. If they find you, I—''

He put his hand lightly over her lips. ''As you always say to me, hush. Let us not concern ourselves.''

He took her into his arms. As they embraced, Aidan was besieged with dangerous thoughts. He had been honest in saying he wished to stay with Peri, yet staying together went against all their Clan instincts. Only in the lowest castes were permanent relationships allowed, even encouraged. And then merely to ensure the maintenance of a population numerous enough to provide personnel for all the services necessary to the warrior caste and for the industries scattered among the Clan planets. One of

Nicholas Kerensky's principal intentions was that no essential facet of Clan life be understaffed.

The higher castes had no trouble maintaining proper population levels. The scientists, for example, kept their ranks at optimum levels through casual procreation among themselves. Peri had told Aidan that once she was fully qualified in the caste, it was expected she would breed with various of her colleagues at the station.

"Does that not disgust you?" Aidan had asked.

"No. Why should it?"

"Peri, you were once a warrior, belonging to the highest caste possible. Not only that, but because warriors do not have to create or bear children, you would never have been made to carry a child in your womb, you would never—"

Seeing that Peri was laughing, Aidan stopped.

"Aidan, you forget, we are no longer warriors."

"I never forget."

"Yes. Your problem. Definitely a problem for you. But, remember, I did not come as close to becoming a warrior. I am settled with my new life, just as you are not. I do not detest the thought of bearing a child. I even look forward to it."

With an unpleasant feeling starting in the pit of his stomach, Aidan no longer wanted to discuss the subject. It seemed to him as foul, as obscene, as listening to laborers speak in contractions or Watson referring to others as his children.

"Aidan, you perhaps will someday want to create your own child, you—"

"Do not even say it. I wish only to leave my imprint in a gene pool."

"Which you never will."

"Peri, how can you talk like this? How can you even look forward to having a child?"

"That is easy," she said, almost mysteriously. "Easier than you might think, Aidan."

"You *have* changed, Peri. In the sibko you would not have had such thoughts."

"This is not the sibko, Aidan."

"No, it is not."

"There is some bitterness in your voice. A surprise."

"Why?"

"You never used to indicate your emotions, at least within the sibko. Perhaps to Marthe alone, but certainly never to me or the others."

"As you say, we are no longer in the sibko."

The conversation so disturbed him that Aidan wondered if he should leave the science settlement, but then the feeling passed. He was becoming used to being with Peri. Feeling the warmth of her now, he could not really understand why it seemed to leave him with a vague sense of guilt.

If the next few days were pleasant, Aidan found that Peri's embraces had taken on a strange hint of desperation. Each time they coupled, she behaved as though he might be gone within hours. It was not long before she was proved right. When they heard the first sound of a heavy VTOL skimming along the top of the nearby forest, they were in each other's arms for the last time.

## 31

**A**idan is apparently going to be uncooperative, wrote Falconer Commander Ter Roshak. Falconer Joanna's report—spoken to me, as I had ordered, so as to leave no written record—indicated that she had caused a bit of an uproar on Tokasha, bullying her way around as she did. I destroyed all her dispatches as soon as I heard she was bringing Aidan back. I have a complaint from a scientist, self-styled Watson (one of those filthy and useless lab-names), which charges that Joanna injured him severely when she confronted him in his office.

I can see her knocking the scientist about, at least until (as she told me) he cried out that it was he who had sent her the communique revealing Aidan's presence at the science station. He is still angry about the way Joanna treated him, and he has sent me a message asking me to reprimand her. I will not, of course. She was acting properly. So, like any communication from a lower caste, even one as important and, by some, exalted as the scientists, I will ignore it. Watson should have known better than to send it anyway. These scientists tend to have stupid ideas regarding ethics. If they lived even a day in a warrior's body, they would think differently.

It was shrewd of Tech Nomad to suggest checking computer records for members of Aidan's sibko. I understand from Joanna that this Peri was quite surprised when her former training officer strode into the lab, demanding that Aidan reveal himself. She told Joanna that Aidan was no longer there, speaking rather smugly, I am told. Sibkin, even those who have progressed out of the sibko, may still retain old ties, I am also told. That may be true. As for me, I never think of anyone from my old sibko.

I would like to have seen Aidan's face as he rushed into the nearby forest, only to encounter Tech Nomad holding a submachine gun on him. They tell me Aidan did not even blink at the sight of the weapon (a part of the story I was, ironically, glad to hear) and that he rushed at Nomad, who had the presence of mind to whack Aidan on the side of his head with the gun instead of pulling the trigger. Nomad said he had to hit the young man two or three times, and that even as Aidan was passing out, he made a grab at the Tech's ankles, knocking him off his feet. He is still limping along, a graphic reminder that Aidan never gives up. That is something I intend to exploit.

Aidan is now being held in an underground weapons vault near here. I did not want to take the chance that someone might recognize him. My plan requires that no one know who he is, or was, especially those with whom he will serve.

Nor must anyone know the complete plan, not even Falconer Joanna, and certainly not Aidan. To Joanna, the annihilation of the freeborn training unit will seem a fortuitous accident. Even if she suspects something, she will never know for sure. As far as Aidan is concerned, his new identity will be a godsend. I know the young man still hungers to be a warrior. I could see it in his eyes on my one visit to the vault.

The freebirths will die in an active minefield. I will claim that Falconer Erica was informed about the mines, but that she obviously did not deign to inform the cadets. Once in the field, it will seem that the freebirths panicked, with only one survivor.

In my interviews with Aidan, at first I gave him the standard disciplinary lecture about deserting his post and all the other standard-manual rigmarole, but even he knew I was going through the motions.

"You do not chase a deserter all over the globular cluster and bring him back without some other reason," he commented drily.

I put my false hand onto his shoulders. He flinched a bit beneath it, but had enough respect to sit still.

"I am returning you to cadet training with another unit," I said.

"Why?"

I admired his unhesitant reply. Everything about him had the makings of a good MechWarrior, even his stubborn inquisitiveness.

"It is my decision. That is all you need to know. Do you not wish to be a warrior?"

"More than anything else in my life," he said fiercely, showing emotion for the only time during our interview. Had any question remained about whether I was going to all this trouble for the right person, the doubts fled now.

"Then you should not complain."

"How can I go into a sibko? They would never accept an outsider."

"That may be true, but it is not for you to worry about. You must trust me. Your new group will accept you. All I need to know at this moment is whether you agree to follow my orders in this regard. When I call you to me next, you will be prepared to reenter training—at a late stage, incidentally—no matter what the circumstances."

"You know I will, do you not?"

"Yes, I do."

"You must have known that even before coming here. Yes, I agree. Is there anything more I need say?"

"Nothing."

He nodded. Satisfied, I left.

Tomorrow I will send the freeborn unit to the obstacle course. I have already laid the charges that will destroy it. I must set them off myself. I can trust no one else.

# 32

There were still seven survivors, besides himself, in Jorge's unit. Freeborns all, they had the audacity common to freeborn cadets, the conviction that they had just as much right to be warriors as the more arrogant trues. Perhaps even more, for the so-called truebirths were merely the products of concoctions placed in vats rather than the fruit of passion and subsequent womb-nurturing. Jorge knew that, like him, his fellow cadets believed that they could prove themselves as good as any warrior. They looked forward to their Trials with as much eagerness, if a shade less expectation, than truebirth cadets. The only drawback was the knowledge that, even if they succeeded, they were destined for assignment to garrison units on the most backwater posts, with no hope of ever engaging in honorable combat against another Mech-Warrior.

No matter, Jorge thought, as his unit marched to its next test. Stepping desultorily at their head was Falconer Erica, their tall, muscular training officer who had made no secret of her distaste for the assignment. The freeborns felt that they had to work doubly hard to learn necessary information because Erica so often neglected to instruct them properly. She frequently disappeared, and the gossip went that she had a good taste for bad wine. Whatever they smelled on her breath in the rare times they were in proximity to Erica, it was foul and suggestive of ephemeral fermentation.

They arrived at their destination, an obstacle course where they had already qualified. Erica explained that they had been ordered to perform a re-test, to verify that their skills had not degenerated in the three months since originally passing through this rather simple set of challenges. There were some mutterings among the freeborns, most of it complaint that they were only being retested because they were freeborns and that no sibko would ever have to endure this. Erica had to quiet them down, bellowing in that distracted way of hers that the sooner they performed the task, the sooner they could leave. She pointed out that neither was she particularly pleased with the situation, which required that she accompany them all over again. Perhaps, thought Jorge, the real test was intended for her. Perhaps her superiors had discovered her drinking habit and wanted to see if she was still qualified to train cadets. He relished the thought that Erica might slip off an overhead ladder into mud, or wind up with her nose twisted in some netting.

As if to insult her own cadets, she managed to get out ahead of them in the first stage of the course. Then she stopped on a hill to rally them with her own special brand of disparagement.

They swung over streams on ropes, went hand over hand along the raised ladder, crawled along a narrow log above a chasm, and climbed over a disabled 'Mech (just the model of one, made of light and flimsy material, Jorge noted this time through) into a fake minefield whose small charges could do no more harm than sting exposed skin. Jorge, whose memory was excellent, took the lead as he ran a path that avoided any of the fake explosive charges.

For a moment, he did not believe the loud blasts behind him, thinking they were some theatrical addition to the obstacle course. The screams convinced him otherwise.

Turning around, he saw the smoke rising, obscuring everyone behind him, then one of his fellow cadets come stumbling out of the smoke, his face already bloody and mangled, an arm dangling at his side, connected to the shoulder by the merest tissue. Jorge did not recognize whoever it was that suddenly fell at his feet. He saw no one else, but some of the bits and pieces flying through the air must surely be parts of bodies.

Something hit his arm, a piece of shrapnel that tore open a narrow wound. His mind churning in confusion, he turned and ran from the dreadful scene. What could have happened? This field was not supposed to be laid with active mines. It was all simulation. Were all the others dead? What in the name of hell was going on? What had happened? What had happened?

He ran right into the arms of someone who seized him, held him tight for a moment, then flung him away. Jorge stumbled across the ground, managed not to fall, and then turned around. The man in front of him, he realized, was Falconer Commander Ter Roshak. What could Ter Roshak be doing here? he wondered. Had he come at the sound of the explosions? But why would he be anywhere near a minor obstacle course in the first place?

"You are Jorge, are you not?" Roshak asked.

Astonished by the question and the fact that his commander knew him, Jorge merely responded: "Yes, I am. Sir."

"I am pleased."

"Pleased?" Jorge grimaced as the pain in his arm grew. He held onto the wound with his other hand and felt blood seep through his fingers.

"Yes. If someone was going to avoid my little sabotage, I am happy it was you. It shows how well I chose for the person who from now on will be you."

"Be . . . me? Sabotage. I do not understand."

"It is not necessary that you do."

Suddenly Jorge saw that Ter Roshak held a submachine gun at his side. Raising it quickly, the commander fired it point-blank at Jorge.

Jorge stared down at his chest. With his good hand, he tore open his fatigue shirt and saw the holes on his chest. The bullets had entered him at six or seven places, little bloody circles that seemed to grow as everything else began to fade out. Before he died, he thought he saw only the six or seven circles, growing larger as he, for the last time, wondered what had happened, what had happened, and then the circles abruptly disappeared.

# === 33 ===

"All right, all right, hawkheads, stuff some bullets in your craw and listen to me," the training officer shouted from the door to the barracks. His name was Falconer Othy, and he had a gravelly voice that went well with his bulky, squat body. By the slovenliness of his uniform, one could guess why he had been relegated to train a freeborn unit.

His charges, the four of them still left at this late stage of training, quieted down gradually, going on a bit longer only to annoy Othy, for whom they held no great respect. Accustomed to their recalcitrance, Othy waited patiently, knowing that soon this duty would come to an end, freeing him from its prison.

"This barracks looks like you have been using it as the Cave. Nobody goes to sleep tonight before the place has been scrubbed down."

The group moaned in protest. Othy knew they would do the job perfunctorily, but at least the top layer of filth would be removed.

"As you know, a tragic accident occurred out on the Number Five Obstacle Run. Some frees were killed— only one survived, in fact. The commander has seen fit to transfer the single survivor to our unit. He will finish training with you four."

Looking at the quartet of sullen frees, Othy pitied the newcomer. If the young man had any potential, it would be disheartening to have to compete with this bunch. But being only a free, what potential could he have? Othy had heard of some freeborns who had distinguished themselves in Clan service, but he had yet to meet one.

"Jorge, get in here," Othy bellowed, stepping away

from the doorway. As the newcomer came into the barracks, the others stood and clustered together, a combined force meant to isolate the intruder. "Cadets, this is Jorge, His scores so far have been impressive, and you should be on your toes."

Othy left the barracks, leaving his last statement as an exit line on purpose. He thought it might stir things up.

Aidan glanced casually around the room, suppressing (as Roshak had instructed him) his distaste for his new companions. He wondered how he would ever get through the weeks ahead. Knowing that his second chance at the Trial came at the end of the time gave him hope and even confidence.

One of the frees, a well-tanned young man with a strikingly handsome face, detached himself from the others and walked past Aidan to the doorway. He looked out for a moment, then turned to the others, saying, "All clear. The old bastard's gone."

Suddenly, the freeborns showed an obvious physical relaxation, an easing of tension in the shoulders, a relaxing of posture, at the news. Two of them even smiled at Aidan, while the remaining one held back, staring at the newcomer from across the room.

The freeborn at the doorway walked to Aidan, holding out his hand. "Welcome, mate. My name is Tom. I'm sort of the leader around here. Not boss, just leader. You want the job, it's yours."

Aidan had been warned that freeborns used contractions defiantly. Even though he had heard them so often around Nomad, it still made him tense. But he had to act the freeborn now, so he must watch his own language.

"I, that is, I'm glad to meet you, Tom."

"So—Hor-hay, that's your name, *quiaff?*"

"Aff. Sometimes they used to just call me George."

"They?"

"The others in my unit. They are . . . they're dead."

"Yes. We heard about it. Tragic."

"Yes, it was. I saw it happen."

"Tell us."

Tom gestured the others over. The two smiling ones came, but the other one still stood at a distance. Tom pointed to him. "That's Horse over there. He's never very friendly. He has a legitimate name that nobody remembers, but he's wild about horses, so therefore Horse. This here is Nigel.'' Tom indicated one of the smilers with a thatch of red hair and the lightest blue eyes Aidan had ever seen, but there was a toughness about his mouth that seemed threatening, especially when drawn into such a tight grin. ''And the other is Spiro.'' The other smiler's look seemed to conceal nothing. He had dark hair, mud-brown eyes, and the most solid physique of the four free-borns.

''About the accident,'' Tom prodded.

''What?'' Aidan responded.

''You were to tell us.''

Ter Roshak had described the incident to Aidan, leaving out the part he had played in causing it. He also briefed him on Jorge's background. Aidan now gave his new colleagues an embellished recounting of the event. They listened with awe (again, with the exception of the one across the room) and seemed impressed with the part describing his own escape from death. He got the impression that each envisioned his own death in Jorge's experience.

As Tom gave him the rundown on the unit's record to date, Aidan was impressed with the pleasantness and politeness of the fellow. He had always expected all free-borns to be as sullen and crude as the ones he had seen in various exercises. Well, Tom was either playing a good role or was different from other freeborns. Most of them were probably like Horse, who remained in position across the room.

Hauling a bunk from the storeroom, Tom and Aidan pushed it next to the other beds. Nigel and Spiro brought out bedding and equipment. Horse did nothing and, in fact, had barely moved since Aidan entered the room.

As soon as Aidan had stowed his gear and finally sat down on the edge of his new bunk, he felt a touch on his shoulder. Looking up, he saw Horse standing over him. Though Horse's face was unextraordinary in its features, his fiercely red complexion the only odd thing about his looks, Aidan sensed something familiar about him. As if to verify his suspicions, Horse said: ''I've seen you before. I don't know where, though. Do you?''

''No, I don't remember you, Horse.''

But, in fact, Aidan did remember the sullen young

man. Though Horse was thicker in body now, more muscular, with more meanness in his face, with longer hair that apparently obeyed current freeborn style, he was the same boy who had been Aidan's opponent on the long-ago day of the first 'Mech exercise. It had been Horse who had planted the mock satchel charge, had sent the 'Mech rocking on its foundation, had attacked Aidan with a homemade knife, and had—before Aidan had wielded a weapon that literally fell into his hands—damn near defeated him. With a catch in his throat, Aidan now remembered the fury in Horse's voice when he had called Aidan ''trashborn.''

# ══34══

Aidan wondered why Ter Roshak had not investigated the past history of this freeborn unit and discovered that it had participated in the same exercise as had Aidan's sibko. Well, the little cosmetic changes that Joanna had insisted on might be helpful, after all. His hair was longer, in the current freeborn style, and combed differently. She had lightened it, too, with some disgusting potion that had remained on his head for several hours, nearly choking him with its aroma. She had also ordered him to grow a thin beard along his jawline, a style adopted by many freeborns. (Spiro, in fact, had an almost identical beard.)

"You look familiar but different," Horse said.

"That covers a lot of ground," Aidan said. "Maybe I look like somebody you knew back home?"

"It was a small village. I knew everyone. You don't look like any of them. No, if it is somebody else, it's somebody I've seen since coming here."

Even though Aidan knew he was not moving a muscle, it felt as though he were squirming under Horse's gaze. Fortunately, Nigel sat down beside him and said, "You probably haunt his nightmares, Georgie. Don't be surprised when you hear him wake up screaming some nights."

"I know one thing you're thinking," Tom said, rejoining the group.

Aidan was startled and wondered if Tom had somehow read his mind, which now was filled with doubt that he could pull off this lunatic masquerade.

"What?"

"You're thinking that you have really drawn a hard-luck duty here. An all-male unit. Well, don't think we regret it any less than you do. Nights are long here since Dominique and Cassandra flushed out at the same time. I hear that some falconers use cadets for their satisfactions. Was that true in your unit, Jorge?''

Aidan's mind frantically assembled the information he had been given by Ter Roshak. What was that falconer's name? Then it came to him. ''No, our falconer was usually too drunk to think much about coupling.''

''Well, it will probably make better warriors out of us in the long run. I hear another unit the other side of the camp has the same problem, except they are all female. We thought of petitioning for at least shared barracks with them, but we know Sourfaced Othy would not approve.''

The others nodded in agreement. Even Horse's face seem to relax at the thought of the shared barracks.

''Othy?'' Aidan prompted. ''Is he pretty tough on you—on us?''

The others seemed to approve of the way he had included himself in the group.

''He's incompetent,'' Spiro remarked. ''Fortunately, we have Falconer Abeth, who is on leave at the moment. She makes up for his mistakes. And she doesn't seem to hate us as much as Othy does.''

''I know what you mean,'' Aidan said, remembering the way the falconer had treated him ever since he had reported in. ''He would barely talk with me on the walk over here.''

''That's Othy, all right,'' Nigel commented.

Looking up, Aidan saw that Horse was still staring at him, apparently searching his memory for a clue to Aidan's familiarity.

''We make a living hell out of Othy's life,'' Tom said, ''or at least we try. We play the role of what he believes freeborns to be, slothful and uncooperative and disgusting and all the rest. Horse says it's stupid of us.''

''It is,'' Horse said. ''If we want to be accepted, we should show them our best. Even Othy.''

''You may be right. But he brings out the worst in us. Abeth knows our true worth. She doesn't much like us either, but she's fair.''

The others muttered approval of Tom's words.

As they told him about their training experiences so far, Aidan was astonished by the camaraderie among them. Until now, he had believed camaraderie to be a singular thing, found only among sibkin and warriors. It had never occurred to him that freeborns could have emotional ties and warm feelings. In fact, he would have to go back to his childhood days to recall a time when his own sibko had displayed the warmth that this quartet of freeborns did. And they all came from disparate backgrounds, which made their camaraderie even stranger.

He had come into the room with his usual disgust for freeborns, wondering how he could ever play the role, yet these first moments were not bad. Freeborns looked all right, acted all right, smelled all right. Perhaps their genetic backgrounds did not supply them with the same skills and traits of sibko members, but they seemed human enough to do many things well.

If it were not for Horse and his obvious suspicions, Aidan began to believe this masquerade was going to be easier than originally expected. But what to do about Horse? Should he wait for a moment alone and kill him? Or just tough it out? Aidan could let nothing and no one interfere with his progress toward a second chance at being a MechWarrior, even one from a freeborn unit. He would have to watch Horse carefully. Very carefully.

# 35

Falconer Abeth was all that the others had said she would be, and certainly the opposite of Othy. She had the competence he lacked, and more. She was not like Falconer Joanna either. Somewhat shorter and plain-faced, with hair cut short and a stocky body, she spoke more gently than any falconer Aidan had ever met. But she acted with a swiftness and efficiency characteristic of all good falconers, and with something of the tenaciousness of the bird that gave the Clan its name. When one of the freeborns erred, Abeth was quick to strike him painfully with a whip or plain staff. She accompanied the blow with no words, and her silence was more effective than long diatribes from others.

Because Aidan had already succeeded at this stage of training, he soon led the freeborn unit in performance. Sometimes he wondered whether he should hold back and attain only at the levels of the others. But even when he tried, he could not contain his abilities. Tom offered to turn over leadership to him, but Aidan told Tom he was doing too good a job. Privately, he wondered why sibkos did not have leaders. He suspected that for beings who were created from the same genetic material, it might be difficult for one to emerge as a leader, but he also thought that his sibko might not have fallen apart so easily in its latter stages if he or one of the others had been a leader.

Aidan eventually noticed that Falconer Abeth was observing him closely. He thought at first it was only the interest typical of a leader for a trainee, but as he achieved more and more, she was almost always, it seemed, scrutinizing him.

Finally, she called him in to her quarters. Her room was different from the few other falconer rooms he had seen or heard about. It was not as spare or as casually kept. Indeed, Abeth's was neat and filled with items. On one wall she had carefully arranged a display of Clan weapons and on another were pictures from Clan history. Papers were evenly piled on a long table. In an open closet, clothes were not only hung meticulously, but arranged according to the type of uniform.

Abeth smiled at Aidan as he entered. He thought that perhaps she had called him here for sex, although the other cadets had told him she never summoned any of them for coupling. She motioned him to a chair at the end of her bunk. She was seated in another chair next to the table with the papers on it, and she picked up a folder that lay open at the top of one pile. She gestured with the folder in his direction.

"Jorge, this says that you led your former group in all categories. Your late falconer reported that you were almost certain to pass in the Trial if you did nothing foolish."

Aidan, not knowing how to respond, curtly nodded his head.

"Since you have joined us, you have also achieved the highest performance record for the group. I am impressed. And bothered. You see, your achievements here exceed what you attained in your former unit. Indeed, significantly exceed it. Can you explain this?"

The tone of her voice was as gentle as usual, but the words felt like the harsh blows she was known to deal out.

"I think," he said, "I think it is the tragedy."

Her brow furrowed. "Tragedy?"

"When . . . when the others were killed, I made a vow to try even harder to become a warrior. I suppose I am doing better because I want to bring honor to them as well as to myself."

What an improvisation, he thought, impressed with himself. The intensity of Abeth's stare had not diminished.

"That is an odd response, Jorge. Almost mystical. I am not used to freeborns, or trueborns for that matter, being mystical."

"I do not understand the concept of mysticism."

"I suspect you do. You even sound different from others, certainly your fellow freeborns."

Aidan's heart was in his throat as he went from pleasure at his improvisation to fear of discovery. If Abeth found him out, it would ruin his chances at the Trial.

"Different? No. I am just new. You will get used to me and I will soon seem like the others."

She put the folder down. "You do not even talk like them. You talk like me, like a warrior. For one thing, you have said several things and not once used a contraction. What kind of filthy freebirth does not use a contraction in normal conversation?"

He struggled to remain calm. "I'm sorry. It's just that—that, when I'm nervous, I kind of, kind of get formal. Do you see?"

"I can see that that could be an answer, yes. But I also take note that you reacted to my comment about contractions with the wrong kind of tension. I called you a filthy freebirth. I have not seen a freeborn yet who would not erupt into visible anger when called a filthy freebirth. Even during the earlier stages of training when they cannot address falconers, I have always noted a flinch in the eyes from any freeborn whom I have cursed like that. What do you say to that, Jorge? Is it not true, *quiaff?*"

Aidan felt pushed against a wall, even though he sat comfortably in a chair. "Aff, Falconer Abeth. But in my former unit we had made a pact not to show emotion when insulted. We became skilled at it. I still retain that skill."

Abeth stared at him a moment longer, then laughed quietly. "You are adept, Jorge, I will give you that. All right then, you are dismissed."

When he reached the door, she said to his back: "I am not convinced by you, Jorge, but I will check you out as best as I can."

On the other side of the door, in a long, dark hallway, Aidan let out a breath he had been holding since rising from the chair in Abeth's room. What would he do, he wondered, if she should find him out and confront him with his fake identity? Would he have the courage to kill her? He was certain he would.

# 36

"**I** remember you now," Horse said suddenly. He and Aidan were engaged in breaking down and cleaning the antiquated rifles that freeborns got to use in training. The parts of each rifle lay on a blanket in front of each cadet. Aidan noted that Horse's rifle was divided into precise parallels and right angles. His were more casually arranged, although organized according to the rifle manual. Both had been pushing a treated cloth though the bores of the weapons. Falconer Abeth demanded cleanliness in every single piece before she would allow a cadet to reassemble the rifle.

Aidan responded, "I don't understand, Horse." His voice was calm, but he was ready to cut Horse's throat when the words of challenge came.

"I know where I saw you. You were in a 'Mech on the First Stage Training Ground. We fought. I had a demolition charge that you got rid of, but not before I almost beat you. You've changed, got stronger, shrewder far as I can tell. No, don't bother to deny it. I know. I *know*."

Aidan examined the cloth, surprised that there was still so much residue from the bore on this, the umpteenth time he had pushed a cloth through. He was also evaluating which of the pieces on the blanket would most swiftly dispose of Horse if it came to a fight. Even as his muscles tensed to spring at Horse, however, his brain noted the serenity with which Horse spoke. When it came to freeborns and trueborns talking together, hostility was the norm, never serenity. "What do you intend to do, Horse?"

Horse shrugged. "Nothing, I expect. If you are so hot

to become a warrior that you'll come train with a bunch of freeborns, then I think you probably should be a warrior. Why are you looking so strange?''

Aidan, now facing a clean cloth, put the bore down on his blanket. Everything was ready for Abeth's inspection. ''I am confused by you, Horse. In a similar situation, a trueborn would do *something,* anything. Turn me in, fight me, strangle me while I was asleep.''

''Why would he do that?''

''Because the code would demand right behavior.''

''And what's right about strangling you in your sleep?''

''It would punish me.''

''And you need to be punished?''

''When the code is violated, yes.''

''Well, here, you take my bore, exchange it with yours. That way you won't get the points and I will. Is that sufficient punishment?''

''Probably not, but I agree to the exchange.'' As they switched bores, Aidan said, ''Falconer Abeth might check to make sure we each have the bore we started with.''

''No, she won't. Nobody inspects that close, not even Abeth.''

And he was right. Horse received praise from Abeth for a job well done, while Aidan was told that he was slipping and better shape up.

Afterward, Horse said no more about the past incident. For a while, Aidan thought he might have to kill the freeborn anyway, in order to protect his secret. That, he knew, is what Ter Roshak had advised. Just calling Aidan trashborn, as Horse had done during the training exercise, would have been sufficient excuse at one time to do away with the young man. But now Aidan was too puzzled by Horse's laconic acceptance of him to want to kill him. He had to know more about Horse and about freeborns, if only to maintain his own freeborn identity. Worse, he had begun to like Horse, a reaction he had never anticipated. He could not kill him. Not yet, anyway. Not until he was a clear danger to Aidan. He would not trust Horse because he could probably never fully trust a freeborn but he could, for the time being, spare him.

Two days later, the freeborns were in the midst of a

marching drill, with Falconer Othy futilely, and in an erratic rhythm all his own, sending them back and forth on a parade ground, just to fill in time because the obstacle course, which had absorbed too much rain overnight, was presently impassable.

An orderly ran up to Othy, waving a paper in his hand. Because the paper was a light blue, Aidan knew it was a command-level communique. Othy scowled when he read the message, then he assembled the freeborns in front of him.

"The message concerns Falconer Abeth," Othy said in his flat voice. "She is dead. An accident in a hovercraft. It exploded."

"Somebody killed her," Aidan muttered, and as soon as he said it, he knew the murder had something to do with Ter Roshak. He looked up and saw the others, including Othy, staring at him. He had not realized he had vocalized his thought.

"What did you say, Jorge?"

"Nothing, Falconer."

"No, you said somebody killed her. Why did you say that?"

"Just an active imagination, sir. It was an accident then, a systems failure or some spilled coolant or something?"

"That is what the report says. But you know something, I can tell. Tell us."

"Really, I know nothing. I am ignorant."

"Come with me."

He took Aidan a few paces away from the others and spoke to him quietly. "Everything has been thrown out of kilter since you arrived here, Jorge. Even your arrival was strange. I cannot remember a case where a cadet was transferred into another unit after he became the only survivor of such a disastrous incident. Wherever there is a falconer alive in a unit, it does not matter if that officer or officers are in charge of only a single cadet. Except under special circumstances, the falconer stays with the group all the way, until it is completely flushed out or until it goes through the Trial. But your falconer was killed in that explosion, too. It was very much like a setup. Abeth told me two nights ago that there was something odd about you and she was checking you out. Now

she is dead. Another suspicious accident like the minefield explosion. Does it not seem strange to you, Jorge?''

''Sir, there is nothing strange. Things happen.
Things--''

''Things happen wherever you are, Jorge. Now I am
in danger, too, *quiaff?*''

''Sir, you are imagining—''

''I am imagining nothing. I am not an imaginative sort.
If Abeth had said nothing to me and you had not whispered that somebody killed her, I would have accepted
her death as a mere accident. But now—''

Aidan became frightened. He felt bad enough about
Abeth. She had seemed efficient, a worthwhile warrior.

But Ter Roshak was up to something, and it had to do
with Aidan. That day when the Falconer Commander had
come to see him, he had merely told Aidan that he had
obtained a second chance for him that required assuming
a new identity. The identity came from a freeborn cadet
who had had an unfortunate accident. Aidan had believed
that Jorge's death and those of his fellow trainees were
the result of some kind of bungling on the part of those
who set the minefield. But of course Ter Roshak had been
responsible, just as—to protect the master plan he had
hinted at—he would be responsible for the deaths of anyone else who got in the way. Like Abeth.

But he could not tell Othy any of this, even though the
slovenly falconer was in danger. He could not even talk
him out of pursuing his present thoughts. If he told him
to stop, then Othy would know there was substance to
his suspicions.

''Sir, I know nothing of this. Permission requested to
return to my unit.''

Othy stared at him incredulously, then he nodded and
murmured, ''Permission granted.'' Aidan could sense,
without looking back, that the falconer was still staring
at him. Othy was a dead man, Aidan thought, unless he
came to his senses and said nothing to no one. He wished
he could tell him to keep his mouth shut.

The mood in the barracks that evening was sullen and
sad. Anyone who spoke got barked at by someone else.
No one said anything about Abeth's death, no one ex-
pressed regret. But an aura of mourning hung over the

barracks just as much as if a gray cloud had seeped in through all the cracks in the building.

The only mention of Falconer Abeth came after they were all in their bunks and Horse yelled out suddenly, "She was all right, Abeth!" The others muttered agreement.

Lying in bed, unable to sleep, Aidan decided he *had* to do something. He wanted that second chance at a Trial more than anything he had ever wanted in his life, but it was not worth getting there Ter Roshak's way.

# ====37====

I was right when I decided to mastermind this second chance for Aidan, wrote Falconer Commander Ter Roshak. He has the grit, the tenacity, the bravery to become a good officer. He even has the guts to stand up to me!

He came to me tonight. I do not know how he was able to steal away from his barracks, how he made it past the innumerable Crash Camp guards to my quarters, how he even knew where my quarters were.

I was asleep, dreaming of, well, a young woman I knew when I was a young man. She has been dead for sixteen years, reduced to a charred mass in a 'Mech coolant accident, yet how vividly alive she is in my dreams. At any rate, I am sure I was tossing and turning with the disorientation of the dream when I woke up suddenly, knowing that someone was in my room.

Aidan was just standing there. He seemed to be staring at my prosthesis, which was lying on a table beside the bunk, where I had put it before retiring. I had an impulse to fit it on, but I do not like to display that particular weakness in front of others. With my good hand, I settled my pillow into a position against the wall and sat up.

"I could court-martial you just for being here," I said calmly. "How did you get in?"

He shrugged. "If you must do something, you find a way to do it. What happened to the real Jorge?"

Being careful not to remove my deformed arm from beneath its cover, I shrugged, too, if it is possible to shrug with only one shoulder. "He died," I said.

"I know that. You told me it was an accident."

"Yes, I did. I told you that."

"But it was not the truth."

I stayed silent. He was going too fast. I was not sure what he could know, what he should know. The look in his eyes was strange, unreadable. It is hard enough to read their expression when he is in a normal mood, but in an odd mood, they are impossible.

"You do not have to say, Ter Roshak. I know Jorge must have been killed on purpose, to make room for my identity. But why the others? Why the rest of his unit? Why his officer? Why Falconer Abeth?"

He caught me off guard with the last, and I am afraid I reacted guiltily to the mention of her name. She had unearthed most of the plot and brought the discovery to me, not knowing that the piece of information she was missing was my participation in it. I regretted having to kill her, but she was obviously the kind of officer to whom loyalty to the Clan was all-important. She would never have understood my motives. Killing her was expedient, and I admit that her death was the only one I wish had been avoidable. But, of course, I could not reason with Aidan about her disposal. I suspected he would not understand the necessity of it. He is too young to appreciate tactics.

"Why?" he asked again.

"There is no answer to that, Aidan. What is done, is done."

"But that whole unit—"

"Jorge's?"

"Yes. They were wasted just so I—"

"Forget them. They were mere freebirths."

"But they lived, they—"

"Do you mean to say you regard a freeborn as having the same right to live as we do, as does anyone created out of the gene pool and therefore superior to—"

"Yes, I regard their lives as valuable."

"Of value equal to ours?"

"I, well, I—yes, why not? They were here training to be warriors."

"Do you feel that a freeborn who succeeds in the Trial is therefore better than you, that he has caste status above you? Well, Aidan?"

"I do not know how to answer that. I am trained to

think otherwise. But is it not true that the freeborn who succeeds at the Trial becomes a warrior of the Clan?''

"Yes, but only in a way. You rarely see freeborns on front-line duty. They are mainly useful in freeing up proper warriors for significant duty. They will never contribute genes to the gene pool and rarely earn a Bloodname.''

"But at least they are warriors. I failed. I became a Tech. Yes, the warrior in the most unpleasant rear-guard duty is to be envied when you are back here as a mere Tech.''

"Techs might argue that point, but I do think that you have been living among freeborns for too long.''

"I have been one! I *am* one!''

"Do not get carried away, Aidan. Whatever you are and whether or not you have succeeded in the Trial yet, you are *not* a freeborn. No matter how much empathy you feel for one of that unfortunate genetic state, you cannot become one. At any rate, I trust that you will do well in your next Trial and all of this puerile discussion will be rendered moot. Why are you here?''

He seemed stunned, not able to speak. I had the sensation of my missing hand grabbing fistfuls of sheet and pulling at them.

"I—'' he began, then stopped and took a breath. "I want to be a warrior, but I want no one killed to promote my success. If this killing is to continue, I respectfully request that you return me to the technician caste, and this time I promise to stay there.''

The words came out in a labored way, and I had to respect his courage.

"There is someone else who knows about your background?''

His answer came too slow. "No, there is not.'' I knew there was.

"Aidan, I will return you to the technician caste if you will answer me just one question.''

He scowled, puzzled. "All right.''

"Do you want to become a warrior? Do you want it more than anything else in your life?''

"That is not fair! It is—''

"DO YOU WANT TO BE A WARRIOR?''

"YES! I WANT IT MORE THAN—''

"Then that is enough. I will not interfere with your progress further. You are completely on your own. I admit to nothing that has happened in the past, and you will never again accuse me. You agree, *quiaff?*"

I became instantly furious when he hesitated. Then he said, quietly, "Aff."

"Very well. You are dismissed. Return to your unit."

For once, I could read his eyes. I saw in them a thousand things he wanted to say, and his resentment at me for blocking them. What I felt at that moment perhaps corresponds to what fathers feel for their children at moments of crisis. But of course I could not become *that* sentimental.

He left, but traces of his presence seemed to linger in the air.

I had lied to him, of course. Anything I can do to facilitate his passing of the Trial, I will do. I will risk the consequences. But I must be more subtle, I suppose. I surmise that the person who has suspicions is the unit's other falconer, the one named Othy. But this one I cannot kill. I must arrange a necessary transfer, and then dispose of him later, after the Trial. It should not be too hard to manufacture his removal.

If he goes, then the unit is without training officers. Someone else must move into the spot. And I know just the logical candidate for the job. I feel the wheels turning. It is always exciting when the wheels are turning.

No reason. Wondered, is all. I mean, since you were announced as our training officer, I thought—

Do not. Saying. Anything about the Falconer Othy came down with—

# 38

**T**heir new training officer, a tough bird named Falconer Joanna, really dislodged the equanimity of the freeborn unit. Louder than the late Falconer Abeth and more demanding than the departed Falconer Othy, she was a martinet who suffered no excuses, forced a cadet to lick up any dirt he had not cleaned up, ran a quicker march, demanded better performance, and seemed to despise every freeborn in the universe. She was especially hard on Cadet Jorge, even though he proved time and again that he could do anything she could dream up for him to do. Indeed, she seemed to get special pleasure from finding new challenges for him.

Aidan thought Joanna was just being herself, and then some. When she first arrived and found an excuse to take him aside, she said: "Make no mistake about it, Aidan—"

"Jorge—I am Jorge now."

"I know that."

"But what if someone overhears?"

"If I say it, it does not matter if someone overhears." She glared at him, but he sensed that she almost smiled. "You understand that, *quiaff?*"

"Aff."

"Let us make this as easy as possible. I am not patient, yes? All right. As I was about to say, I am not happy about this assignment. I am here because Ter Roshak said somebody had to be, especially since Othy came down with that influenza."

"Did he then? I mean, he is all right, is he not?"

"If you call lying under a dozen blankets and delirious with fever all right, then he is just fine. Why do you ask?"

"No reason. Why do you so dislike being here? It is no worse than ordinary training."

"But it is. I cannot stomach being around freebirths all day. How can you?"

"It is not so bad. They are ordinary, friendly—"

She seemed shocked. "Of course they are ordinary. How can you stand *that?* But never mind. They disgust me, and I am only glad that my stay here will be a short one."

"Falconer Joanna, you should give them a chance."

"Stop, I have heard such pro-freebirth talk before and I despise it as much as I despise them. I am going to hit you now. They are watching us."

She did not give him much time to think about it. With the back of her hand, she whacked Aidan hard on the side of his head, dizzying him for a short time. Then she bellowed an order and walked away. When he went back to his fellow cadets, they were all smiling. Thinking of what Joanna had said, and recalling warrior beliefs about freeborns, he wondered if he *should* feel so comfortable with them.

Several days later, Joanna rousted them out of bed before dawn with the announcement that they were marching to a special duty. The march was long and it was well after daylight before they reached their destination. Joanna handed rations around and told them they had been chosen to participate in the first stage of a Trial that would be held in this area in two hours. They would deploy with weapons in the forest a kilometer away and attack the cadets as they came through. The weapons were equipped with stun potential, as were the weapons of the cadets taking the Trial.

"It is a chance for you to observe a Trial in action and provide a valuable service for the trainees, sharpening their instincts and presenting them battle conditions before they reach their 'Mechs. Any questions?"

Looking around him, Aidan suddenly recognized the area. It was the same one where he had taken his own Trial. He could see the tips of the hills beyond the forest.

When Joanna was finished and the others were wolfing down their rations, Aidan approached Joanna.

"Yes, Cadet Jorge?" she asked.

"Permission to speak with you privately, Falconer."

She glared at him briefly. His request was against procedure, especially during duty, but she knew that Jorge was regarded with such admiration by the others that they would believe whatever explanation he invented.

When they were a sufficient distance away from the others, Joanna said, "Ter Roshak does not want you to participate in the exercise. When I have deployed the others, you will come with me as if to be placed on the other side of the course as a sniper. Then we will get you clear of the main action. When it is over, you will return. That way, you will—"

"Stop it, Joanna! You lied to them. You told them both sides were equipped with weapons set at stun. You know as well as I do that only the freeborns have the weak weapons. They can be killed."

"That is the risk, yes. Only a few do wind up dead, however."

"But that is murder."

Joanna looked away from him, her face showing disgust. "Ter Roshak must be mad to back you. I have no idea what it is about, but I wish I was not under orders to see that you get through."

"I thought you said you were not to interfere."

"Another of my lies. Forget that. Just do what you are ordered. You will never become a warrior with your rebellious attitudes and softheaded emotionalism. You must strip away both." She took a deep breath. "It is not murder. It is a part of training. Like other phases of training, the risk of death is always present. You saw others in your own sibko die, and the risk is the same for freeborns. If they die, so be it. If they survive, it is because they have shown some mettle, despite being freeborns. Your orders are to accompany me and stay out of the action. Why should you even consider the fate of these foul freebirths? You killed five freeborns in your own Trial. Ponder that for a while. That is all. Return to your unit."

Aidan wanted to say more, but he knew Joanna would not allow it. As he returned to the others, he considered telling them what to really expect, but that would mean revealing his cover and he could not do that. Nobody would gain from it. He would not get his second Trial and the unit would still have to risk their lives in the forest.

"Looked from here like you two were having an argument," Tom said.

"No," Aidan replied, "I was just proposing extra rations for tonight after the long march back."

He hated every word of the lie. It seemed to tie him in a tight chain to the lies of Ter Roshak and Joanna. Looking around, he saw Horse watching him intently. Suddenly the magnitude of his lies struck Aidan. Horse knew who he was and was keeping quiet about it, while Aidan's lie was setting the other cadets up to possibly be killed. Was that what it meant to be a warrior? To make hard decisions coldly, to sacrifice friends when necessary, to order allies into battle with the odds against them? The lessons the sibko had learned from Dermot tended to support such views.

Joanna would say that Aidan must turn his back on Horse and let the young freeborn shift for himself. Perhaps she was right. But it was hard for Aidan to be unfair with someone who had been so fair to him. Pretending he needed to make a weapons check, he walked away from the group. Only Horse seemed to notice.

After Joanna had found strategic positions for the others, she led Aidan away, ostensibly to select his deployment.

"This will be far enough away from the action," she said after they had walked about fifteen minutes. She indicated a small open area where he could sit with his back comfortably against a tree. "Stay here and relax. I have other duties in this Trial, and I hear the personnel carrier arriving."

As she walked away, he, too, heard the arriving vehicle. Laying his head back against the bark of the tree and shutting his eyes, he remembered himself, Bret, and Marthe arriving for their Trial, the anticipation he had felt, the wild dash through the forest and (as Joanna had so astutely pointed out) his killing of so many freeborns, the exhilaration of being in the 'Mech, the thrill of the battle, even the despairing excitement of failing. For the first time in a long while, he recalled the sensation of sailing through the air in his ejection seat—the ground coming up to meet him, the landscape extending far in all directions.

Opening his eyes, he noted how peaceful the forest seemed. Above him a branch bobbed lightly. At first, recalling his Trial, he thought it was a sniper. Somewhere in the foliage a small bird must be traveling along the branch. The bobbing stopped and another branch moved. He got a glimpse of some blue and white feathers between a pair of leaves.

Suddenly he could not sit still either. It felt wrong to sit here while the others were in danger. In spite of Joanna's orders, he at least wanted to be nearer the action. Hiding out for his own safety was simply not in his nature. Even Joanna should have known that.

Moving cautiously, he went back the way he had come with her. His survival training had instilled in him an instinct for noting geographical features and remembering particular trees. It did not take too long to find a location near where the members of his unit were hiding. Going to ground, he crawled back to the edge of the forest. In the clearing there, he could see the hovercraft, landed and quiet. Nearer were a group of training officers, and among them, the two trainees about to take their Trial, a male and a female. They looked as much alike as he and Marthe had. Both were tall, about the same height, and both held themselves with a kind of eager pride that reminded him, not only of himself and Marthe, but of several of his sibkin. For a moment, he saw his sibko as it had been when they had first arrived on Ironhold and played their ludicrous game of team tussle in front of the scornful officers. Perhaps the sibko of this pair of Trial candidates had been similarly foolish on their arrival before going through the long stages that had whittled their group down to this duo. The sibko experience might be identical for all. He would never know that. Most would not have cared to know, and he wondered why he did.

He could see that the course officer was about to give the signal to start, so he edged back into the forest. Standing up, he tried to retrace the path to his comrades. It amused him to think of how furious Joanna would be to know he used that word for them even in his thoughts. But this time his tracking instincts failed him. He could not remember just where Joanna had positioned any of them. He would have to wait until the Trial started and watch for events to develop.

Returning to the wood's edge, he looked out from behind a tree. He was further down the course now and had a different angle on the scene. The signal was about to be made. The two candidates were more eager than ever for the Trial to start.

At the signal, both broke into a run and disappeared into the forest. Aidan worked his way toward where they had entered the forest. He spotted the male candidate and tracked him, a difficult task because the cadet moved so fast.

Aidan had to stay far enough behind so that he did not become a target himself. In a particularly dense part of the woods, he lost sight of the cadet.

Ahead of him was a slight rise. He ran to it, hoping for a better view. What he saw surprised him.

Falconer Joanna was in the forest and moving stealthily away from him. She could not have seen him. Using trees as cover, he worked his way toward her. Because she was moving slowly, he was able to get quite close.

They had reached an open area, one he recognized now as the place where Joanna had assigned Horse. What was she up to? Did the falconers observe their charges from positions inside the forest? He began to doubt that possibility when he saw her draw a laser pistol and hold it tight against her side.

Looking beyond her, Aidan saw Horse leaping out of his hiding place onto the back of the male cadet, who apparently had been ripe for ambush. The two wrestled briefly and Horse came up with the candidate's weapon, a short-barreled rifle that could be worn in a holster. Horse immediately pointed it at the young man's face and looked as if he was going to blast the trueborn's head off.

At the same time Joanna raised her pistol, and Aidan realized she intended to kill Horse. That was against all the rules of the Trial. An officer could not interfere with any part of it, not even to protect the primary candidates.

Leaping from his hiding place, Aidan's hands brushed against Joanna's arm just before she fired, and her shot streamed high into the air. He looked into the clearing. Apparently Horse had not been aware of Joanna's ambush, so intent was he on his own. The cadet had made a futile grab to get his weapon back, but Horse had merely kicked him to the ground. He shifted his aim from the trueborn's head to his legs and shot him there. The cadet grabbed his right leg in pain. Hurling the rifle away, Horse quickly vanished into the forest. The true-born tried to stand up, but his leg collapsed beneath him. Aidan could appreciate the look of disappointment on the young man's face.

"You rotten freebirth!" Joanna muttered. "You had no right to deflect my aim. What are you doing here anyway? I told you to stay—"

"You have no right to rebuke me, Falconer. I may not have followed orders but what you were doing was worse. You would have killed him, is that right?"

"Of course I would. He is only a freeborn. Why should I care about killing him? After all, he was going to kill a trueborn, a potential warrior."

"Not any more." He indicated the trueborn's sad, weary crawl out of the clearing. "At any rate, I do not believe you. You were not protecting the candidate. That was just a convenient excuse. You were here to kill Horse."

"Do not be ridiculous. Horse had the cadet's gun, a *live* weapon. I was just protecting—"

"Save your excuses. I know what it is all about. I do not know how Ter Roshak discovered it but—"

"Ter Roshak had nothing to do with it."

"Another lie of yours. I told him I would abandon the warrior training if he interfered again. He has interfered again. Another convenient accident, with Horse the victim, and the Trial a fine place to create an accident."

"You cannot abandon—"

He held up his hand to stop her talking, for once giving his own order. "Take this message back to Ter Roshak. In a way he has won. I will go on. I realized in coming here today that I need to be a warrior too much to allow someone like him to drive me away from it with his manipulations. Tell him there is no need to interfere again. I will not fail this time."

The two stared at each other for a long while. Aidan despised the hint of victory in Joanna's eyes.

''Goodbye,'' he said suddenly and began walking away from her.

''Where are you going?''

''There is something I want to see.''

Along the way, he found Horse and the two ran to the other end of the forest. At the rim, they were joined by Spiro and Tom.

''Nigel was killed,'' Tom said softly. ''Blown up by a grenade. The woman had a grenade.''

Nobody said anything else.

Aidan pointed forward. They could just see the female candidate running up a hill toward her 'Mech. She took long strides and Aidan marveled at the grace of them.

They watched her scale the heights of her 'Mech and then get it operational. They watched her rapidly initiate its trip up the hill. They watched the 'Mech take strides that were not as lithe as its pilot's, but had a certain grace of their own. They watched the 'Mech reach the crest of the hill and begin to descend the other side. Gradually, the legs, then the torso, then the head vanished behind the hill.

Aidan and the others stayed at the edge of the forest and listened to the sounds of battle. They could see some of the firing streak high through the air. Finally, they heard a 'Mech fall and were agreed in their hope it was not the female cadet's.

Later, back at barracks, Aidan stayed awake while the others slept—fitfully, it seemed. He was sorrowful. Now Nigel had been added to the list of victims scattered over his trail on the way to becoming a warrior.

# =39=

The freeborn unit reached the Trial without any further loss of personnel. The last weeks of training were an odd combination of anticipation and boredom for Aidan. Having been through it all previously, the repetitions irritated him, as they were useful only for honing his skills. Even then, he had to pretend a difficulty he did not feel. Still, with each task accomplished, he was that much closer to once more occupying the cockpit of a Trial BattleMech.

During the fitting for his neurohelmet, he was disappointed that someone other than Alexander gave him the instructions. The new voice was not nearly as gentle and persuasive.

The last days came and went, and then the unit was loaded onto a skimmer and taken to the Trial field. Examining the maps they were given, Aidan was glad to see that he would confront a different area, a different terrain. There would be no run through a dense woods, just a race across an open field to the 'Mech and a trip across a river into hilly country, where they could expect to find their opponents. There would be no freeborn ambushes, they were told by Falconer Joanna. Freeborns were not wasted in the Trials of other freeborns.

Though Aidan was relieved that he would not have to face the duplication of the killing of freeborns from his first Trial, he deeply felt the insult, the knowledge that trueborn officers regarded freeborn cadets as so inferior that they were not allowed the complete Trial. From his previous life as a cadet, Aidan knew that freeborn candidates had a higher failure rate in the Trial. At that time, he, like the others, blamed it on the inferiority of the freeborn. Now, having seen the way freeborns were treated, he knew that the failure rate was as much lack of inadequate preparation and, as now, the selection of a more difficult site for their test. The system declared that freeborns were just as eligible to become warriors as trueborns, but the system saw to it that freeborns became warriors with only the greatest possible difficulty.

Or perhaps the system was not stacked against freeborns as much as Aidan thought. Perhaps they were the victims of trueborn attitudes. Trueborns were always in charge; therefore, the desultory preparation, the shoddy conditions, were not the result of malicious intentions but merely of deep-seated antagonisms.

At the Trial site, they drew lots. Spiro and Tom would go out in the first wave, while Horse and Jorge had to remain behind, waiting out the long time period before the first Trial ended and theirs began.

As Tom and Spiro raced to their 'Mechs, Jorge and Horse watched from a vantage point next to the skimmer that had delivered them to the site.

"Where'd Falconer Joanna disappear to?" Horse asked.

"I suspect she might be taking out one of the opposition 'Mechs. She's a fine pilot, I've heard."

"You don't have to use the contractions around me."

"I've gotten used to them. If I get in a trueborn Star, I will have to remember to drop them."

After a pause, Horse said: "I've looked for the proper moment to thank you. I think this is it."

"What do you mean?"

"I know what you did for me back at the other Trial site."

"You did? How? It is not possible."

"I am not blind. I saw the shot that went astray. After I ran out of the clearing, I doubled back and came upon you arguing with our honored falconer. I was tempted to take a potshot at her, but I figured the unit could not survive still another training officer. So, as I said, my thanks."

Aidan reddened. "Well, after all, I owed you a favor. You kept my identity secret."

Horse nodded. In the field the 'Mechs were moving. Soon they were out of sight.

This time they only heard the sounds of battle—sites were designed so that the waiting Trial candidates could get no advantages by studying what their predecessors did. And they did not hear many sounds. The engagements were over quickly.

Aidan and Horse endured the long wait until the Trial results were announced. Both Tom and Spiro had been defeated. Spiro had been hurt. He would lose a leg, someone said.

"That certainly adds to my optimism," Horse said. "I wish they'd start us."

"Horse?"

"We might be able to prevail if we formed a team."

"Isn't that against the rules? I mean, aren't we supposed to fight individually, in good Clan style?"

"That is custom, but not a rule. What if we stay close together instead of competing? What do you say?"

"I don't know. But I'm scared enough to try it."

"Good."

Just then, an officer walked up to tell them that it was almost time for the signal to begin.

out, too much weight encumbrance. Maintaining a balance was a real effort in this terrain, and Aidan for the millisecond became the Aidan who faced Falconer Joanna—

# 40

The *Summoner*s strutted into the hills side by side, almost shoulder to shoulder. There was no commlink between the two 'Mechs, but Aidan and Horse had quickly worked out their strategy while awaiting the signal to start. Aidan thought it possible the cooperative plan had been tried before, but their opponents, all seasoned warriors, might not anticipate it from what they perceived as a pair of freeborns. If Joanna was in one of the 'Mechs—and he fully expected her to pilot the first one to be set against him—she would have the added surprise and shock of knowing it was a trueborn cooperating with a freeborn.

A mist had settled near the ground, giving the place an eerie, dreamlike look. Aidan watched the feet of Horse's 'Mech lift out of the mist and then step back into it, and knew that, to Horse, Aidan's 'Mech was doing the same.

All his weapon systems were ready. When making his systems check, there had been no failures, no indications of mechanical dysfunction or jamming. Unlike his last outing, he had not been able to make minor reconfigurations of his 'Mech, although the one he piloted had a short-range missile system instead of the usual LRM in its left torso. He also had an extended-range small laser slung under the PPC in his 'Mech's right arm. Aidan assumed that the same alterations had been made in Horse's *Summoner*. Apparently the ability to choose one's own configurations was another trueborn privilege denied to freeborns. Oh, well, he thought, that does not matter. In hilly terrain like this, we are better off traveling light. He felt he could maintain balance better without too much weapons encumbrance. Maintaining balance was a real effort in this terrain, not only for the hilliness but because the heavy mist forced them to maneuver via computer-generated geological diagrams.

The first challenge came rather quickly. Coming over a hill and looming from the mist, three 'Mechs—a *Hellbringer,* a *Warhawk,* and an *Executioner*—appeared slowly. The *Hellbringer* continued to advance until it was more than 600 meters ahead of the other two 'Mechs of the trio, as if to show contempt for the freebirths, as if to say only one 'Mech was needed to take one on. When the *Hellbringer* gestured toward Aidan, he lifted both of his 'Mech's arms up and down to indicate acceptance of the engagement. A formality only, one of those odd bits of courtesy used in tests but rarely in battle, where there was no time for etiquette.

Aidan pondered the familiarity of the situation, as he again faced a *Hellbringer* to begin his Trial. But there would be no impulsive action this time, no jumping over the heads of his three foes. This time there would, in fact, be a delaying action rather than a sudden one. Swiveling his 'Mech's torso an eighth of a turn, he placed it so that it seemed to lean toward Horse's *Summoner.* Horse's 'Mech remained still, waiting for its adversaries to appear.

The *Hellbringer* seemed to hesitate. Aidan suspected it was field procedure to allow the Trial cadet to fire first, but he also knew any tactic was fair and that he could not trust the *Hellbringer's* pilot to remain polite for long.

He glanced toward Horse's 'Mech. Suddenly it raised its arm and pointed to its left. His opponents had now made their appearance, arising from a deep gully. He also had drawn a *Hellbringer* and a *Warhawk,* but the third 'Mech was a *Dire Wolf,* the same type Aidan had faced, but not engaged, in his first Trial. The *Dire Wolf* was the largest of the Clan OmniMechs. As in Aidan's trio, a *Hellbringer* broke off from its group and contemptuously advanced some 600 meters to face Horse alone and unsupported.

Using a prearranged signal, Aidan rotated his 'Mech's torso another eighth of a turn, then returned it to its original position. Horse's 'Mech made the same precise rotations. Aidan smiled, knowing that the movements no doubt looked odd to the other 'Mechs in the field, and also to those observing from safe havens. It might have resembled a kind of 'Mech calisthenic. First one did the exercise, then the other.

Since both trios of opponents were entering the fray at about the same plane instead of at angles to the Trial cadets, Aidan's and Horse's 'Mechs lined up side by side, as they had agreed to do if the attack came in this fashion.

The arm of Horse's 'Mech pointed down at an angle for a moment, then came up level, the signal that he and Aidan would begin to walk their 'Mechs straight toward the pair of *Hellbringers*, each of which was now detached from the others as the first to engage the cadets. Aidan noticed some scorch marks on the *Hellbringer* in front of him, which made him think this must be the same 'Mech that had finished off Tom or Spiro in the earlier Trial. He drew this conclusion because the other two 'Mechs were shiny and untouched. He also assumed the *Hellbringer*'s pilot was probably feeling pretty cocky, because the 'Mech itself had hardly been damaged. Horse, on the other hand, had drawn a *Hellbringer* that apparently had not been involved in the first battle, showing that one of the freeborns had probably inflicted some damage on his opponent.

Neither side had yet fired. Aidan wondered how long the warriors in the rival cockpits would wait to commence the battle. He did not have to wonder for long. A grid on the side of his primary screen showed that the *Hellbringer* was trying to lock onto him at cockpit level with its Targa-7 fire-control system. A good move, Aidan noted, for it forced him to dodge sideways, away from Horse, breaking their even line. They had expected to have to continually adjust in order to remain close together, and Horse's move toward Aidan might even have looked cowardly to the other 'Mechs.

They had agreed there would be no signal to fire. Whichever of them decided to strike first would do so.

Aidan, figuring the pilot in the *Hellbringer* would make another attempt to lock on with the Targa, aimed and set off a volley of short-range missiles toward it. The missile's arc was true, but the *Hellbringer* picked them off, as expected, with a burst from its anti-missile weapons system. What its pilot did not foresee was that another missile would come swooping in, fired by Horse. It hit the *Hellbringer* at mid-torso and sent armor flying.

As his opponent reeled from the hit, Aidan rapidly turned his attention to the *Hellbringer* facing Horse's *Summoner* and shot at it with his extended-range PPC. Catching that *Hellbringer*'s pilot by surprise, Aidan got in several shots very near the *Hellbringer*'s cockpit. Horse, reacting quickly, knowing that the pilot in that cockpit must be disconcerted by Aidan's hits, turned his attention back to the foe intended originally for him. Aidan glanced quickly at his long-range scanner. The other heavier 'Mechs were now released and advancing quickly to support their comrades. Horse and Aidan had less than a minute to finish off their opponents.

Alternating adversaries, heedless of the damage being inflicted on them, the two *Summoner*s strode steadily toward the *Hellbringer*s. A cluster round hit Aidan's 'Mech in the lower part of the torso, just above the left leg, while Horse's foe penetrated his armor in a long line of fire that nearly bisected the 'Mech's torso. But none of the havoc was significant. The two *Summoner*s continued their march forward without either one falling behind. Frequently their crossfire seemed to confuse the *Hellbringer* pilots, sending their assaults off target.

It was a real showdown, as Aidan had planned. The two *Summoner*s took on the pair of *Hellbringer*s simultaneously, working together against them. The *Hellbringer* pilots, used to fighting single battles according to bidding procedures, had difficulty adjusting to the unClanlike assault.

Aidan knew he would take criticism on two accounts. First, that he violated the rules by persuading Horse to fight their opponents in tandem (of course, to Ter Roshak and Joanna, Aidan's violation of rules would be no surprise). Second, they were using up their firepower drastically against their initial opponents, thus removing any chance of winning a higher rank by defeating a second 'Mech. This time, Aidan's strategy was pure and simple: to win and become a warrior. Having failed once because of ambition, he did not want to ruin this chance. In his first trial he had been greedy and had lost because he overextended himself. Now he would concentrate on defeating just the single opponent. One for him and one for Horse, and they would both be warriors. Any complaints from Clan officers would be easy to endure. And, anyway, were not he and Horse freeborns? What good could trueborns expect from freeborns, after all? They would all go back to their bunks tonight muttering about how lousy freebirths always ruin everything, while he and Horse would sleep tonight as warriors.

Seeing that his *Hellbringer* opponent was severely weakened, he helped Horse finish off his enemy. Concentrating fire from two directions, they forced the enemy 'Mech to its knees, then pierced the last shreds of armor protecting the 'Mech's fusion reactor. Aidan almost whooped when the *Hellbringer* pilot, endangered by the collapsing magnetic bottle containing the miniature sun that drove the BattleMech, ejected. They did not even watch the 'Mech fall, turning their attention to the remaining *Hellbringer*.

Aidan's barrages had ruined all the laser weapons on the *Hellbringer*'s torso, and it was firing the PPCs in each arm almost desperately. Horse and Aidan spread apart as they continued their assault on the 'Mech, which was now rocked by each blast. Aidan nearly made a fatal mistake, however. He had not realized the *Hellbringer* had one SRM salvo left, and it came flying directly at his cockpit. Suddenly, the massive arm of Horse's *Summoner* blocked his view. The SRMs detonated, engulfing the arm in a ball of flame. Aidan's *Summoner* wavered dangerously with the concussion and the shrapnel bouncing off its surface.

It was time to finish off the *Hellbringer*, and he and Horse moved in on it relentlessly, hitting it with shot after shot, missile after missile. Smoke began pouring out of the enemy cockpit and Aidan's heart stopped as he realized the pilot might be unconscious, unable to eject. Certain that the pilot had to be Joanna, he suddenly realized that, no matter how much he disliked her, he did not want to spoil his Trial by killing her. His body mimicked the eject procedure as he mentally urged the opposing pilot to get out of his or her 'Mech.

Another cross-barrage and the 'Mech toppled, falling backward onto the ground, with an impact that sent tremors through Aidan's *Summoner*. The two cadets, so much of their firepower spent on the pair of victories, immediately ceased their attack.

Though Aidan knew he should be concentrating on the *Warhawk* coming toward him, he could not take his eyes off the fallen *Hellbringer*'s cockpit. Finally, through the smoke, a figure appeared. The pilot came out of the cockpit and, running, got clear of the 'Mech. As the pilot took off her headgear and shook out her hair, Aidan saw that it was a woman. But it was not Joanna. It was Marthe. And she was all right.

He turned his attention to the *Warhawk,* knowing that the rest of the Trial would be routine, as long as he was careful to protect himself and not foolishly get injured or die. Checking his systems, he saw he had little response to offer the *Warhawk.* He used it until his *Summoner* took the hit that would disable it completely, then the new warrior signaled defeat and ejected from his 'Mech.

# Epilogue

For a time after the Trial, Aidan experienced events in a daze. He was a warrior now and that was all that mattered. He had avenged his failure, shown Joanna and Ter Roshak what he could do, and in the bargain had helped Horse along, too.

Horse thanked him energetically. "Never thought when we were struggling on that primitive 'Mech that fate'd bring us together and—and look what did happen."

"No such thing as fate."

"Are you sure?"

"No, I am not sure about anything right this moment."

True to form, Joanna refused to praise him. "That was a pretty shoddy performance out there."

"It worked, did it not?"

"But it was not Clanlike."

"Are you sure? Is not the point to win?"

"But single combat is the ideal of the Clan warrior."

"Will we always encounter enemies willing to divide themselves up and fight us on our own terms?"

"If they have honor, yes."

"When we return to the Inner Sphere, we might not be so fortunate. We may have to battle on their terms, not ours. It is good for us to face one another on unknown terms, without a defender declaration, without a bid. I did that today."

Joanna gave him her usual glare, although he thought perhaps it contained a hint of amusement. "Aidan, I think you have been with stinking freebirths for so long, you are beginning to think like one." She whirled around and left without waiting for a reply.

Beyond the border of the Trial field, Marthe ran up to him from behind and whirled him around.

"It *is* you."

"I was the one who sent your 'Mech—"

"I know, I know. What are you doing here?"

"Becoming a warrior."

"It is illegal to compete with an assumed identity."

"It may be. Will you report it?"

She shook her head. "No, of course not."

"Thank you, Mar—"

"No, not for you. For the sibko, but not for you. I do not allow personal favors. You won and that is enough."

She went away from him as quickly as she had appeared. It was the last he was to see of her for several years, and he carried that memory with him.

Ter Roshak called Aidan to his office. He was impressed with the young man as he walked into the room with a warrior's gait. There was a new arrogance in his face, replacing the old look and improving on it.

"In both Trials, Aidan, you overreached your—"

"I do not care about that. This time I achieved the goal. You should be satisfied."

"I am."

"Enough people had to die to satisfy you. I hope you have no more killings to—"

"Stop. I want to explain my reasons to you."

Aidan's face became hard. It very much resembled a warrior's defiance. "You are my commanding officer. If you wish to explain anything, I must listen. But, as I must tell you, I would prefer not to hear it."

"You will, you piece of filth. You will."

Ter Roshak smiled as he spoke the insult. Then he told Aidan about Ramon Mattlov, all his memories of the man, and how he had manipulated events in tribute to his former comrade. He tried to convey some sort of emotion, but expressing emotion was not his forte and the story came out, he knew, cold and dispassionate. At the end of it, he looked at Aidan and said, "Well?"

Aidan shrugged. "It is a good tale. Why do you not petition to have it inserted into *The Remembrance?*"

Then he stood silently, stoically, and Roshak knew he could not convince the new warrior that it had been respect for Aidan that contributed to his decision to take a hand in his success. He could have tried to say more, but instead changed the subject: "You know, then, that you must retain this identity? That you are still, in the eyes of others, a freeborn, albeit a freeborn *warrior?*"

"Joanna explained that to me just moments ago. I had hoped otherwise, but I belong to the Clan, especially now. I must serve the Clan however I can, in whatever identity I can."

"Then you also know you have no hopes of serving in the front line of battle?"

"I am told that, yes."

"And many of your assignments will not be pleasant, *quiaff?*"

"Aff."

"And you will not earn a Bloodname, for that would be a lie, too, *quiaff?* Why do you not answer?"

"I wish to earn a Bloodname."

"But you are freebirth now. You cannot."

Roshak noted the tightening of Aidan's shoulders at the word freebirth.

"If you clam to be otherwise at any time," Roshak continued, "I will have you killed. If others found out what I have done in your cause, it would threaten my position, taint my own Bloodname. Your former identity may never be revealed. You are Jorge, now and forever. Is that clear? Is that clear, warrior?"

"Yes. It is."

"Good. Dismissed."

As Aidan left, Ter Roshak wondered if he could count on Aidan to remain silent. The young man's volatility ran deeper than Roshak had suspected. Well, the risk had been taken, the risk would have to be taken.

He sat back in his chair, rested his prosthetic hand upon the table, and thought back again to the times when he had piloted a BattleMech in combat beside Ramon Mattlov.

On Tokasha a warrior-to-be was going through its first Trial, and a long, hard one it was. Sliding through liquid and skimming along wet surfaces, it pressed forward, always struggling to achieve its goal. Around it, surfaces expanded and contracted, pushing the warrior-to-be forward. It was a long Trial, conducted in darkness. But gradually light came and grew larger. With a final effort, the warrior-to-be shot forward, suddenly bursting into the light and seeming to hang in air for a very brief moment, and then settling into the hands of a waiting collaborator in the Trial. The warrior-to-be heard voices but could not understand the words.

"What? What? Tell me, Watson. Please."

"It is a girl, Peri. Healthy. Fiercely healthy, from the look of her."

Other voices made sounds that the warrior-to-be did not realize were utterances of approval for her.

"What will you name her, Peri?" one of these people said.

"Diana," she said.

The voices sounded their approval of what they deemed a lovely name.

Peri was thinking that she had hoped for a boy, which she would have named Aidan, thus revealing the identity of the father to all. As it was, the cleverer among them might realize that Diana was an anagram for Aidan.

Listening to the satisfying cries of the newborn, Peri leaned back and fell into an exhausted half-sleep. In one dream she gleefully told Aidan about the baby.

# Glossary

## AUTOCANNON

This is a rapid-firing, auto-loading weapon. Light auto-cannon range from 30 to 90mm caliber, and heavy autocannon may be 80 to 120mm or more. The weapon fires high-speed streams of high-explosive, armor-piercing shells.

## BATTLEMECHS

BattleMechs are the most powerful war machines ever built. First developed by Terran scientists and engineers, these huge, man-shaped vehicles are faster, more mobile, better-armored, and more heavily armed than any 20th-century tank. Ten to twelve meters tall and equipped with particle projection cannons, lasers, rapid-fire autocannon, and missiles, they pack enough firepower to flatten anything but another BattleMech. A small fusion reactor provides virtually unlimited power, and BattleMechs can be adapted to fight in environments ranging from sun-baked deserts to subzero arctic icefields.

## BLOODHERITAGE

The history of Bloodnamed warriors of a particular Bloodright is called the Bloodheritage.

## BLOODING

This is another name for the Trial of Position that determines if a candidate will qualify as a Clan warrior. To qualify, he must defeat at least one of three successive opponents. If he defeats two, or all three, he is immediately ranked as an officer in his Clan. If he fails to defeat any of his opponents, he is relegated to a lower caste.

## BLOODNAME

Bloodname refers to the surname of each of the eight hundred warriors who stood with Nicholas Kerensky during the Exodus Civil War. These eight hundred are the foundation of the Clans' elaborate breeding program. The right to use one of these surnames has been the ambition of every Clan warrior since the system was established. Only twenty-five warriors, which corresponds to twenty-five Bloodrights, are allowed to use any one surname at one time. When one of the twenty-five Bloodnamed warriors dies, a trial is held to determine who will assume that Bloodname. A contender must prove his Bloodname lineage, then win a series of duels with other competitors. Only Bloodnamed warriors are allowed to sit on the Clan Councils or are eligible to become a Khan or ilKhan. Most Bloodnames have gradually been confined to one or two warrior classes. However, certain prestigious names, such as Kerensky, have shown their genetic value by producing excellent warriors in all three classes (MechWarriors, Fighter pilots, and Elementals).

Bloodnames are determined matrilineally, at least after the original generation. Because a warrior can only inherit from his or her female parent, he or she can only have a claim to one Bloodname.

## BLOODRIGHT

A specific Bloodname lineage is called a Bloodright. Twenty-five Bloodrights are attached to each Bloodname. A Bloodright is not a lineage as we define the term, because the warriors who successively hold a Bloodright might be related only through their original ancestor. As with Bloodnames, certain Bloodrights are considered more prestigious than others, depending largely on the Bloodright's Bloodheritage.

## BONDSMAN

A captured warrior, called a bondsman, is considered a member of the Laborer Caste unless and until the capturing Clan releases him or promotes him back to Warrior status. A bondsman is bound by honor, not by shackles. Custom dictates that even Bloodnamed Warriors captured in combat be held for a time as bondsmen. All bondsmen wear a bondcord, which is a woven bracelet. The base color of the bondcord indicates to which Clan he belongs and the striping indicates which unit captured him.

## CLANS

During the fall of the Star League, General Aleksandr Kerensky, commander of the Regular Star League Army, led his forces out of the Inner Sphere in what is known as the Exodus. After settling beyond the Periphery, the Star League Army itself collapsed. Out of the ashes of the civilization Kerensky's forces tried to create rose the Clans.

## DROPSHIPS

Because JumpShips must generally avoid entering the heart of a solar system, they lie at a considerable distance from the system's inhabited worlds. DropShips were developed for interplanetary travel. As the name implies, a DropShip is attached to hardpoints on the JumpShip's drive core, later to be dropped from the parent vessel after in-system entry. Though incapable of FTL travel, DropShips are highly maneuverable, well-armed, and sufficiently aerodynamic to take off from and land on a planetary surface. The journey from the jump point to the inhabited worlds of a system usually requires a normal-space journey of several days or weeks, depending on the type of star.

## ELEMENTALS

The elite battlesuited infantry of the Clans. These men and women are giants, bred specifically to handle Clan-developed BattleArmor.

## FREEBIRTH

This epithet, used by trueborn members of the Warrior Caste, is a mortal insult to another trueborn warrior. It generally expresses disgust or frustration.

## FREEBORN

An individual conceived and born by natural means is freeborn. Because the Clans value their eugenics program so highly, a freebirth is automatically assumed to have little potential.

## JUMPSHIPS

Interstellar travel is accomplished via JumpShips, first developed in the 22nd century. These somewhat ungainly vessels are made up of a long, thin drive core and a sail resembling an enormous parasol, which can be up to a kilometer wide. The ship is named for its ability to "jump" instantaneously from one point to another. After making its jump, the ship cannot travel until it has recharged by gathering up more solar energy.

The JumpShip's enormous sail is constructed from a special metal that absorbs vast quantities of electromagnetic energy from the nearest star. When it has soaked up enough energy, the sail transfers it to the drive core, which converts it into a space-twisting field. An instant later, the ship arrives at the next jump point, a distance of up to 30 light years. This field is known as hyperspace, and its discovery opened to mankind the gateway to the stars.

JumpShips never land on planets, and only rarely travel into the inner areas of a star system. Interplanetary travel is carried out by DropShips, vessels that attach themselves to the JumpShip until arrival at the jump point.

## LASER

An acronym for "Light Amplification through Stimulated Emission of Radiation". When used as a weapon, it damages the target by concentrating extreme heat on a small area. BattleMech lasers are designated as small, medium, and large. Lasers are also available as shoulder-fired weapons operating from a portable backpack power unit. Certain range-finders and targeting equipment employ low-level lasers also.

## LRM

This is an abbreviation for Long-Range Missile, an indirect-fire missile with a high-explosive warhead.

## PERIPHERY

Beyond the borders of the Inner Sphere lies the Periphery, the vast domain of known and unknown worlds stretching endlessly into interstellar night. Once populated by colonies from Terra, these were devastated technologically, politically, and economically by the fall of the Star League. At present, the Periphery is the refuge of piratical Bandit Kings, privateers, and outcasts from the Inner Sphere.

## PPC

This abbreviation stands for Particle Projection Cannon, a magnetic accelerator firing high-energy proton or ion bolts, causing damage both through impact and high temperature. PPCs are among the most effective weapons available to BattleMechs.

## QUIAFF/QUINEG

This Clan expression is placed at the end of rhetorical questions. If an affirmative answer is expected, *quiaff* is used. If the answer is expected to be negative, *quineg* is the proper closure.

## REMEMBRANCE, THE

*The Remembrance* is an ongoing heroic saga detailing Clan history beginning with the Exodus from the Inner Sphere to current time. *The Remembrance* is continually expanded to include contemporary events. Each Clan has a slightly different version reflecting their own opinions and experiences. All Clan warriors can quote whole verses of this marvelous epic from memory, and it is common to see passages from the book lovingly painted on the sides of OmniMechs, fighters, and even BattleArmor.

## SEYLA

This word roughly means "unity." It is a ritual response voiced in unison by those witnessing certain ceremonies. Seyla is the name of a Clan Wolf freebirth warrior who sacrificed herself in combat to protect Khan Jerome Winson during the Right of Absorption and Trial of Refusal against Clan Widowmaker.

## SIBKO

A group of children of the warrior caste eugenics program who probably have the same male and female parents and are raised together is known as a sibko. As they mature, they are constantly tested. Additional members of the sibko fail at each testing, and are discarded to the lower castes. A sibko is made up of approximately twenty members, but usually only four or five remain when they are given their final test, the Blooding. These tests and other adversities bind the surviving "sibkin" together so closely that they form bonds of mutual trust and understanding that often last for life.

## SRM

This is the abbreviation for Short-Range Missiles, direct trajectory missiles with high-explosive or armor-piercing explosive warheads. They have a range of less than one kilometer, and are accurate only at ranges of less than 300 meters. They are more powerful, however, than LRMs.

## STAR LEAGUE

The Star League was formed in 2571 in an attempt to peacefully ally the major star systems inhabited by the human race after it had taken to the stars. The League prospered for almost 200 years, until civil war broke out in 2751. The League was eventually destroyed when the ruling body, known as the High Council, disbanded in the midst of a struggle for power. Each of the royal House rulers then declared himself First Lord of the Star League, and within months, war engulfed the Inner Sphere. This conflict continues to the present day, almost three centuries later. These centuries of continuous war are now known simply as the Succession Wars.

## SUCCESSOR LORDS

Each of the five Successor States is ruled by a family descended from one of the original Council Lords of the old Star League. All five royal House Lords claim the title of First Lord, and they have been at each other's throats since the beginning of the Succession Wars in 2786. Their battleground is the vast Inner Sphere, which is composed of all the star systems once occupied by Star League's member-states.

## TRUEBORN/TRUEBIRTH

A Trueborn or Truebirth is born as a result of the Warrior Caste's eugenics program.

**Type:** Adder
**Mass:** 35 tons
**Chassis:** Endo Steel
**Power Plant:** 210 XL
**Cruising Speed:** 64.8 kph
**Maximum Speed:** 97.2 kph
**Jump Jets:** None
    **Jump Capacity:** None
**Armor:** Ferro-Fibrous
**Armament:**
    1 Flamer
    16.25 tons of pod space available

## ADDER

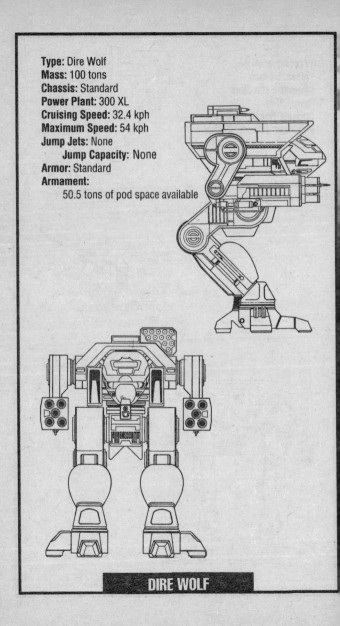

**Type:** Dire Wolf
**Mass:** 100 tons
**Chassis:** Standard
**Power Plant:** 300 XL
**Cruising Speed:** 32.4 kph
**Maximum Speed:** 54 kph
**Jump Jets:** None
    **Jump Capacity:** None
**Armor:** Standard
**Armament:**
    50.5 tons of pod space available

**DIRE WOLF**

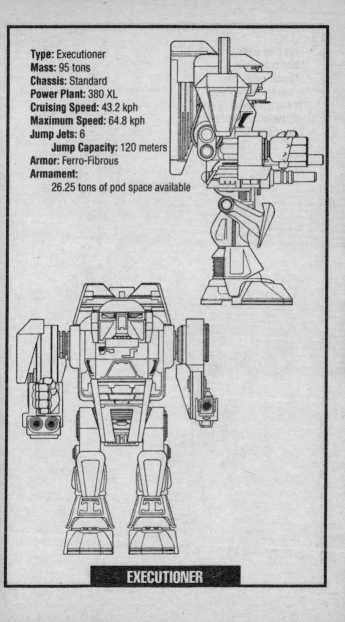

**Type:** Executioner
**Mass:** 95 tons
**Chassis:** Standard
**Power Plant:** 380 XL
**Cruising Speed:** 43.2 kph
**Maximum Speed:** 64.8 kph
**Jump Jets:** 6
    **Jump Capacity:** 120 meters
**Armor:** Ferro-Fibrous
**Armament:**
    26.25 tons of pod space available

**EXECUTIONER**

**Type:** Fire Moth
**Mass:** 20 tons
**Chassis:** Endo Steel
**Power Plant:** 200 XL
**Cruising Speed:** 108 kph
**Maximum Speed:** 162 kph
**Jump Jets:** None
　　　**Jump Capacity:** None
**Armor:** Ferro-Fibrous
**Armament:**
　　6.75 tons of pod space available

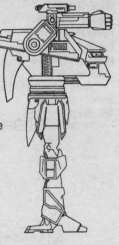

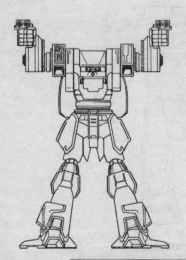

## FIRE MOTH

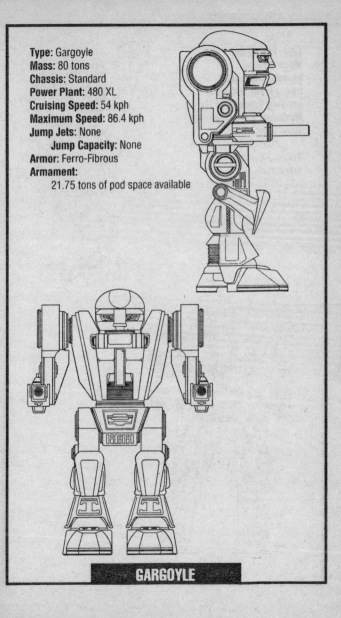

**Type:** Gargoyle
**Mass:** 80 tons
**Chassis:** Standard
**Power Plant:** 480 XL
**Cruising Speed:** 54 kph
**Maximum Speed:** 86.4 kph
**Jump Jets:** None
    **Jump Capacity:** None
**Armor:** Ferro-Fibrous
**Armament:**
    21.75 tons of pod space available

**GARGOYLE**

**Type:** Hellbringer
**Mass:** 65 tons
**Chassis:** Standard
**Power Plant:** 325 XL
**Cruising Speed:** 54 kph
**Maximum Speed:** 86.4 kph
**Jump Jets:** None
    **Jump Capacity:** None
**Armor:** Standard
**Armament:**
    28.75 tons of pod space available

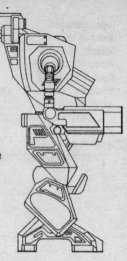

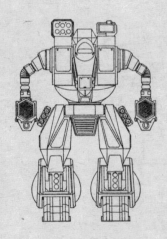

**HELLBRINGER**

**Type:** Ice Ferret
**Mass:** 45 tons
**Chassis:** Endo Steel
**Power Plant:** 360 XL
**Cruising Speed:** 86.4 kph
**Maximum Speed:** 129.6 kph
**Jump Jets:** None
   **Jump Capacity:** None
**Armor:** Ferro-Fibrous
**Armament:**
   9.75 tons of pod space available

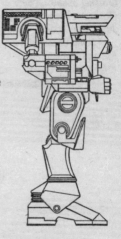

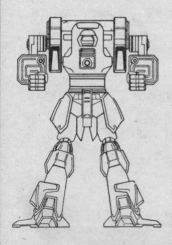

**ICE FERRET**

**Type:** Kit Fox
**Mass:** 30 tons
**Chassis:** Endo Steel
**Power Plant:** 180 XL
**Cruising Speed:** 64.8 kph
**Maximum Speed:** 97.2 kph
**Jump Jets:** None
    **Jump Capacity:** None
**Armor:** Ferro-Fibrous
**Armament:**
    16 tons of pod space available

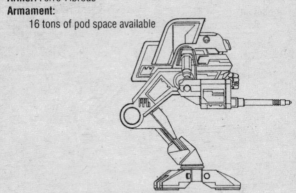

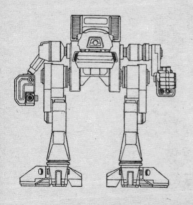

**KIT FOX**

**Type:** Mad Dog
**Mass:** 60 tons
**Chassis:** Standard
**Power Plant:** 300 XL
**Cruising Speed:** 54 kph
**Maximum Speed:** 86.4 kph
**Jump Jets:** None
    **Jump Capacity:** None
**Armor:** Ferro-Fibrous
**Armament:**
    28 tons of pod space available

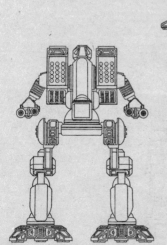

**MAD DOG**

**Type:** Mist Lynx
**Mass:** 25 tons
**Chassis:** Endo Steel
**Power Plant:** 175 XL
**Cruising Speed:** 75.6 kph
**Maximum Speed:** 118.8 kph
**Jump Jets:** 6
    **Jump Capacity:** 180 meters
**Armor:** Ferro-Fibrous
**Armament:**
    8.75 tons of pod space available

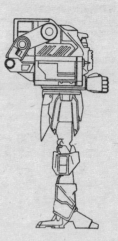

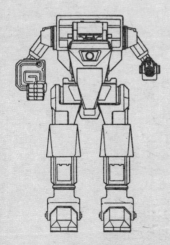

**MIST LYNX**

**Type:** Nova
**Mass:** 50 tons
**Chassis:** Standard
**Power Plant:** 250 XL
**Cruising Speed:** 54 kph
**Maximum Speed:** 86.4 kph
**Jump Jets:** 5
    **Jump Capacity:** 150 meters
**Armor:** Standard
**Armament:**
    16.25 tons of pod space available

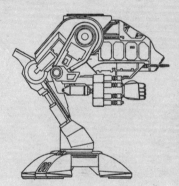

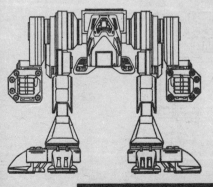

**NOVA**

**Type:** Stormcrow
**Mass:** 55 tons
**Chassis:** Endo Steel
**Power Plant:** 330 XL
**Cruising Speed:** 64.8 kph
**Maximum Speed:** 97.2 kph
**Jump Jets:** None
    **Jump Capacity:** None
**Armor:** Ferro-Fibrous
**Armament:**
    23 tons of pod space available

## STORMCROW

**Type:** Summoner
**Mass:** 70 tons
**Chassis:** Standard
**Power Plant:** 350 XL
**Cruising Speed:** 54 kph
**Maximum Speed:** 86.4 kph
**Jump Jets:** 5
    **Jump Capacity:** 150 meters
**Armor:** Ferro-Fibrous
**Armament:**
    22.75 tons of pod space available

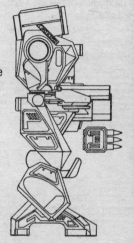

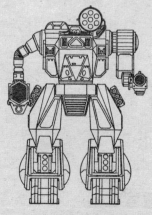

**SUMMONER**

**Type:** Timber Wolf
**Mass:** 75 tons
**Chassis:** Endo Steel
**Power Plant:** 375 XL
**Cruising Speed:** 54 kph
**Maximum Speed:** 86.4 kph
**Jump Jets:** None
    **Jump Capacity:** None
**Armor:** Ferro-Fibrous
**Armament:**

    28 tons of pod space available

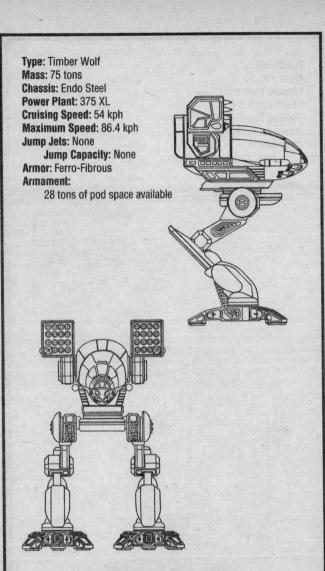

**TIMBER WOLF**

**Type:** Viper
**Mass:** 40 tons
**Chassis:** Endo Steel
**Power Plant:** 320 XL
**Cruising Speed:** 86.4 kph
**Maximum Speed:** 129.6 kph
**Jump Jets:** 8
    **Jump Capacity:** 240 meters
**Armor:** Ferro-Fibrous
**Armament:**
    8.75 tons of pod space available

**VIPER**

**Type:** Warhawk
**Mass:** 85 tons
**Chassis:** Standard
**Power Plant:** 340 XL
**Cruising Speed:** 43.2 kph
**Maximum Speed:** 64.8 kph
**Jump Jets:** None
    **Jump Capacity:** None
**Armor:** Ferro-Fibrous
**Armament:**
    32.5 tons of pod space available

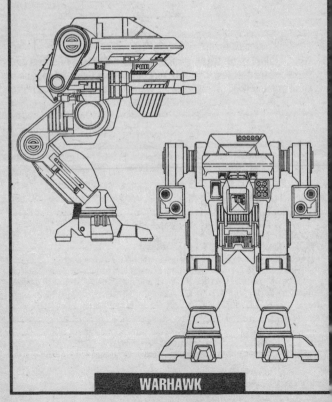

**WARHAWK**

# SENSATIONAL SCIENCE FICTION

If you and/or a friend would like to receive the *ROC Advance*, a bimonthly newsletter featuring all the newest and hottest ROC books and authors, on a complimentary basis, please fill out this form and return it to:

### ROC Books/Penguin USA
375 Hudson Street
New York, NY 10014

**Your Address**

Name _____

Street _____ Apt. # _____

City _____ State _____ Zip _____

**Friend's Address**

Name _____

Street _____ Apt. # _____

City _____ State _____ Zip _____